# The Chase

*Brides of Beadwell*

# By Sara Portman

**LYRICAL PRESS**
Kensington Publishing Corp.
www.kensingtonbooks.com

Lyrical Press books are published by
Kensington Publishing Corp. 119 West 40th Street New York, NY 10018

First Electronic Edition: November 2017
eISBN-13: 978-1-5161-0051-4
eISBN-10: 1-5161-0051-4

First Print Edition: November 2017
ISBN-13: 978-1-5161-0054-5
ISBN-10:1-5161-0054-9

Printed in the United States of America

# Chapter One

The ache was setting in again. Michael Rosevear had been on the road less than two hours and already, his leg was troubling him. The night had not been restful enough to erase the stiffness of the previous day's torturous travel. It seemed a clear message that no part of him, not even his damned leg, desired to go to London.

He shifted his weight. The adjustment did not bring relief. Even the velvet cushions in his father's wheeled palace of a traveling coach could not make him comfortable. Yet here he was, the dutiful son, making his miserable way to town in response to his father's summons.

He glanced out the window. The sky was foul as well. There was no end to unmistakable signals that he belonged, not rattling along the London Road, but back home at Rose Hall, overseeing the next day's brew or tangled up with Delia or some other warm and willing woman. Instead, he was trapped inside this cushioned prison with no one to provide company or comfort, save Gelert.

Michael looked at the hound. Sensing he was the subject of his master's unspoken thoughts, Gelert lifted his head and regarded Michael with only modest interest.

"You're no better, you mongrel. You're shamefully obedient, coming when you are called, no matter how miserably I treat you." Michael reached out as he spoke and teased his fingers in the wiry brown and black fur between Gelert's ears. The dog pushed his head upward into the scratch.

Michael pulled his hand away and Gelert sighed, lowering his head to rest once more atop his front paws. He stared at Michael still.

"Don't call me a liar," he grumbled at the animal. "I don't coddle you. And don't become accustomed to these plush cushions either."

The dog released another huff of air as though to confirm he had, in fact, already become accustomed.

The carriage rattled into a particularly rough patch of road and one wheel caught a rut that jarred the conveyance and its occupants all the way to Michael's teeth. He winced as the pain along the back of his leg intensified.

The dog lifted his head, questioning.

Michael pressed his fingers into the underside of his leg and kneaded the muscle, as firmly as he could bear, until the ache dulled to a tolerable level. He had only just stretched the leg onto the cushioned seat when the carriage dipped again, this time into a rut on the other side. The jarring motion clenched the muscle all over again and sent a sharp spike of pain shooting from his knee to his backside.

Michael cursed.

Gelert released a plaintive whine.

*Damn.* Not even two hours. It was unmanning. Michael gritted his teeth and lifted one fist to rap loudly on the roof of the carriage. The vehicle slowed in response.

Once they had stopped completely, the coachman appeared at the window. He opened the door.

"Stop at the next town, Albert," Michael said. "I need to stretch my leg a bit."

To Albert's credit, he did not question the decision to break so early in their journey. He should have. Any man of sense would. If they halted every pair of hours to stretch his infernal leg, this day's travel would be even slower than yesterday's. Their arrival would be considerably delayed.

*Yet another reason I should turn around and never see London again.*

Michael looked at the dog. "I don't know what you're so happy about. London will be no fun for you either."

\* \* \* \*

Juliana tucked herself deeper into the shadow under the jutting second story of the Bear & Boar coaching inn and watched the road. With each moment that passed, regret grew for the poorly considered decision to allow the mail coach to depart without her.

She had been so certain of her plan. She had only paid the fare from Beadwell to Peckingham, as she couldn't spare the coins to go the rest of the way to London on the mail coach. More importantly, she would be easily intercepted on the mail coach, if her father decided to come after her. In what had seemed a clever plan at the time, she had determined that she would approach a traveler in Peckingham and request aid in the form of a ride. She was clean and unthreatening in appearance. Surely, someone would be charitable and invite her into their coach for the remainder of the journey to London. She knew the distance was less than a day from here.

Less than a day, that is, provided she departed soon. She had been waiting for more than three hours and had not yet approached anyone to pose her request. Traffic had been lighter than expected. Travelers had come through, but none had been of a sort to draw Juliana from her hiding spot under the jetty and behind a bush. There had been two lone riders on horseback, who were, of course, no use to her at all. There had also been two loud young men out for a joyride in an open curricle. They had been followed by a demanding matron traveling with a beleaguered younger gentleman who Juliana guessed to be her son. The latest arrival was a large family who seemed to possess a secret compartment in their traveling coach, for far too many occupants emerged from the carriage as should have fit inside. They had not yet departed, but she had already dismissed the family as a possibility. There could not conceivably be room to include her in their crowded vehicle, and besides, the children—all daughters—had bickered incessantly from the moment they'd arrived.

She pulled her shawl more tightly around her shoulders. Even sheltered from the wind, the day was unseasonably dark and cool. When she had decided upon her present course, she had not counted on inclement weather. She had envisioned a sunny day and a kind, older woman in a comfortable carriage, traveling with a quiet maid and perhaps a floppy-eared lap dog. She had thought to appeal to the woman's pity and her desire for company on the balance of her journey.

She could now admit it was a wholly unrealistic vision. Aside from the uncooperative weather and decided lack of pleasant older gentlewomen, Juliana knew herself to be horrid company. She never knew what to say to anyone, primarily from lack of practice. Making conversation for hours with a kind but talkative stranger was nearly as distasteful a thought as enduring hours listening to the family of sniping sisters. The comparison was of no consequence, however, as the kindly old woman of her imaginings never appeared. The unhappy family, however, was still inside.

Juliana looked to the sky, growing darker despite the midday hour, and wondered if she shouldn't reconsider and at least inquire. Perhaps, despite their disagreements with each other, they would be charitable enough to share their limited space. And if they were willing to endure the discomfort of an extra person, surely she should be willing to endure the bickering. It was, after all, better than returning to Beadwell.

Just as she released a breath meant to bolster her commitment and courage, she heard the sounds of another carriage. She craned her neck to study it as it came into view. It was a large traveling coach of glossy black with a blue and gold coat of arms painted on the door. It was the richest looking coach she had ever seen. She watched as it slowed and the coachman guided it to a halt in front of the Bear & Boar.

Breathless to see who might emerge, Juliana waited as the coachman lowered himself from the box. He stopped and looked up to assess the sky, but she could not see well enough in the shadow of the darkening clouds to make out his expression. Then he moved to open the carriage door and her attention was fixed upon another profile.

Despite the fervency of her prayers, it was not a kindly old woman who descended with the aid of both coachman and cane. The fabric billowing around the occupant of the vehicle was not a woman's skirt, but a man's greatcoat, dark and voluminous.

The lord of the crest-emblazoned coach did not pause to evaluate the skies, as his coachman had done, but walked purposefully, relying on the support of his cane, toward the inn. As he drew nearer to the door, and thus to her, her view of him was obstructed by the shrub. She wanted to see him more closely but dared not rustle the branches for fear of being discovered when she had not yet decided whether to emerge.

Fortune was not smiling upon her today. If the threatening clouds brought rain, she would be left, cold and wet, waiting outside the Bear & Boar with nowhere to go and no funds to spare for a room. Once the rain stopped, she would be wet and bedraggled, thus even less likely to convince a traveler to take her in. On the other hand, she mused, if her intent was to inspire charity, she would certainly appear more pitiful. More than appearing so, she would actually *be* more pitiful. She sighed and the door of the inn opened again, sending the unhappy family spilling out into the yard.

"Why do I have to sit next to Mariah?" a plaintive voice asked from within a cluster of pastel-clad females. "She can't be still and keeps poking me with her elbow."

"I do no such thing," came another voice from group. "And how would you even notice? You'll have your nose buried in your novel the entire time."

"It's not my fault reading in a moving carriage makes you ill. Why shouldn't I read if I am perfectly well?"

"I don't know how Beth can read anything when Emily snores so loudly," another of the girls observed.

"It's quite simple," the reader responded. "If she starts snoring, I just pinch her. She always stops snoring then."

"How dare you pinch me!" the snorer squeaked.

"Well, of course she'll stop snoring if you wake her, but then she'll start right up again once she falls asleep."

"Just pinch her again."

The speaker must have chosen to demonstrate, for her statement was followed by a sharp shriek. Or perhaps, Juliana mused, the snorer had retaliated. She rather hoped that was the case.

Either way, she couldn't fathom there was space for her inside that coach.

Which left only the cane-carrying lord of the fancy carriage. Indecision gripped her. Was she bold enough to importune a gentleman for an unchaperoned ride to London—even a lame, older gentleman? She glanced at the door to the inn and again at the family, who were settling themselves back into their carriage. She heard a high-pitched squeal from inside.

Juliana knew two things in that moment: The first was that she absolutely would not fit in that carriage. The second was that courage grew from desperation. One thing she had never been in her life was bold, and she did not feel particularly bold just now. But neither was she willing to face defeat and return to her father's house in Beadwell. She had come this far. If she failed, she would not let it be for lack of courage.

\* \* \* \*

Unwilling to make a show of stretching his uncooperative limbs in front of an audience, Michael made do with pacing along the property behind the inn for several minutes after letting himself out the back with the excuse of using the necessary.

What he needed was a full day outside the confines of the blasted carriage. When he could walk or ride, his leg remained loose and ailed him very little. But he could not walk all the way from Yorkshire to London. He paced a few minutes longer then looked at the sky. For the very little relief his paces were achieving, the effort was likely costing him dearly in rapidly dwindling hours of travel-worthy weather.

Leaning slightly less heavily on the cane for the time he had invested, Michael went back through the rear door of the inn to collect Albert.

The coachman considered him with an openly assessing eye. "Are you sure you're ready to continue?"

"I am sure delays help very little. There is no way around this journey but through it. We can be in London before the day is out of the weather is merciful. Let's be on our way."

Albert nodded and preceded him to the front door, holding it open as Michael passed with his cane. He hated the blasted thing, but so many days shut up in a box left him more crippled by his injury than usual. As he limped across the yard toward his father's coach, he vowed this would be the last summons from his father that would see him traveling the full length of England. He would marry this woman his father had found for him and he would give her the choice to either return to Yorkshire with him, or stay in London. He would be returning to Yorkshire and remaining there the balance of his days, father be damned.

And he would watch the blasted cane burn in the fire.

"Don't coddle my leg with your speed, either, Albert," he added. "I am impatient to be done with this journey and slowing its pace is not a kindness."

"Understood, sir."

Michael walked to the rear of the coach as Albert walked to the front. As his coachman saw to the horses and readied them for departure, Michael made himself useful, inspecting the luggage. He tested the ropes securing the trunks and cases, ensuring they were still secure.

"I beg your pardon, my lord."

The feminine voice halted Michael in his task and he turned to find its owner was a young woman standing a few paces away, eyes lowered, gloved hand clutching her shawl tightly at her front. The shawl was thin and worn and his first thought upon seeing her was that there was not enough weight to her to combat the unseasonably cool wind, despite being covered from boot to bonnet. She must be freezing.

She didn't have the look of the women who hovered around coaching inns, making their living either begging from or offering themselves to the men who stopped. If she had, he would have turned her away immediately. Aside from the threadbare shawl, she seemed tidy and respectable. He couldn't see the face underneath the brim of her bonnet, as she'd chosen to address his boots for some reason, rather than his eyes.

"Yes?" Michael asked.

"I…I wonder if I might prevail upon you for your aid, my lord. I…"

She paused and he had the sense she was summoning the courage to continue.

"I must find my way to London, my lord, and I have…I have missed the mail coach. It will not come again until Friday, and I cannot wait."

Practiced beggar or no, when she had begun by soliciting his 'aid', he had expected her to ask for coins. He would not have predicted she request an invitation into his coach to accompany him on his travels. Perhaps she was a whore after all? He peered more closely at her. There was nothing in her look or manner that suggested it. Did she understand what she was asking?

"You want to know if I will take you to London? Alone? In my carriage?" She was daft. If she had any reputation at all, it would be ruined by what she asked. Not to mention the tangle for him if anyone knew. He was not going to be compromising any young misses this day.

"Yes, my lord, I..." She lifted her head. Deep green eyes went round as they met his, and pale cheeks flushed pink. "Oh," she breathed.

She stared at him, lips parted in hesitation and he had the distinct sense that he was not what she had expected, which made no sense at all because *she* had approached *him.*

*His* surprise, however, was quite reasonable. She was young, but not a girl, and she was striking in an unearthly sort of way. Her features were an odd collection of contradictions. Watchful green eyes fringed with long, dark lashes, and delicately pale skin, clear of any freckle or blemish, framed with wisps of auburn that swept beneath the coverage of her bonnet.

"I...I'm sorry, my lord," she stammered. "I thought...that is...I didn't consider..." Her words trailed off and her eyes drifted to the cane in his right hand.

He understood then. She had seen him from behind. With his high-collared greatcoat and hat, she had only the cane for a clue and she had erroneously surmised he was a much older man, as opposed to simply a lame one.

His mouth tightened. "It appears you have made an error in judgment, miss. I bid you good day." He turned from her, bent on continuing his task, but stopped when a small, gloved hand rested tentatively upon his forearm.

"Please, my lord."

He faced her. She was very near now, gazing directly up at him. "It is imperative that I depart for London today. I shall be no trouble at all and I promise that you shall never hear from me again once we reach town." She made her plea then stared up awaiting his response, eyes wide with entreaty, jaw squared in determination.

He looked down to where her hand still lay on his coat sleeve.

She followed his gaze there and slowly withdrew her hand. "I beg you, sir."

It may have been the waver in her voice on the last word she spoke that made up Michael's mind. More likely it was the fact that here stood a mystery and unraveling it in the hours between Peckingham and London would be a welcome distraction from the ache in his leg. Or maybe he was simply restless. Whatever the reason, and even as he knew he should not, Michael slowly lowered his head into a nod of assent. "Very well, miss. I shall see you to London."

She took a sharp intake of air and he could not tell if she was relieved or frightened by his agreement.

"But we leave momentarily," he added. "If you have things to collect, I suggest you do so, and hand them over to my coachman."

She glanced over his shoulder and Michael saw that Albert had completed his preparations and now stood as audience to his reckless decision making.

"I have my things, my lord." As evidence to this claim, she lifted a small satchel that could not have contained more than a precious few items.

"Very well, then. Let us not delay."

Michael turned and caught the questioning lift of Albert's brow.

He ignored it. "We have a lot of road to cover," he said gruffly. "Let's get to it."

Albert nodded and led the young woman to the carriage door where he pulled down the step to help her in.

\* \* \* \*

Aside from the painted crest, the traveling coach was glossy black, cloaked in as much of the dark color as its owner and just as intimidatingly sized. Juliana took a deep breath and attempted to steady her roiling nerves as she accepted the coachman's hand and climbed into the vehicle. As she did, her attention was immediately drawn to the source of a low groan from the far side of the rear-facing bench. A large canine head lifted, short ears erect, watchful eyes trained intently upon her. The sound it emitted was not a growl, precisely, but given the size of the animal, threatening enough to halt her in her ascent. She swallowed and returned the animal's stare.

"Don't mind the dog, miss," the coachman said from behind her, accurately surmising the reason for her hesitation. "He's a right lamb, I promise you."

She exhaled and continued cautiously into the coach, staring all the while into the black eyes of the animal and sensing his own wariness. His wiry fur was dark, with mottled splotches of gray and black and brown. Far from lamb-like, he was the sort of animal one would expect to see pacing a darkened alley for scraps, not lounging on the velvet-covered cushions of an aristocrat's carriage. As she settled herself on the seat across from him, his dark eyes followed her intently from beneath an eyebrow-like veil of more wiry fur.

From outside the coach, the beast's master tossed his silver handled cane onto the seat next to the dog. The cane had tricked her. She didn't know what the man's injury was, but he was not in the least frail—and young enough to be both dangerous and highly improper. She looked down at her lap as he climbed in and sat on the rear-facing seat next to the dog. She wanted to look again, to judge him more closely now that she was at his mercy, but she hadn't the courage.

She didn't know which frightened her more, man or animal. The coach was the grandest she'd ever seen, but both he and his dog seemed to consume more than their fair share of the available space. His heavy black boots rested on the floor very near her own feet. She peered at them, as they and the accompanying breech-covered knees were the only parts of him she could study without looking up and directly facing him.

She had mistaken him for someone altogether different, and he had known it.

She never would have asked him to take her to London if she'd understood, and he knew that as well.

But she was desperate to get there—so much so that she had accepted the offer anyway. And this, too, he knew.

He already knew too much of her and she nothing of him, save his size and youth and possession of an equally intimidating canine companion. The exhilaration she'd experienced at stealing away from her father's house that morning had been weathered by the uncertain hours outside the Bear & Boar. What remained was thoroughly extinguished as she sat, trapped and vulnerable. She knew exactly why she'd importuned this man to transport her to London. Too late, she'd thought to consider why he'd accepted.

The man lifted an arm to rap sharply on the roof of the coach to signal his readiness for departure. The vehicle lurched into motion. She clutched her satchel and pressed herself deeper into the seat.

# Chapter Two

"What is your name?"

Juliana started at the sudden interruption to the silence. She had known there would be questions, but they had gone a fair distance with nothing. In the small space his voice was large—masculine, unfamiliar, and much deeper than her father's, as though it rumbled forth from a place low within him.

She lifted her attention from his boots to the front of his coat, not ready yet to meet his eyes. "My name is Craw…Crawley. Miss…Ana…Crawley." She had not considered the matter before, but now that she was here, at the mercy of a stranger, giving her true name seemed reckless and unnecessary.

The dog released a huff as though he recognized the lie. She looked at it again. It was looking back at her, which she found disconcerting.

He must have noticed the direction of her gaze. "Do you have an aversion to hounds?"

Her attention shifted back to the man across from her and, finally, she lifted her eyes to face him, determined that he should not understand the extent of her trepidation. Hat removed despite her presence and broad shoulders slouching against the plush brown cushion, he, too, looked wild, with his hair strewn into disarray by the wind. His eyes were as dark as his companion's and just as wary. "I am not averse." She glanced at the dog again. Why was it watching her so closely? "I am merely… unfamiliar, my lord."

He considered her response with no outward reaction. "There are no dogs where you are from." He said it as a declaration, she knew, to better illustrate the dubiousness of the idea.

"None in my household," she answered, willing her eyes not to cast nervously again at the dog as they so wanted to do.

"And what sort of household is that?" He asked the question flatly, but she knew despite his tone he was pouncing on her mistake in referring to her home and inviting his inquiry.

"The sort without dogs," she said impulsively, unwilling to reveal more. She realized too late it had been a second miscalculation. Her obfuscation revealed entirely too much.

His coal eyes narrowed, full of questions, but he didn't voice them.

The dog's head lowered again to rest upon his outstretched front paws. They were sizable paws.

Silence stretched between them again for a time, but it was not a respite for Juliana. She was aware that he was watching her. He studied her for a long time, eyes flitting uncomfortably over every inch of her as though there may be clues to read in any spot on her person. If she'd had a cape, she'd have pulled the thing over her head and hidden beneath it, so exposed she felt to his inspection.

The carriage bounced in a rut and he winced. The expression disappeared quickly, but she had seen it. He must have known she saw and disliked it, for he looked away, ending his examination of her person. He shifted in his seat, causing her to wonder at the nature of his injury. She couldn't stare the information from him so she looked down as well, to ease his discomfort as much as her own. In the silence, she played her fingers in the nap of the brown velvet upholstery, leaving tracks that remained after her fingers moved away.

"Are you averse to dogs *and* conversation?" he asked sharply, breaking the miserable quiet.

She lifted her eyes to his again. "I am not well familiar with either, my lord."

Her response only brought the return of his scrutiny and she regretted it.

"Not familiar with conversation? How can that be so?"

She had no intention of sharing the details of her life thus far and so gave the simplest answer she could devise that might prove acceptable to him. "I've led a very quiet life, my lord."

He sighed heavily and pursed his lips as though considering just what to do with her. Finally, he said, "Allow me to make it simple for you then. I shall ask questions and you shall provide answers. What say you to that?"

She wished fervently to decline. She intended to be careful with the answers she gave, but he made her anxious with his probing looks and intimidating shoulders. She could not refuse him, however, given the circumstances, so she gave a slight nod. "As you wish, my lord."

"Where in London is your destination?" The first question came with the speed of a slingshot that had been stretched back, waiting for release.

She hesitated, wondering just how much she should share. Would it matter if he knew the purpose for her journey? Would he take pity on her, or would he believe, as most men would, that she should be returned to her father without delay?

"You shall have to tell me that much at least, Miss Crawley. I cannot deliver you to your destination if you will not name it."

"Number 48 Hardwick Street."

He blinked. Twice. "And what will we find at Number 48 Hardwick Street?"

"The offices of Hammersley, Brint and Peale, Solicitors," she offered, as he would know that much eventually.

"You have urgent business with Hammersley, Brint and Peale?" He picked a piece of dog hair from his black sleeve and waited for her response.

"I do, my lord."

His brow arched. "So urgent that you would place your reputation— and frankly, your person—in considerable danger in order to arrive there two days earlier?"

She stilled at his words and her heart seemed to slow. Should she panic at this point? She studied him intently, needing to find some answer in his eyes and expression, but found nothing. The dark eyes and square jaw were not blank, but guarded and unreadable like looking into darkened water—the surface revealed nothing, but the depths could hold all sorts of threatening creatures. She tried to put aside her imaginings of poisonous eels and venomous snakes as she asked, "Have I, my lord? Put my person in considerable danger?"

His brow arched. "Haven't you?"

She stared at him only to find him inspecting her just as closely. How was *she* to answer that question?

"I am thoroughly familiar with my own character, Miss Crawley, so *I* know the answer to your inquiry. It is not lost on me, however, that you do not. Thus, I am able to surmise that whatever awaits you in London is of critical importance. Or, conversely, whatever you leave behind is a considerable threat." He crossed his arms, his assessment unrelenting. "Which is it, Miss Crawley? Are you hurrying toward something or running away?"

*Both.* She weighed her options in responding. "You have not answered my question, my lord. Have I placed myself in danger?"

His mouth quirked. It was the closest she'd seen to a smile from him, but it was mocking rather than kind. "You are safe from harm, Miss Crawley, but not from interrogation. As I am charitable enough to convey you to London, the least you can do is answer a few simple questions."

Except they were not simple questions at all. And hours remained in their journey. That meant many questions, not few. How could she confide in him? Even if she believed he would not harm her, how could she know that he would be sympathetic to her? He was lord of whatever peerage was painted on the side of his coach. He had already been high-handed enough to point out that she was entirely at his mercy. If she admitted that she had saved pennies for more than a year to flee her father's house and, more importantly, his control, he seemed the sort to believe she had been wrong to do so. Would he refuse to take her farther? Or worse, would he insist upon returning her?

Juliana resolved to correct her earlier mistake of appearing to guard secrets. She willed her tense frame to relax and attempted what she hoped was a pitiful smile. "I am sorry to disappoint, my lord, but if you anticipated that my story would provide hours of distraction on the London Road, you were mistaken. I am quite uninteresting."

It was not a lie. What did her life consist of, but seeing to her father's orders and wandering around their house as though she were haunting the place? He rarely allowed her to leave. She had no friends to speak of.

"I believe I shall judge my own disinterest, Miss Crawley. I have answered your question and now you shall answer mine. Is it something in London that has you hurrying to arrive, or something back in Peckingham that has you running away?"

"I have nothing to fear in Peckingham, my lord." As the statement was true, she was able to deliver it with a modicum of nonchalance. "My future awaits in London and I am impatient to begin it." She tried her best to appear optimistic and unconcerned, but she had no practice at such artifice.

He was unconvinced.

"Where shall you go after your visit to Hammersley, Brint and Peale, Solicitors?" he asked, adding dramatic inflection to the name of the business office. "Have you family in London? Connections there?"

She did not like how solidly he had the upper hand and so she said, "Indeed I do. In fact, I grew up as neighbor to a woman who is now a duchess. She is in London with her husband." For good measure she added, "The duke." The connection was tenuous as they had spent virtually no time together and her father had attempted to blackmail the duchess to gain her property thus ensuring she would consider herself an enemy of any with the name Crawford, but she kept that bit to herself.

"A duchess?" he asked, his lip twitching in amusement. "Is that so?"

It occurred belatedly to her that her companion, as a nobleman, may well know her neighbor, Lady Emmaline, now Duchess of Worley. To stave off any inquiry as to the specific duchess of her acquaintance, she summoned the courage to pose a question to him. "And what may I know of you, my lord? May I know the identity of the gentleman who has come to my aid?"

There was a telling pause and she continued. "You need not fear that I will appear on your doorstep, claim that you've compromised me, and demand that we wed—if that is your concern."

"Are you already married, then, *Miss* Crawley?" he asked, stressing the miss that she'd assigned herself.

"I am not, but I have no desire to be so."

"I think you would find, Miss Crawley, that in the matter of compromised young ladies, their desires are rarely taken into account. It is not the young ladies one must fear, but their gravely offended parents."

She couldn't help the bitter laugh that escaped. She could not imagine her father ever taking grave offense on her behalf. "My father doesn't wish to see me married any more than I do, my lord. Besides, it wouldn't matter if he did. Judging by the crest decorating the side of your coach, even without your identity I could determine that my family would find themselves quite powerless against yours."

She realized as she finished her speech that he was staring at her, the most puzzled expression upon his face.

"Have I confused you?" she asked.

"Quite."

"How so?"

He scooted forward in his seat, bringing an alertness to his posture and straining the sleeves of his snug-fitting frock coat. "Why the devil would your own father not want you to marry? Isn't that what all fathers want for their daughters? To see them settled and supported?"

Juliana schooled her expression, trying not to show her frustration. She'd done it again. Without thinking, she had revealed more than she intended. Most fathers probably did want to see their daughters settled and supported. It certainly seemed the sort of thing a caring father would pursue. That was not the situation into which Juliana had been born. "My father is unconventional," she said, and tried to smile to make the description seem a compliment.

"Unconventional?" He scoffed. "I think most would call him irrational. How does he intend to see you supported after he is gone?"

Juliana felt certain her father wasted no thought whatsoever on what might happen to anyone after he was gone—particularly not his daughter.

"I appreciate your concern for my future security, my lord, but as we will only spend this one day together and as I've already promised you shall never hear from me again, it should not matter. If you do not wish to tell me who you are, I understand and will not press you further." It was a bolder speech than Juliana had ever given. She hoped her false confidence and her attempt to redirect attention to his secrets might stop the line of inquiry.

She was not so fortunate.

"Miss Crawley, the few things you have told me about yourself, when taken together, do not make sense. In my experience, tales that do not make sense are rarely true." He crossed his arms and gave her a look that dared her to prove him wrong.

She could only stare mutely back at him. She had no response that would not seem to be a confirmation.

"You may keep your secrets," he continued, watching her closely. She was aware of every place in her body that became the subject of his examination and willed it to be still. He could interpret any movement, any tick, any outward reaction whatsoever, as her confession. "But know this, Miss Crawley. You are correct in one respect—that crest you spied on the side of this coach is that of a marquessate. I am on my way to London to meet the wealthy heiress who shall become my bride. There is enough money and influence between the two families that there is very little you could do to trouble us. There is, however, a great deal we could do to trouble you, if you give us cause."

Juliana opened her mouth to respond, but was caught when no answer came. Her instinct was to be as she had always been—to reassure him that she would be no trouble to anyone and then sink quietly into her corner of the coach, as far from man and beast as she could be. But for some unaccountable reason, she sensed the only power she retained in that moment was the last trace of fear and mistrust that he held for her. She could not bring herself to erase it.

"If you mean to remind me of your close friendship with a duchess, do not," he continued. "I am not so stupid as to believe that a woman who consorts with duchesses wears a threadbare shawl and lacks fare for the mail coach."

"But I told you I missed the…"

He lifted a hand, halting her objection. "Do not. I overheard the innkeeper in Peckingham talking with my coachman. The mail coach will pass again tomorrow, not Friday as you claimed."

Juliana's breath caught. He had known. He had known the very first claim was a lie the moment she'd spoken it, and still he'd taken her in.

Now she was left to wonder at his reasons. Still, he had not harmed her yet. And every moment they sped along the road was a moment closer to London and farther from Beadwell.

"I was dishonest," she admitted, feeling the need to explain the lie. "About the mail coach. I have no funds until I reach London, and even then I am not certain how quickly I will be able to access my money. Until then, I am forced to make economies."

One brow arched elegantly. "Economies such as accepting passage from strange men while unchaperoned?"

"Precisely," she said, ignoring the doubt and censure in his question.

He nodded slowly. "Thus the reason your first stop in London shall be the solicitor's office."

"Yes."

He had continued to dig and she had continued to reveal, despite his assurance that she could keep her secrets. She did not want to play any more guessing games about her future plans. She would not allow an arrogant lord to decide whether she was on the right course and determine he might be entitled to change it.

They needed another topic of discussion. A benign one. She knew, despite her shortcomings, she must engage in conversation. Reticence on her part was only encouraging his interrogation.

She nodded toward to the dog, lounging comfortably at his lordship's side and considered the animal carefully. "Does it have a name?" she asked finally, meeting the dog's dark eyes.

The dog showed no discomfort with the inspection.

"Gelert," his master said. "His name is Gelert." Reminded of the dog's presence he reached out his hand and buried it into the mottled, disordered fur on the dog's back. The dog sighed.

"Gelert." She tested the name. "It is an odd name for a dog."

"It is an honorable name for a dog."

"How so?" The dog did not look honorable. It looked like a stray. A very large, potentially vicious stray.

"Gelert is legendary," he explained.

"Legendary?" Juliana inspected the animal with renewed curiosity.

His lordship cleared his throat. "*This* Gelert is not legendary. The original Gelert is the hero of a Welsh folk-tale."

She nearly smiled. A story. How perfect. She hoped it was a long one. In an effort to delay even further she asked, "How does your dog come to have a Welsh name?"

"I have a Welsh grandmother. She liked to tell stories."

"I should very much like to hear Gelert's story."

"Would you, Miss Crawley?" He tilted his head and a stray lock of dark hair fell onto his brow. "I should caution you, it is not a delicate one."

However gruesome the tale, it was better than interrogation. "I am not squeamish, my lord. And you have piqued my curiosity."

"Very well." He slouched more deeply into his seat for the telling of the tale. "The first Gelert was a gift to Llywelyn, Prince of Gwynedd, from King John. A favored hunting dog. As the legend tells, for one hunt the dog did not respond to his master's call and Prince Llywelyn hunted without him. When he returned from the hunt, it was to find his infant son missing, the cradle overturned, and the dog's mouth smeared with blood."

He had not misled her. The story was indeed upsetting. "I don't understand. There is no honor in killing a child," she pointed out, her attention now riveted to the present Gelert. As though to aid her imagination, the dog chose that moment to lift his muzzle and lick his paw. She could not help but envision him calmly cleaning blood from his fur. She shivered.

"Prince Llywelyn must have agreed, for as the story is told, he immediately drew his sword and ran the dog through."

Juliana cringed. Indelicate indeed.

"Over the sound of the dog's dying yelp, however, he heard a baby's cry. When he lifted the overturned cradle, he found, underneath it, his unharmed infant son and, behind it, the body of a dead wolf."

She gasped and stared up at the storyteller. " Gelert was not the villain, but hero? And he was killed for it?"

His lordship nodded.

"Was Llywelyn remorseful?"

"He was. The dog was buried with great ceremony. It is said the prince could hear the dog's dying yelp for the remainder of his days and never smiled again."

Juliana exhaled, hoping to expel the disturbed feeling the story had settled upon her. "What an awful tale. Why would you burden your pet with such an unhappy legacy?"

"It is a legacy of great honor. Gelert's loyalty and fierce protectiveness are legendary."

She looked to the dog again. He'd been calm through their journey thus far, but very watchful. Though he had not displayed it, she could easily believe in his ferocity. Would he, if called upon, rise to the legacy of his eponym? She was no threat to Gelert's master, but could she trust an animal to know it?

Perhaps the story had not been a wise way to pass the time after all. She decided silence might be better for a while, if his lordship would allow it. She sat very still in her seat, lowered her eyes to her lap and made no more attempts at conversation.

Even with the cooperation of her companion, the silence was fleeting. Within minutes it was broken by a violently loud clap of thunder, followed closely by the insistent rapping of rain buffeting the roof and walls of the carriage. Juliana's heart fell. Of all things, a storm.

# Chapter Three

The storm brought her worst fear.

"We shall have to stop," his lordship said, calling out to be heard above the racket caused by the pelting storm.

"Already?" she asked, his simple observation sending a thread of panic through her despite the fact that she had known it already.

He looked out at the heavy rain, falling in torrents around them. "A half-hour of this and the roads will be impassable. Better closeted at an inn than stuck in the mud. Either way, our progress is halted."

"But we've barely covered any distance. Are you sure you want to stop?"

He turned his attention to her. "No. I am quite sure I do not want to stop, but the weather requires otherwise."

She was revealing herself again, but she couldn't help it. They were not far enough. *She* was not far enough. If she were taken to cursing, she would have cursed the vindictive weather. She craned her neck to watch out the carriage window.

"Albert shall know to stop at the next town," he clarified. "There is no help for it."

She shouldn't have waited. If she had importuned the angry matron and her beleaguered son, she would be an hour closer to London by now. They may have stayed ahead if the weather altogether.

Alas, she had not approached the matron. It seemed only a few moments passed before she felt the carriage slowing, marking their approach to the next village. "How long do you think we shall have to stay here before continuing?" she asked.

He shrugged. "I am no more able to predict the weather than you are, but if the rain ceases before nightfall, the road should be passable by the morning."

Her eyes flew to his. "Tomorrow?" She looked at the scene again and back to him. "Do you mean to stay the night here?"

He peered at her, making her feel as though he found her very odd. She was used to being found odd, so it did not quell her questions. "Do you think such a delay is wise?"

"I am not choosing to delay," he said, impatience rising in his tone and tightening his jaw. "The choice has been made for us. If you are concerned about the cost, do not be. I shall arrange for your room as well as my own."

Her own room.

They were definitely not far enough from Beadwell for her to have her own room. She could be quite easily found here, especially if she drew attention to herself by arriving unchaperoned in a fancy coach with an oversized, highborn lord who paid for her stay. The night stretched long before her, sitting in a strange room by herself, listening to every noise. She would be like an animal caught in a trap, with nothing left to do but wait for the arrival of the hunter.

"I…I could…" What could she do?

She could curl up in the corner of his lordship's room and feel much more secure there. She looked up at him. She couldn't very well propose such a thing. Then he would certainly believe—if he did not already—that she was trying to snare him by compromising her reputation. He had not, after all, divulged to which marquessate his family belonged. And yet, how could she endure the entire night alone, knowing she was trapped prey?

The noise from the rain was riotous in their small space. It was raining very hard. Perhaps with the roads washing out, there wouldn't be two rooms available and they would have no choice but to stay together. Or, better yet, perhaps there would be no rooms at all and they should be forced to continue. Heartened by this thought, Juliana fortified her courage for their arrival. When the coachman appeared at the door, she allowed him to assist her down from the passenger compartment under the shielding cover of his cape, which he held over head. Stepping gingerly to avoid the rapidly forming puddles, she hurried with him toward the entrance of a small stone building from which candlelight beckoned, warm and golden, in the windows.

Despite the cozy warmth that enveloped her inside the dimly lit inn, when the coachman drew the cape from above her head, she felt nothing but cold. She needed only a moment to see the room was empty, save a young, aproned girl who wiped a rag across a table in the corner. The picture before her could not have been more opposite to her prayers.

The door opened again behind her, allowing in a great gust of rain-filled wind. She turned to see that her companion had entered, gripping his cane in one hand, with Gelert, more horse than dog, at his side.

"I'll see the horses, sir," the coachman said, giving Juliana the nonsensical concern that he'd overheard her thoughts. Of course he hadn't. Seeing to the horses was the logical thing. He rushed to exit and closed the door behind him.

His lordship stood there, dark and dripping, and she marveled that she had ever mistaken his profile for that of a feeble, elderly man. Despite the cane, he stood erect—intimidatingly so—and he was quite tall. She was not particularly small, but this man was two head above her. Intelligent eyes surveyed everything in the room, her included, and unruly locks of dark hair clung, damp, around the edges of his face. In the brightness of the warm candlelight, she thought she saw a thin scar edging along his chin. As though obliging her curiosity, he reached up, doffed his hat, and shook it, sending a shower of droplets radiating from it. The dog sidled away from the spray, then proceeded to shake himself in very much a similar manner to rid himself of the results of the rain.

Juliana had realized the dog's large scale even lying across the generous seat of the traveling coach, but upright the animal's head reached the man's elbow. They were both threateningly large, ragged, and dark.

Even as she feared them both, however, she felt an odd comfort in the menacing image they presented. There was no sense in it. Neither the man nor the animal had any duty to protect her. Still, she vowed to stay close to them—as close as her courage would allow.

"Ho there," called a booming voice, and Juliana looked up to find a man with a broad smile and equally broad waist descending the stairs to greet them. His smile faltered only briefly at the very image upon which Juliana had so recently been musing before he steered himself directly toward his lordship and clapped the much taller man roughly on the back. "You are fortunate today, my good man. You are the first to arrive and you've your pick of rooms. With the washing we're getting, we'll be full up and turning them away within the hour I'd say. Excellent timing, sir. Very lucky."

*Lucky, indeed,* Juliana thought. No part of this journey had gone in her favor.

"If my luck were that good, sir," her companion responded flatly, failing to return the innkeepers joviality, "the sun would shine and we would be in London before nightfall. As that is not our fate, we shall instead take two of your rooms and a hot meal."

The innkeeper's attention immediately shifted to Juliana upon the announcement that their party would require two rooms. She chafed under his thorough assessment and had to prevent herself from exhaling in relief when he finally turned back to his lordship.

"Which shall you require first sir, meals or rooms?"

"Meals first. Rooms second," came the reply.

"Very good, sir. Very good." The innkeeper nodded but did not move to arrange for either request. Instead he peered uncomfortably at Gelert. His mental deliberations played clearly across his face as his attention shifted from dog to master and back again. He didn't want the dog in his common room. Neither did he want to offend his lordship. While the dog may cause trouble or damage, the fancy lord represented significant income. In the end, his mercenary nature won out. "I'll have to charge a supplement if ye plan for the dog to stay inside. Otherwise, it's in the stables with the other animals."

"Understood," was his lordship's only response. He made no move toward removing the dog from the common room and the innkeeper seemed quite pleased with this decision. He had not, Juliana realized, quoted the amount of the supplement.

It was painfully clear to Juliana, as the innkeeper led their odd party to a table in the corner of the room, that her intent to avoid drawing notice had failed miserably. She had thought to be unremarkable so that the innkeeper would not recall her presence in the event anyone arrived to inquire after her. Instead, they were the only travelers in an empty room and she was a lone woman traveling with a wounded lord, who was clearly not her husband, and his horse of a dog.

* * * *

Michael lowered himself stiffly onto the wooden bench and pointed to a spot at his feet upon which Gelert obediently lay. Supplement, indeed. The dog was likely better mannered than most of the travelers who passed. As though proof of Michael's thought, the front door opened again, sending in a gust of damp air they could feel even seated at their table some five yards away. The newcomers who arrived with it received no more than a passing glance from Gelert, who remained quiet. They, on the other hand, did not. The four men were loud and complaining and one of them bellowed loudly to call the innkeeper when he did not immediately appear.

His annoyance with these new arrivals only added to his already black mood, attributable to the ache in his leg, his hunger, and his annoyance at the delay. He needed to get to London and cooperate with this ridiculous betrothal so he could be allowed to return to Yorkshire. He had responsibilities there. If the storm were not raging so fiercely, he would go for a long walk, rain or no, to relax both his limbs and his frustration.

Instead, he turned his attention to his enigmatic travel companion. She had proven disappointingly ungenerous in her willingness to satisfy his curiosity, applying both avoidance and outright lies. Did she really expect him to believe that she didn't know how to converse properly? Or that, at the same time, she was personal friends with a duchess? The two claims were equally preposterous whether taken together or separately. The only truth he suspected he had received was the address to which she desired to be delivered in London, but even that could be inaccurate, provided it was in the vicinity of her true destination.

One wouldn't guess it to look at her. Despite the boldness of her lies, she had the odd habit of falling into the meek posture of a mistreated servant, all hunched and quiet. He didn't like that either. She was considerably more interesting when she lifted her attention and engaged in conversation.

He attempted to spur her to do just that. "Are you sullen, Miss Crawley, or just intrigued by the tabletop?"

She lifted her face partway, but retained her guarded expression. Her hooded, half-raised eyes surveyed the gradually filling room as she answered. "I am neither, my lord."

"Then what is the reason for your quiet?"

"I have no reason," she said. "Though I do wish the weather had not delayed us." She gave an almost imperceptible shrug before returning her attention to the scarred wooden table.

Given her surreptitious glances around the room, Michael doubted the truth was so simple, but he was distracted from further questions by the arrival of a serving girl with the promised meal. She bent to set a plate of fragrant meat pies between them and Michael decided his hunger was a greater priority than his curiosity in that moment.

His attention to his appetite prevented him from noticing immediately that she did not help herself to a share of the food. "Are you not hungry, Miss Crawley?"

Her cheeks blushed beneath lowered lashes and he was again reminded that, for all of her odd manners, she was pretty in an uncommon sort of way.

She opened her mouth and replied in an unintelligible mumble. The population of the common room was growing and, with it, the din of conversation.

"I'm sorry, I didn't hear you," he said.

"I can't pay for food, my lord." Her color deepened.

"Is that all?" he asked. Did he honestly appear so monstrous as to deprive her of a meal? "Eat for pity's sake. I've offered. I'll not accuse you of picking my pocket." His attempt to be gracious likely missed the mark given his overall frustration, but her refusal was silly after all. "Eat," he repeated when she did not take action after his first request.

She did, reaching hesitantly out to take one of the pastries. She brought it to her mouth and ate gingerly. She ate nearly half of it before setting it in front of her and lifting her head—only partway again. "Thank you for the meal, my lord."

He nodded.

To his surprise, she did not return to studying her lap, but gave a delicate cough and continued speaking. "I am not accustomed to particularly fine accommodation, my lord. And I am imposing upon you enough already. There truly is no need for the added cost of a second room."

He frowned. "While I appreciate your frugality, Miss Crawford, I will not be spending the night sitting up in this public room while it fills with unhappy and intoxicated travelers. And I am not so unchivalrous as to leave you to do so while I slumber peacefully in my private chamber."

Her eyes widened. "I couldn't stay here by myself, my lord. I shall be frightened enough alone in a room."

He peered more closely at her, noting how her hands fidgeted in her lap. "Frightened? What reason have you to be frightened?"

She swallowed. "Only knowing that I am alone and unprotected and the inn is full of strangers," she said and he knew it for a lie—or at least an incomplete truth. Where was her paralyzing fear of strangers when she had walked up to him in the yard of the Bear & Boar in Peckingham?

"The door will be locked," he reasoned.

"Locks are not impenetrable." Her lips pressed into a grim line after delivering this truth.

He looked at her—the way she held her arms close to her body, her shoulders rounded forward, her eyes always darting. Realization dawned on him. She was not submissive. She was fearful. Into what had she entangled him? He was curious, surely, but more than that, he deserved to know from what or whom they were running—if it in fact posed some grave form of danger.

"You are truly frightened to stay alone?" he asked, considering.

She closed her eyes and gave an almost imperceptible nod.

"All right," he conceded. "If you are frightened, Gelert will stay with you in your room."

She said nothing but tilted her head to look below the table where the dog lay.

He nearly laughed at her expression. He had his answer. The threat was not so sinister. Clearly, the prospect of the dog's company frightened her more than being alone. "I only consider your peace of mind, Miss Crawley," he said, folding his hands as he set his elbows on the table. "I will be happy to keep him in my room, if that is more comfortable for you."

She peeked at the dog again then picked up the uneaten half of her pie. It did not receive her full attention but, in fairness, neither did his. He watched her as he ate, just as she watched the people in the room. The door to the common room opened again and both of them turned to take in the new arrival. This time, two men, large and roughened, joined the growing assembly. They stood at the entrance, dripping from the rain, and surveyed the room with an inspection more thorough than necessary to simply assess the size of the crowd.

Miss Crawley turned back to her plate and lowered her eyes. She drew one delicate hand slowly up and tested the knot of auburn hair at the nape of her neck, the action having the effect of tilting her face away from the door. "Do you know," she said, her voice just a bit higher pitched than he recalled it, "With so many arrivals, it seems rather uncharitable for me to claim a room for myself at all." Her eyes darted everywhere except to meet with his. "I'm sure we could make some other arrangement. I could ask after a place with the maids, or I could...I suppose I could even sleep on a pallet in the corner of your room, my lord."

Michael halted, his mug of ale halfway to his lips. "Sleep in the corner of my room?"

"Like a page might," she offered.

He gaped at her. "A page? Do you mean like my attendant?"

She swallowed. "Of a sort, my lord."

Michael set his mug of ale onto the weathered table and considered his companion. "What of the fact that I'm not a medieval knight and not in need of a squire, Miss Crawley?"

Her mouth curved into a nervous smile that was gone as quickly as it appeared. "No. Certainly not. I only meant that I should be no trouble at all and would be out of your way. In the corner."

Michael watched her: hands in her lap, eyes cast downward, shoulders rounded forward. Was she so meek, or did she fancy herself a clever actress? Was she truly so frightened that she would prefer to stay in the room of a stranger? Or was she playing a game? She could not be a fugitive. She was not wily enough to be running from the authorities. But was she wily enough to believe she could trick him into compromising her? She'd already denied it, but that could be a lie. It would not be the only one she'd offered him.

His gaze shifted once more to the two men whose arrival had so discomfited her. They had taken seats and food, but the dark-haired one, with a bulbous nose and a scar above his left eye, continued to scan the room as he ate. Their presence didn't bother Michael. He knew his own appearance was sometimes intimidating to strangers and so rarely judged others based solely upon a hard-worn look. He supposed, however, if he considered the men from Miss Crawley's perspective, they might seem rather menacing. Their habit of checking the room did lend an air of more sinister purpose. If one were a slip of a girl, alone in a strange place, letting one's imagination wander as to the intent of men such as these, he could imagine that would be very frightening indeed.

Michael considered his pretty and mysterious companion. Empathy with her plight may be admirable, but he could not risk such softheartedness— not when he had yet to understand her purpose. "No, Miss Crawley. You shall be just fine in your own room. And that is the end of it."

# Chapter Four

By the time the meat pies were gone, the public room was crowded to the point of discomfort and so loud that one could not even think. Michael suggested they pass the remainder of the evening in the rooms upstairs and Miss Crawley was enthusiastically in favor of this proposal. She lowered her head as soon as she rose from her seat and kept it thus as she walked—briskly—in the direction of the stairs. Still stiff from days of travel, Michael followed at a more relaxed pace, with Gelert at his side. Whether due to his size or his canine companion, he drew more attention in crossing the room than Miss Crawley, and it occurred to him that she had intentionally hurried ahead to avoid that very notice.

The upstairs hall was narrow and paneled with dark wood. At its far end were two rooms, on opposite sides of the hall that had been assigned for their use. In Michael's experience, coaching inns varied greatly in cleanliness, so when he opened the doors to each in succession, he was pleased to discover two clean, if not spacious, chambers that were essentially mirror images of one another. Each contained a neatly made bed tucked under the low sloping ceiling of one exterior wall, a small fireplace, a pair of chairs, and a window that looked out over the increasingly chaotic yard of the coaching inn. The windows were large enough such that, on a brighter day, they likely allowed a cheery amount of daylight into the rooms. That was not the case this day, however, as the storm had darkened the skies earlier than usual for the night. As he inspected the rooms, Michael lit candles in each to add to the glow from the low fires that had been set for them.

"You may have your choice of room, Miss Crawley," Michael said once they had completed their investigation and stood in the hall between the two open doors.

She hesitated, looking back down the narrow hall toward the noise that echoed from below. "I…It doesn't matter," she said. "That is, either would be fine, my lord. Thank you."

Since there was no difference between the rooms, Michael simply shrugged and said, "Very well. You shall take the right and I shall take the left." He handed her the large iron key that had opened the door on the right. "I believe Albert will be up shortly with your things."

She looked down at the key he'd given her, drawing his attention to where she held it. It looked very large in her small hand. She stared down at it for moment as though she wasn't quite sure what to do with it.

"Is there a problem, Miss Crawley?"

"No." Her attention shifted from the key to the dog and then again to the far end of the hall from which they had come.

"All right, then," he said. He turned toward the left door and signaled to Gelert to follow.

"I've changed my mind," she blurted, then proceeded to say the last thing in the world he would have expected. "I accept your offer. Regarding the dog. I would like for him—" she cast another furtive glance at Gelert, "—to stay with me, in my room."

Michael halted. He pivoted slowly on one heel and faced her, making no effort to hide his surprise. "Are you sure?"

She swallowed. "Yes, if that is still all right."

He was convinced she was not at all sure, given how she continued to stare at the dog as though he might lunge at her without notice, but he gave a slight nod anyway. "Of course. If that is your preference."

"It is, only—" her brows furrowed as she looked more closely at Gelert, "—if he is to stay with me, what shall I do for him? What does he require?"

"He shan't require anything. He ate this morning and he has been outside."

"He only eats in the morning?"

"Only in the morning," Michael confirmed.

"He must eat a great deal."

"A fair amount, Miss Crawley." Michael peered at her. He knew almost nothing about her and found her nearly impossible to decipher, with one exception: She was without question terrified of dogs. For the entire ride in the carriage thus far, she had not allowed more than ninety seconds to pass without verifying the dog's present position and state. He knew with absolute certainty that he had not misjudged her fear of the dog. It was indeed palpable. What he had not considered, however, was that her fear of Gelert might pale in comparison to a still greater threat. From whom had she fled? What misery chased her?

He could pose the question, but she would not answer. Instead he said, "The dog requires nothing, so would you like him in your room or no?"

"Yes," she said, though she looked a bit sickened by the decision.

"Very well, Gelert will be your companion for the evening," Michael said, then he gestured to Gelert, who lumbered calmly through the doorway to the right.

She watched him as he went and stared into the room as though hesitant to enter herself.

"He shall be fine, Miss Crawley, and so shall you," Michael said, but when she followed the dog into the room, closing and locking the door behind her, he remained in the hall, puzzling over the woman. He considered the locked door and turned his attention to the bend in the hall that led to the stairwell. Just who might be ascending those stairs in search of her? Had that very person been in the common room as they'd eaten? Without knowing what threat chased her, Michael had no way of knowing if the threat loomed nearby—perhaps even now in the public room below.

He shook his head in an attempt to clear his mind of the thoughts. Was paranoia catching? Why had he always been one to champion the weak and wounded? Why should he offer his protection when he knew not from what he protected her? He may simply be protecting her from a sound thrashing from her parents and a lecture not to run away again. What if he was aiding her in something wholly rash and irresponsible and she was better off, in fact, to be discovered?

The shape of a man rounded the shadowed bend in the hall and startled Michael from his thoughts. Almost immediately, however, he recognized the brawny shape and stalking gate of Albert.

"Is anything amiss, sir?" he asked, approaching Michael with an odd, assessing look.

Alarm at Albert's question drew him a step toward the stairwell. "Amiss? Why?" he asked, tilting to head in an attempt to peer around the corner. "Is there some reason to believe so?"

The curiosity in Albert's expression grew to confusion. "Only that you're lurking about in the hall, sir."

Michael stepped back again. He straightened his shoulders and tugged at the front of his waistcoat. "I do not lurk."

Albert shrugged.

"I was only thinking," Michael insisted.

"Too much of that's a dangerous thing, I say." Even in the dim light, Michael saw the corner of the coachman's mouth tip into a wry smile.

There was too much wisdom in the declaration for Michael's comfort. Now that his thoughts were consumed with possibilities as to the threat that chased his female companion, he would not be at ease until he learned the truth. "I'm afraid I agree with you, Albert."

Albert cocked a questioning brow. "I suspect there's a meaning in there, sir."

"There is. It means I've acquired a room for you."

"For me?" The coachman's expression could not have been more stunned at this announcement.

In truth, Michael was a bit surprised himself. He had not realized he had made the decision until he'd said the words. "Yes," he said, lowering his voice. "Miss Crawley and I shall be passing the night in the same room. For her protection only," he was quick to add.

The coachman's eyes narrowed in judgment. "Do you think that's wise, sir?"

Michael stared mutely back at Albert. No, he did not. It was likely a terrible decision on his part. But it had been her idea, hadn't it? She had *asked* to stay in the same room as he did, then proceeded to behave as though the prospect of staying alone frightened her beyond reason. She could be a brilliant liar and hoping to make sure she was thoroughly compromised by the night's end. Or perhaps she was a thief. Then again, he'd looked at her hands—half the time she'd been nervously wringing them in her lap. No. She was no thief. A liar, perhaps. But he could not seem to ignore the fact that she was not lying about her fear.

Michael stepped forward and spoke quietly, so the subject of their discussion would not overhear. "She is running from something."

"How do you know?"

"I can see it in her. We have been in war, Albert." Michael's voice softened as he mentioned that time in both of their pasts. "We have seen men killed and we have watched others with the same memories be asked to go into battle again. I never understood what real fear looked like until I looked into the face of those men." Michael shook his he continued, "This woman fears something or someone that much. I recognize it in her and you would too, if you spent any time in her company."

Michael did not add that what intrigued him beyond the need to know the origin of her fear was her strength against it. He had witnessed the sort of fear that took root in the very soul and held a person, planted, unable to march forward. He'd seen strong men—prideful men—crippled by it. Unlike those men, she had not crumpled into a heap of begging desperation, too ashamed to meet his eyes. She'd looked into his face and asked for the protection of an animal she feared nearly as much.

Michael looked at the door and again down the corridor.

If her fears were justified…

"Who is she?" The coachman asked.

Michael sighed. "I have no earthly idea who she is."

"She gave you a name, didn't she?"

"Indeed. But she hasn't given me *her* name." He shook his head. "She's as much Ana Crawley as I am."

"I don't trust a woman with secrets, sir," Albert said.

Michael looked to the door again, wishing he could not only see into the room but into the woman's head. He didn't trust a secretive woman either. He wanted to know what those secrets were, particularly if they placed her in any danger. "That is probably wise, Albert. I've tried to glean why she is traveling to London alone, but her reasons don't fit together."

"But she's not traveling alone, is she sir?"

Michael paused and lifted his head.

"I wonder at just why she's traveling with you." Albert crossed his arms in front of his chest and leaned one shoulder against the paneled wall. "It's good of you to help a woman in distress, but that common room is fair to overflowing with witnesses if she wants to be certain she's found in the wrong room, sir. Or the right room, depending on how you see it." He pursed his lips briefly before he continued. "I wouldn't want you to find your charity is more costly than you expect is all."

Michael nodded slowly. "Your point is well taken, Albert. The innkeeper knows that we have taken two rooms. If we are discreet, no one need know which rooms we occupy." Albert lifted one shoulder in unconvinced acceptance of Michael's theory.

"And if I am wrong," Michael felt the need to add, "It won't matter. I won't be forced into anything. There may be a hassle, but not a wedding, I promise you." Michael ignored Albert's continued skepticism in the face of this assertion and turned to rap gently on the door to Miss Crawley's room. When he received no response, he knocked again. "Miss Crawley?"

The door opened—only a crack at first and then the rest of the way. Expectant green eyes stared back at him.

"The crowd below stairs is becoming unruly," he said. "For your safety, I suggest we pass the night in the same room."

For a moment, she only blinked up at him, then she exhaled her obvious relief. "Thank you, my lord." She lowered her eyes again and bit her lip—drawing his eyes to her mouth.

He cursed inwardly. Perhaps Albert was right. She was a bit too dramatic and mysterious to even be believed. If he was being pulled into some manipulative game, he deserved his consequences, whatever they may be. "The privy is outside and it will be full dark soon. I suggest you make use of it now," he said, more sharply than he had intended. "Albert will show you there."

She looked over his shoulder at Albert, then gave a brief nod. Michael moved from the doorway and she stepped into the hall.

Albert bore a displeased look but said nothing to him as he handed Miss Crawley's satchel and a bag of Michael's things over to Michael. "This way, miss." He paused only briefly then strode toward the stairwell, Miss Crawley hurrying to stay close behind.

Michael walked into the room and considered it. Gelert stood at attention near the fireplace, watching him. He tilted his head to one side.

Michael set the bags on the bed and scowled at him. "You should know your place as well." Whether or not his decision was a wise one, he did not need his dog or his coachman questioning his reasons.

*Damn.* They had *him* questioning his reasons. Why did she have him so intrigued? Was he over-imagining her need for protection? Maybe his mind was as plagued as his leg by the days spent on the road. Just who the hell was she anyway? What the hell was she running away from?

He looked down at the bag of her things. It was worn and too small to contain enough for a journey of any significant duration. What did she have in there? What sort of person rifled through another's things?

*One who had a right to know just whom he was harboring.*

He plunked the bag onto the bed and untied it, irked as he did so that she'd turned him into a snooping busybody.

\* \* \* \*

As the rain still fell, though not as violently as before, Juliana saw to her needs quickly. She also did not want to encounter others and the sooner she returned to the upstairs room, the lesser the chance of that occurring. She was grateful beyond measure that she would not pass the night alone.

Now that some moments had passed, however, the relief was mingled with apprehension of another sort. She had interacted more today with his lordship than she had with any man in her entire life, save her father. Now she would be spending the night in the same room. The thought made her anxious. Oddly, it also made her a little curious—excited even. No doubt her father would have much to say about the matter if he knew.

*You're just as wanton as your mother.*
*I always knew you would turn out like her.*

Juliana took an odd, defiant pleasure in knowing that her father would object. A small smile curved on her lips.

"What has you traveling to London, miss?" The coachman's question pulled her from her thoughts and cleared her smile. The question was given casually enough but Juliana noticed the way he slowed his pace, awaiting her answer, not willing to continue until he received it.

She had never interacted with anyone's coachman before, other than seeing one now and again when the duchess visited Beadwell, but they had always seemed to mind their business. Apparently this coachman was not of that sort.

"I must see a solicitor about some arrangements that have been made for me," she said, despite feeling quite certain his lordship's coachman was even less entitled to explanations than his employer.

The man peered at her. "Seems to me," the coachman said, "if someone went to the trouble of making arrangements for you, they might have included the arrangements for your travel."

Though she did not feel it, Juliana chose confidence as a tactic. She lifted her chin and met the man's gaze directly. "Yes, it would seem that way, wouldn't it?" Then she turned and stalked toward the stairs, cheeks warming as she marched.

She knew he followed because she heard his footfalls on the stair treads behind her, but she did not look back. She proceeded directly to the room at the end of the hall in which a strange man and his monstrous dog awaited to spend the evening with her. She found the door unlocked and went inside, not bothering to bid the coachman good night.

She turned after closing the door behind her to find her companion for the evening standing over her satchel, unashamedly perusing its contents.

"What are you doing?"

He looked up, unabashed. He didn't even pull his hand out of the bag. Surely any person with a conscience would have pulled his hand away. Even her father would have pulled his hand away if caught, and he had no conscience whatsoever.

"My coachman advises me not to trust you," his lordship said matter-of-factly.

Of course he does. "I don't care what your John Coachman thinks of me," she said with more pique than she'd ever in her life delivered aloud.

His eyes narrowed and he stepped toward her, making her want to step away but she did not. "My 'John Coachman' has a name," he bit out. "He is Albert Finn and he served his king and country under Wellington, so you would do well to speak of him respectfully."

Juliana paused, startled by his vehemence. Didn't all the aristocracy call their man John Coachman? Who was this man who demonstrated enough arrogance to unapologetically search her possessions, yet not only knew his coachman's given name, but insisted she know it as well? "I meant no disrespect to Mr. Finn, my lord," she said slowly, wondering where his mood may go next. "I only point out that he knows even less of me than you do sir, and you,"—she glanced pointedly at the satchel, "—are presently going through my things."

He let out a dismissive huff of air. "If you mean to imply that I have gleaned a greater understanding of you by viewing the contents of your bag, you are mistaken. Your possessions are a collection of pointless objects. Let us evaluate." He returned to the bag, lowered his head, and rummaged again. He produced one of her novels and held it aloft. "A book," he announced.

"To pass the time on the journey," she explained, though she imagined that should be quite clear to anyone.

He dropped the book onto the bed and pulled another object from the bag. "A rag."

She stared at the bit of worn fabric clutched in his large hand and felt her cheeks warm. "My underclothes, my lord," she said through gritted teeth. Did he think everyone could afford silks and weekly trips to the dressmakers? Every single garment she owned had been hard won through an unpleasant conversation with her father about the insufficiency of her previous garments for her changing body. That particular garment was at least eight years old.

He tossed her worn chemise onto the bed with the book and produced her hairbrush. "A hairbrush with a broken handle."

"It's perfectly functional."

"And my personal favorite," he continued, in a sing-song tone that bristled up her spine. "A wooden spoon."

Her shoulders stiffened as he lifted the large wooden spoon, worn smooth from years of use, and she carefully schooled her expression. "For courage, my lord."

He looked from her to the wooden utensil and the back again. "For courage?" he asked, his expression dubious.

"For courage," she repeated.

He set the spoon down and came around the bed. "If this is a game, Miss Crawley, you will not win it."

She looked at him in genuine confusion. "I don't know your meaning, my lord."

"As I suspect you well know, this night spent together in one room would see any gently-born lady well and truly compromised, regardless of the fact that I have no intention of touching you. If it is your fantasy that we shall be discovered and I shall be honor bound to rescue you from your pitiful life via a hasty marriage, you should redirect your efforts elsewhere. I am not lord of anything, my 'honor' is weak at best, and I will not marry you no matter who discovers us."

She gaped at him. "That is preposterous. You think this is an elaborate ruse to see myself married to a stranger? You think I lay in wait all morning because I knew that you would stop in Peckingham?" The pitch of her voice rose as she spoke, but she could not stop it. Indignation pushed her forward. "Tell me this, my lord, once I convinced you to take me in, how do you think I brought about the storm that necessitated our stay here?" She spread her warms wide, lifted her palms upward and glared at him. "Do you think I recited some incantation to open the skies and call forth the rain?"

"Don't be absurd," he snapped, but he looked at her, dark eyes full of questions, and she wondered if he wasn't considering it.

She lowered her arms. She softened her tone when she spoke again and despite her best efforts to control it, her voice wavered. "I am not a witch." Her strength grew with the words despite their tentative delivery. She was *not* a witch. Nor was she mad or odd or unnatural, though her own father called her all of those things and more. This man would be her companion for only one more day. She would never see him again and his opinion of her mattered not at all.

She turned away and faced the fire, cursing inwardly at the knowledge that his questions stung all the same. Perhaps the sting would not smart so fiercely if she had not been so comforted by his gesture to allow her into his room. He'd sensed her fear—she'd been unable to hide it—and agreed to protect her. She had felt a wave of gratitude, but there had been more. She had not expected to feel so drawn to his protection, as though the closer she stayed to the fire, the better to keep out the cold.

Then he had doused the warm glow inside her with a frigid gale of accusations.

*Marry him. Never.* Marriage would not be his trap, but hers. Why would she trade one owner for another less than a day after she'd gained her freedom? She had not spent the past years plotting—pilfering pennies one at a time because her miserly father would notice more—only to become prisoner to another man.

"Very well then, Miss Crawley," he said, scooping her possessions from the bed and placing them back into the bag. "Let us assume you have no agenda other than to arrive in London. You have not, however, been fully truthful."

"Neither have you."

He crossed his arms and mulishly waited for her to explain.

"You said you are not lord of anything."

"I am not."

"I have called you lord from the beginning and you've not corrected me."

Just one of his massive shoulders shrugged, as though the observation was not significant enough to warrant the commitment of both. "That is your mistake, not my dishonesty."

She advanced on him. "Why do you travel in a lord's coach?"

"It is my father's coach."

"You are a younger son?"

"I am a bastard son." He stared at her after this declaration and there was so much challenge in it, she could hear the taunt. *If you thought I was a prize to be caught, you were wrong.* She could feel how he dared her to judge him for it.

"If you travel in his coach, you are acknowledged if not legitimate."

"I am acknowledged when it is convenient," he said, tilting his head to one side, "just as you are confiding when it is convenient."

*Drat.* They were back to her again. He was much better at this than she. "I can no longer call you my lord," she pointed out. "What do I call you?"

He paused at this and she congratulated herself for at least causing some disruption of his relentless interrogation. He stared at her with an unsatisfied sort expression, as though he were making an assessment and displeased with the result. He sighed. "Very well. I am Michael Rosevear."

She gave a slight nod. "Mr. Rosevear."

His expression pinched a bit, as though he didn't quite like her speaking his name. "You have your wish now, Miss Crawley. You have my name. And, I think more significantly, you have the protection of both myself and Gelert. I believe now would be an excellent opportunity to explain why such protection is required."

She had made another irreversible blunder. She had been so transparent with her fear that she could no longer deny it. She struggled for an excuse. "I am merely frightened because I have led a sheltered life and I am a woman on my own. I am certain my fears are foolish."

He shook his head. He didn't believe her. She was not surprised. She had not felt particularly confident in her delivery.

"Who do you fear?" he asked.

"I don't have reason to fear anyone," she insisted.

He stepped forward. "Who would follow you?" His tone was louder, more insistent. "If there is no one, then I can only assume your fear was a ruse after all, designed to trap us together in the same chamber."

Juliana's face grew hot in anticipation of what she knew she must reveal. He would not be satisfied without an answer and she could not, in the moment, devise a credible lie. Telling him could be the end of it. Despite his suspicions of her, he'd offered his protection, but would that be withdrawn when he knew the truth? Would he, as most men would, believe she had no right to defy her father? He could march her down to the common room with a clear conscience and announce her identity in the hopes of being rid of her.

Worse still, he could see the weakness in her. She was a grown woman. Admitting to sneaking away from her father's house was also an admission of all the years she had endured until now—all the years of meek acceptance.

She lowered her head, lacking the courage to watch Mr. Rosevear's reaction, hating that he would inevitably be disgusted with her—whether for her past subservience or her present defiance, she would not know until she spoke.

"My father. I suspect my father is pursuing me."

# Chapter Five

*Her father?* "Because you have run away?" Michael asked.

She looked up then. "I have not run away, precisely."

He cast her a dubious look.

"Running away is for children and criminals. I am neither. I am a woman of five and twenty and well capable of charting my own course." She said it with such force, he wondered if she were attempting to convince only him, or both of them. "I am traveling to London because the rest of my life begins there. I will not return to my father's house."

Michael watched her and measured his response. She was defiant enough in the moment to finally deliver some truth, if only he provoked her enough. "My apologies," he said. "You are *traveling* away. Either way, if you believe your father may want to find you and return you home, that does not seem particularly sinister to me."

And that was the trick apparently, for the flash of spirit awoke fully, removing the last of the veil over her now expressive green eyes. Her spine straightened. Her fists clenched at her sides. "If he is pursuing me, it is not out of fatherly concern. It is only because he finds it unacceptable to have been abandoned by both his wife and his daughter."

Now they were getting somewhere. Her mother had left before her. "He pursues you out of pride, then," he offered.

Miss Crawley shrugged and turned to face the fire, her flash of spirit disappointingly short-lived. "That and now he has lost his housekeeper."

"He cannot afford to keep servants?"

Her shoulders were wooden and her back straight. She delivered her response to the flames. "He chooses not to incur the expense."

"That is not the same," Michael said, his voice softening.

She turned, then, and faced him. "Yes. I know."

Gone was the meek, subservient posture he had seen in the common room and just moments before when she'd first mentioned her father, but also missing was the burst of indignation. She stood, spine straight, with quiet dignity in the face of this admission.

He nodded. "An indication, I suppose, of why your mother chose to leave."

"We had a housekeeper, then, before she left."

Gelert chose that moment to brush his large body against Michael's leg.

"Did you?" He asked, absently reaching down to stroke the dog.

She eyed Gelert cautiously as she answered. "Yes. Her name was Mrs. Grace Sanderson. My father released her on the twenty-second of September, eleven days after my mother's departure."

Michael's hand stilled atop Gelert's fur. She remembered the precise day. "Were you very close to your housekeeper, then?" he asked, his voice soft and cautious, not wanting to close the gate that he'd opened. He deserved answers, didn't he? Deserved or not, he chose not to dwell on why he wanted them so badly.

"No."

Had she averted her eyes or otherwise appeared discomfited, he would have interpreted the response as a protective one. But she met his gaze directly, brow furrowed in confusion at his question. She had him doubting his own common sense. He felt compelled to explain.

"I only ask because you recall the day so clearly. I assumed it bore some significance."

Her gaze drifted away then. "He wrote her a letter of dismissal. It was dated."

"Still," he pressed. "It was months ago."

"It was years ago."

He realized his error, then, in presuming she referred to the past September. "How old were you when your mother left?"

"Eleven."

"And where did she go?"

She lifted her green eyes to his again and spoke firmly. "London. That's why I must go to London. I go to my mother."

"I see," Michael lied. If she'd known where her mother was all along, why hadn't she gone before now? Why hadn't her mother taken her daughter in the first place? Or sent for her? Or arranged for transport to London? Was she to meet her mother at a solicitor's office? None of it made sense. In his experience stories that did not make sense, were generally untrue. That bit about the housekeeper's dismissal letter sealed it. She had to have pulled the date out of the air. Liars, he knew, often over-embellished details.

He'd believed her when she discussed her father, but this bit about her mother—it was false. The more she confounded him, the more determined he became to make sense of her.

Thunder sounded and Miss Crawley's eyes widened. She immediately went to the window. "Do you think the storm is strengthening again?"

How the devil was he to know that any better than she? "I certainly hope not."

Perhaps it was the frustration in his tone that drew her attention away from the rapidly blackening night. She looked over her shoulder at him. "You are as anxious to reach London as I," she observed.

"For several reasons, yes."

He spoke sharply and she understood his implication, for she gave a small, silent nod of acceptance that she was now one of these reasons. She lowered her eyes and he felt a stab of guilt for his insensitive comment. He then attempted to immediately retract the emotion, chiding himself for his weakness. Why should he feel guilt for identifying the inconvenience she presented? He was providing a considerable service in conveying her to London and she was repaying him with dishonesty. When she importuned him in Peckingham, she'd not clarified that she required protection as well as transport, had she?

She had not. *She* was the one who should feel apologetic.

"You said Mr. Finn served under Wellington. Did you as well?" she asked, stepping back from the window.

"What?" He had heard her question. He simply wasn't sure why she'd asked it.

"Did you fight in the war?"

His lips pressed into a grim line. It seemed an odd and, frankly, personal, change of topic.

Her explanation was delivered in a rush. "I only wonder about your injury," she said, "if it makes your journey more difficult. Did you acquire it in service to The Crown?" He considered her carefully, mused upon the fact that she was not entitled to inquiries of her own, and then, to his great surprise, answered anyway. "I was shot, yes. 'In service to The Crown' as you say. Or to my father, however one views it."

"In service to your father?" she asked, glancing down at his leg.

"My father purchased the officer's commission. Albert was one of the men under my command. He dragged me to safety after I was shot. The bullet was removed, but the muscle was damaged."

"I am sorry for your injury, my lord."

"I do not require your pity, Miss Crawley. I am not typically so affected, but days of confinement have taken their toll and I am unusually stiff, making the cane a necessary concession." He couldn't fathom why it mattered that she knew that—knew that he was, in fact, a capable person—but for some reason he felt compelled to clarify. As punishment for his vanity perhaps, he became presently aware of the tightness in the back of his thigh.

"I see," she said.

Michael crossed the room, lowered himself to the chair near the fire, and stretched the offending limb out before him. He faced her, indicating the smaller chair, and she came to sit across from him. He considered this stranger he harbored. She sat primly, hands in her lap. They were small and pale. She was pale enough that as the room darkened, her skin—her hands, face, throat—seemed to reflect the glow of the fire, giving off an unearthly light. Everything about her, even her appearance, seemed impossible to believe.

"Where did your journey begin?" she asked, just as he was about to launch into more questions of his own.

"Yorkshire."

"It is a long way between Yorkshire and London," she observed. "Do you travel it often?"

He sensed she was asking questions to prevent him from doing the same, but he provided the answer anyway. "No."

"Is Yorkshire your home?" she asked.

For one who claimed not to prefer conversation, she seemed rather bursting with it, now that he was the topic. He looked to the fire. Was Yorkshire his home? It was and it wasn't. He'd been at Rose Hall for three years. He'd brought considerable change there—improvements to the estate, the addition of the brewery. Rose Hall was his in all but one minor aspect. "Rose Hall is my father's estate," he said, turning back to her, "but I live there, yes."

"Rose Hall." She said it as though she were attempting to imagine it, though he couldn't fathom how she would. He'd given no description other than its location. "You do not travel between London and Yorkshire on the same schedule as your father?"

Michael couldn't stop the bitter exhale of laughter that escaped at her question. "My father does not travel to Yorkshire and I am rarely summoned to London."

In response to his declaration, she tilted her head to one side and peered at him with open curiosity. "Your answers only beg more questions, Mr. Rosevear."

He met her eyes. "I am familiar with the frustration."

He won the challenge. Her gaze shifted to her lap before she continued, ignoring his reference to her own lack of detail.

"If your father's estate is in Yorkshire, wouldn't he travel there regularly?"

"Rose Hall is not my father's primary estate." When Michael had arrived there, the estate had been sorely neglected and the nearby village suffered as a result. He had made changes, returned prosperity to the estate. No one had granted him the authority to do so, but no one had paid attention enough to object either.

"You seem very fortunate to have your father's acknowledgement."

Michael scoffed. "I am acknowledged when he finds it convenient.

"You said that before. What do you mean by it?"

Michael didn't hesitate in informing her. She may as well know for certain that he was not a prize to be caught. He slouched further into his chair, noting the spots of uneven padding as he did. "I mean precisely that," he said. "I am acknowledged when doing so serves a purpose for my father. There is a pattern to our interactions. I am summoned when I am needed and sent away again when I am not."

She sat very still, watching him with eerily perceptive eyes. "When you are needed?" she prompted.

Michael obliged her with an explanation. "I told you my father purchased my officer's commission. He didn't do so out of duty to his bastard son, I promise you. When my father felt someone should represent the family in the war effort, I was the ideal candidate—recognized but illegitimate, thus conveniently expendable. When I returned,"—he glanced down at his leg—"imperfect, I was banished to Yorkshire in the same manner I was sent away to school as a young boy."

"Banished?"

He shrugged. "No one wants their by-blows lurking about, do they? Especially not when he has a wife and real son to be concerned about."

Her expression was careful, but curious. "Is Rose Hall comfortable?" she asked, and he thought it an odd response.

"Very." It had been neglected when he arrived but wasn't so anymore.

"Perhaps banishment is not the worst of all scenarios."

"Perhaps not, Miss Crawley." He sat forward, resting his elbows on his knees and studied the contrast between her blank, placid expression and her busy, darting eyes. She was full of contradictions—meek then defiant, quiet then curious, pale yet striking. He couldn't puzzle her out. Her comment made him wonder what sort of worse scenarios she was imagining.

She did not show pity for his complaints and he preferred it. Gaining her sympathy was not his purpose in answering her questions. There was a salient point she was better off to understand. "The significance," he told her, "is not that I was sent away, but that I have been summoned again. This time to be married."

This drew surprise from her. "Your father dictates that you marry?"

"My father has chosen her."

"Why do you allow him to choose?"

He lifted a brow.

Her hands fluttered up from their place in her lap and then lowered again. "It is just that…well, you don't seem the sort not to have your own thoughts on the subject."

"I do have thoughts on the subject," he assured her.

She leaned ever so slightly forward in her chair and he knew she waited to hear.

"My only thought is that I want Rose Hall."

Her face registered confusion at his words and he explained. "I am wiser today than when my father summoned me to take an officer's commission in the army. If my father wants something more from me, I will ask for something in return."

"Rose Hall."

"Indeed."

"Can he give it to you," she asked, "if you are not his legitimate heir?"

"It is not entailed. My father has no interest in it. The generally accepted story is that his grandfather won the property in a game of cards and renamed it Rose Hall so that it seemed to have always belonged to the Rosevear title."

"So he has given you the family name. You are Rosevear and he is Rosevear."

"Not precisely. The family surname is Brinley. I am not Michael Brinley." Rosevear as a surname was simply a made up name—a way of acknowledging a connection, but not a legitimate one.

She nodded, but her eyes held more questions. "There is one part of your bargain I don't understand. I can surmise why you would want Rose Hall, but why does your father want to choose your bride?"

"For the same reason all members of the aristocracy choose their mates—wealth. He must preserve his by supplementing it. His heir is too young to be married, and he would not align his legitimate son with a merchant's daughter anyway. And so he offers me. In addition to what she brings to me with the marriage, her father settles an amount on my father and in return they have connections to the aristocracy, even if it is on the wrong side of the blanket."

"His legitimate son? You have a brother?"

"The future Marquess of Rosevear is currently twelve." Michael had only met the boy once. He didn't think of him as a brother, but he supposed he was.

She watched him closely, likely finding the traces of bitterness in his carefully guarded expression. "So you see, Miss Crawley, I am a desirable match for only one woman—my father's heiress. If I were to marry any other woman,"—he met her eyes, not allowing her to look away—"she would acquire only a penniless bastard who has lost his father's support."

She did not retreat from the challenge in his gaze. Instead she straightened her shoulders and said quite calmly and firmly, "It is fortunate, then, that I don't wish to marry you or anyone else, Mr. Rosevear, as I have already explained."

Michael found himself smiling at her response, for it was delivered entirely without pique this time. He preferred pragmatism. He didn't believe her, of course. Even if she had no designs on him, surely she intended to marry at some point. There was no other security for a woman.

He leaned back in his chair and marveled at how, after hours in her presence, he still had no way of anticipating her. "You must admit you've not been particularly forthcoming about yourself, Miss Crawley. Your unwillingness to give the details of your purpose only leads my imagination to darker and more fanciful images of the truth.

"Perhaps you are *not* a gentlewoman bent on forcing me to the altar. Then again, you may not be respectable at all and you mean to seduce me then rob me of all I have. You cannot blame me for my suspicions. You were, after all, discerning enough to make your plea to a man in a very fine coach."

"I consider neither intent to be respectable, Mr. Rosevear." Then she blushed, and softened her voice. "And I assure you, I am quite incapable of seduction."

"Are you?" he asked, causing her eyes to widen in surprise.

Was she? Her modest rag of a dress was no paramour's costume and she had not flirted with him at any point, but she was rather fetching in a mysteriously haunting way, blush staining her pale cheeks. The firelight flickered in her now uncertain green eyes, giving them flashes of gold and amber. He realized one benefit of having her in his room was that she would remove her bonnet and it occurred to him that he very much wanted to see her hair without the hat.

"As neither of us possesses any seductive intent, Miss Crawley, perhaps it is relevant that we discuss sleeping arrangements for the evening."

She swallowed and managed to lose the frightened mouse expression his mention of seduction had inspired. "There is no need for discussion. I shall sleep by the fire."

"On the floor?"

"On a blanket."

"A blanket that is lying on the floor."

She nodded. "Yes."

"That is your plan?"

Her brow furrowed in confusion. "Yes."

He sighed. "The trouble with your plan, Miss Crawley, is that I am not an ass."

She blinked.

"I cannot consider myself a gentleman of any sort if I sleep in the bed and require you to sleep on the floor next to the dog."

That caught her attention. She immediately dropped her eyes to where the dog lay on the floor near his chair. Then she looked at the space immediately in front of the fireplace, making an unveiled assessment of the distance between these two locations. She lifted her attention to Michael again. "I shall be perfectly comfortable in front of the fire."

*Damn.* Michael sighed heavily and pushed himself up from his chair. "I shall sleep on the floor. You shall sleep on the bed."

She shook her head and rose as well. "Thank you, but no. I get quite cold at night and will be more comfortable near the fire. It truly is my preference."

Michael pursed his lips. "Are you usually this stubborn, Miss Crawley?" She had refused to even say the words 'on the floor' as though calling it 'near the fire' would make it more palatable.

"I am not being stubborn. Only honest. It is my preference to sleep here." She opened her hand to indicate the space at their feet.

No it wasn't. No one preferred to sleep on the floor. There wasn't even a rug. But if she insisted upon stubbornness what was he to do? "Very well, Miss Crawley," he said, shaking his head. "You may help yourself to as much of the bedding as you would like. I will make do with whatever is left."

She nodded and walked around him to the bed. She peeked under the drawn up quilt, presumably to assess the condition and quantity of the bed linens. Then she efficiently flipped the top of the quilt back. She quickly folded it in half and then quarters before draping it over her arm. She took one of two pillows that rested near the headboard. "This is all I will need."

She returned to the spot in front of the fire and he moved away, clearing the space for her. He made no attempt to hide the fact that he watched her as she unfolded the quilt and refolded it lengthwise, thus to provide both cushion underneath her and warmth above. She shook it with a snap and bent forward to lay it on the floor between the chairs and the fireplace. She set the pillow at one end of the blanket before placing her hands on her hips to briefly survey her makeshift sleeping pallet.

Michael walked to the bed and saw that she had left him a thin coverlet that would be more than sufficient, as he was usually too warm in the night. He unbuttoned his frock coat and removed it, draping it across the side of the bed that would remain unused. He did the same with his buff-colored waistcoat and untied his cravat. When he glanced back at Miss Crawley, he found her watching him, her bonnet removed and resting on the chair upon which she had recently sat.

Her hair was very auburn—darker in shade than he would have guessed given the paleness of her skin. He wondered how long it might be and how she would look with it down around her shoulders. Even still knotted at her nape, the effect of having it fully uncovered brightened the green in her eyes and the contrast of her dark lashes.

They stood a moment, watching each other, before she averted her gaze. She pushed her bonnet aside and sat on the edge of the chair to remove her shoes. Then she straightened her skirts, lowered herself to the floor and quite neatly slid into the pocket she'd created with her quilt.

Michael sat on the bed and removed his own boots. He pulled the hem of his shirt loose from the waist of his trousers. He left both garments on, considering that he should offer her the coverlet as well, given how overdressed he was for sleeping. He didn't, though. He walked to the room's one table and blew out the candles there before returning to the bed, pulling back the coverlet, and stretching himself out for the night.

He peeked at Miss Crawley as he did so. She had turned on her side, facing the flames. When he lay his head on the pillow and closed his eyes, he saw her still. He decided her coloring was appealing, even if it was unconventional. She was far from buxom, but as he'd watched her thin and nimble form move about the room, he'd decided he rather liked her shape as well. And she'd been intently watching him as he removed his clothing. Damn it. She *was* capable of seduction, even if not overtly so. She had not flirted with him or touched him. But then there was nothing so alluring as a mystery was there? Bollocks. It seemed a part of him rather hoped her intent was seduction. The fleecing may well be worth it.

He dismissed the thought and sternly reminded himself the part of him that wished for seduction was the not the part that should be allowed to make decisions. Her appeal derived from the mystery, nothing more. He had only to unravel it and this irrational attraction would fade.

He opened his eyes and lifted himself onto one elbow. "Shall we have a bedtime story, Miss Crawley? You still haven't explained your purpose in London."

She twisted inside her blanket to face him, rolling to rest on the opposite shoulder. "You said in the coach that I could keep my secrets."

"That was before I discovered you were smuggling wooden spoons," he teased.

He watched her pink lips tip up at one corner and he was glad he'd nearly coaxed a smile from her. She had not produced a single smile in all the hours of their acquaintance so far, now that he thought on it. She'd intermittently moved between meek silence and verbal gamesmanship to evade his search for answers, but all the while she'd been deadly serious. The expression seemed even more fleeting in the inconsistent firelight. He found he wanted to coax another smile from her—a laugh even—just to know if he could.

"What do you think the innkeeper thinks of our odd little party?" he asked.

She looked at him and for a moment, he half expected her to roll away again or say something along the lines of *I'm sure I don't know, Mr. Rosevear,* but then her lips curved and she spoke.

"Since you bring your dog into your bedchamber and splurge on private rooms for your coachman, I am sure he finds you quite eccentric."

Michael laughed. "And not you?"

She shook her head. "As I've not been introduced, nor our relationship clarified, I can only hope he assumes I am your wife. If he believes so, I've done nothing for him to consider abnormal."

Michael considered this. He had not introduced her, had he? "I suppose that could be true."

"Of course," she said, eyes glinting in the firelight, "yours is a very fine coach, as you've pointed out. And your clothes, though rumpled from travel, appear of high quality. So, if I am your wife, you've been rather miserly with my allowance," she said, briefly opening her blanket pocket to reveal her drab dress.

"Have I?"

She nodded. "Indeed. That is in awfully poor taste, given how you spoil your dog and your coachman."

He laughed aloud. Where had this wit been hiding? "So again, it is my eccentricity?"

"I am afraid so, Mr. Rosevear."

She smiled fully then, a wide smile that rounded her flushed her complexion and set her eyelids fluttering briefly closed as she rested her check upon the pillow.

Yes. Entirely worth a fleecing.

He forced himself to lie back and gaze at the ceiling. How had he distracted himself from his purpose? If he did not solve the mystery of Miss Ana Crawley soon, he would be completely enamored of her by the time they reached London.

# Chapter Six

Michael wasn't sure what caused him to wake in the night, but the dark and the quiet told him it was still very much night as opposed to morning. He turned his head to find Gelert, upright and alert, sitting on his haunches and staring across the room.

Michael stilled. An intruder?

As slowly and quietly as he could, he turned his head and as little of his body as possible to peek at what had Gelert so intent.

It was her, cast in the dim light of the moon.

She sat on the floor like a child with her legs crossed, a long, thick braid snaking down her straight spine. She was holding something in her lap, but he couldn't quite make it out.

Saying nothing, he rolled his body enough to consider her more thoroughly. Realization dawned. She was sitting up, eyes trained on the door to their chamber, holding the damned wooden spoon.

For courage, she'd said.

His eyes quickly surveyed the rest of the room to assure himself only the three of them were present. The door was still shut and locked. The window intact. Nothing was out of order, save her increasingly strange behavior. He sighed audibly and sat up, swinging his legs to the edge of the bed. This gained her attention and she turned, eyes wide in the moonlight.

"What the devil are you doing?" he asked.

She swallowed. "I couldn't sleep."

He peered at her. "So you thought you had better sit up all night and watch the door like some unarmed sentry?"

She only stared back at him.

He rose from the bed, trying not to wince as he put weight on his leg. He waited a moment to gain his stability then walked stiffly to where she sat. Her eyes, round and uncertain, followed him on his path until she stared up at him from the floor as he towered over her. He held out a hand to help her rise.

She took it, placing her bare hand in his. It felt small. She rose, in one fluid movement and immediately tugged at the hand he held, but he did not release it. He held her there, facing him, mere inches separating them.

"I'm only watching," she said quietly. "You...you can't know who might be lurking around this place."

"And if we are attacked, you will defend us with a wooden spoon?"

She blushed at his remark and he regretted the tease. The spoon was a poor sword however

"You don't need this," he said, taking the spoon from her grasp. "While you are traveling with me, you are under my protection." He cast a glance over his shoulder. "And Gelert's."

At his words, the veil of inscrutable expression that seemed to guard her every thought fell away. She looked up at him with the wide wondrous eyes of a child and he was nearly overcome by the naked emotion in them—a startlingly bald combination of relief, gratitude, and hope that made him feel intoxicatingly heroic.

"Do you mean it?" she asked, her voice a trembling whisper.

"I always say what I mean." And because it seemed the thing to do next, he pulled her to him and held her, as his mother had held him as a boy and soothed the fears of a bad dream.

He half expected her to pull away from his embrace, but she did not. She burrowed her face into his shoulder and clung to the comfort and reassurance he offered. He could feel the tiny quakes in her body as she still shivered from the fear that had kept her on edge and on guard all through the night.

He ran his hand along her back to soothe her until the shivers began to subside. When she no longer shook with fear, he was left holding a woman up against the full length of him—a mysterious and appealing woman who'd gazed at him like a hero. Awareness of their contact moved gradually through him like a tangible thing—a serpent that slid, unhurried, from his shoulders to his feet, awakening the sensation of each place it roamed until he was alive with the pleasure of having this woman pressed against him.

He probably should have let her go then.

No. He should *definitely* have let her go.

Instead, he placed his chin atop her hair and allowed his hand to continue stroking, up and down, rhythmically, along the length of her back. Each time he reached the gentle inward curve at the base of her spine, it teased him, tempting him lower. But each time he halted there and forced his hand to slide back upward.

Then she sighed—a blissful, melting sigh that blew warm breath onto his chest through the thin lawn of his shirt.

While one hand kept her firmly pressed to him, he placed his other hand beneath her chin and gently lifted her face to his view. He knew the kiss was inevitable the moment his gaze met haunting green eyes and lips parted in question.

*I am going to kiss you.*

He didn't say it, but allowed his attention to linger on her delicate mouth in such a way his intent could not be mistaken. He waited so she would have every chance to pull away, turn her face, deny him. When she did not, a boyish victory swelled in him and he lowered his lips to hers.

She didn't pull back from the touch of his mouth on hers. For a moment, she offered neither resistance nor effort of her own. He trailed his tongue along the part in her lips and deepened the kiss, allowing her no choice but to participate.

She did—hesitantly, at first, and then meeting his fervency with unpracticed enthusiasm as the kiss continued. Slender though she was, she felt very much like a woman—curving and soft—up against him. She tasted like a mystery and, too quickly, he was drunk on the brew. In his intoxication, he gave in to temptation and allowed his wandering hand to dip below that teasing curve in her back and graze lightly over the round of her backside. She made a sound—a quiet mewling sound—and he liked it too much.

Somewhere in the room, Gelert whined and Michael heard it as a warning. He had to stop. If he gave in to each successive temptation, how far would he go? He was taking liberties he shouldn't take, barely a moment after he'd told her that he would protect her. He lifted his mouth from hers and stepped back, slowly but firmly putting a pace of distance between them.

She stared up at him, bewildered, catching her breath as he did. They looked at each other for a long, questioning moment and then she brought a hand to her lips, as though testing that they were the same lips as before. "Why did you do that?" she asked, her voice wavering and hesitant.

As he had no good answer, Michael answered with a question of his own. "Do you want to know why I kissed you, or why I stopped?"

Dark lashed fluttered onto flushed cheeks. "The first."

He gave the answer for the second. "I stopped because I didn't have a good enough reason to kiss you. And there are several good reasons why I should not have done it." He said it firmly, to impress the point upon them both. He was damned if he understood why he had kissed her. And he had lost control so easily. He was not in the habit of being overset by the simple act of kissing an attractive female. Somehow her complete lack of feminine wiles had managed to utterly beguile him.

She nodded. "Yes. I think you are probably right." But she touched her fingertips to her lips again, belying her words.

"Why did you?" he asked. "Why did you let me kiss you?"

She stared at him a moment, then she shook her head. "I…I don't know. I think it was because no one's ever touched me like that before."

"No one's ever kissed you?"

"No…that is, well, yes, no one's ever kissed me,"—her gaze lost its courage and fell to the floor—"but I meant before that. When you were… were…holding me."

"You've never had a man hold you before." He expected as much. Her response to his kiss had been alluringly sweet, but not practiced. The alternative, he supposed, was that she was extremely practiced, but played the part of the ingénue.

"I have never had anyone hold me before."

He shook his head. She said the most ridiculously improbable things. "Surely when you were a child…"

She simply stared.

"Not even your mother? During a terrible storm or after a frightening dream?"

She gave a small shake of her head. "Not that I can remember."

How miserably awful, if that were true. His own mother was not a perfect woman by any means. She had made mistakes in her life. But she had held her frightened child, for Christ's sake. He was beginning to suspect Miss Crawley had good reason to flee her father's home. "If your parents never comforted you, they were cold people. Is that who you watch for? Your father?"

"I am not going back." The statement was quiet but firm. She had said the same before.

He considered her. He had many more questions, but his curiosity was a dangerous thing. He was too intrigued by her, this girl who would only be in his life for one more day. Their kiss proved it. He shouldn't need to know more, and she likely wouldn't tell him more anyway. Still, he pressed.

"Is there only your father?" he asked. "You said your mother awaits you in London, but that isn't true, is it?"

She shook her head. "No. I'm sorry."

He had identified the lie the moment she had spoken it, so it shouldn't have bothered him to have it confirmed, but it did. They had just kissed, after all. "If not your mother, who will see to your safety in London?"

Her chin lifted. "I shall do well enough on my own."

"On your own?" He shook his head. "If you hope to hide from your father, London is large but may not be large enough. Besides, there are other dangers in town."

"I don't intend to stay in London."

"Where will you go?"

She looked at him and he could see the calculation behind her expression. She was weighing whether or not she would tell him the truth.

"Boston."

"Did you say Boston?" She had clearly decided to no longer tell him the truth. Her decision triggered more anger than it should have, but had he not just comforted her? Had he not just promised her his protection? She was silent.

"As you did not have the wherewithal to get to London without my help, forgive me if I find it unlikely that you have arranged passage to cross the ocean."

"I...I haven't arranged it exactly, but there is a woman I know, she is married to a shipping merchant..."

Michael cut her off. "Is that so?"

"Yes. He sails to Boston."

"Oh, how convenient," he bit out.

"I'm sorry?"

He had no patience for her stricken looks. "Does your sea captain know the duchess, by chance?"

She paled, eyes wide with hurt at his sharply spoken words, but why shouldn't he be angry? Why should he consider her tender feelings when she disrespected his so freely, continuing to feed him lie after lie? This was no entertaining parlor game in which he tried to tell the truths from the falsehoods. She had asked for his protection this night and he had committed it. One moment she behaved as though she feared for her very life in a rural coaching inn and the next she flippantly declared she would do 'well enough on her own' in London—a city teeming with miscreants and criminals.

*He* would do well enough to stop worrying a damn about whether she told the truth or what she planned to do after they parted company.

"He is not a sea captain," she said, her voice becoming very small, her shoulders once again rounded forward.

"What he is, Miss Crawley, is a figment of your imagination."

"But...I...he's..."

Michael lifted one hand to halt her stammering explanations. "Never mind, Miss Crawley. Go to bed."

She nodded gravely before bending to retrieve the wooden spoon and crossing the room to lay down on her makeshift pallet. She pulled the blanket over herself and turned her body toward the fire.

She had obeyed and that made him even angrier, irrational as that was. She did not merely comply, but skulked to her bed the way Gelert would after a reprimand, with his tail tucked between his legs. Of all the strange things she'd done and said, Michael found this propensity of hers the most disturbing. She had been evasive, she had been indignant, and she had been bold enough to approach him in the first place. But between all that, she'd intermittently fallen into moments of what he could only call quiet obedience. When she did, she appeared more mistreated servant than gentleman's daughter. It had seemed pitiful at times, but in the face of her dishonesty, it seemed nothing more than playacting and he had no patience for it.

Michael tried to shake his questions from his head. She was his concern for only a few more hours and the only bit of information he truly needed was the location to which she should be delivered in London. She'd already given him that.

Perhaps he could take a lesson from her style of obedience. He had answered his father's summons. He was dutifully making his way to London to meet the bride of his father's choosing. Yet here he was kissing strange women. Whether he believed she'd maneuvered it or not, he couldn't go around compromising young misses. Not when obedience would win him Rose Hall. Miss Ana Crawley with her haunting looks and wooden spoon was not part of it. He needed to get her to London and to whatever business she had with Hammersley, Brint & Peale—if they even existed—and then he would never see her again.

\* \* \* \*

Juliana lay on her makeshift pallet with her back to Mr. Rosevear and stared into the blackness of the corner. She would never, ever marry. She was swiftly learning that there were ways for men to be cruel without whipping or calling names. She would not be lured again into his gentle offers of protection. He was neither her friend nor her ally. If she were found by whomever her father had sent to chase her, Mr. Rosevear would likely be more than thrilled to hand her over and be rid of her. She could not let her guard down again.

# Chapter Seven

Michael awoke the next morning feeling decidedly unrested. He should have at least been relieved to look out the window and observe not only blue sky, but also Albert in the yard of the coaching inn, already readying the coach. They were both distinct signs that this damned journey would finally be reaching its end and should have buoyed his mood, yet he felt only annoyance at the reminder that he would soon be delivering Miss Crawley to her mysterious fate. She was supposed to have been a distraction from his own inevitable misery, but instead she had been an endless cause of frustration, as Michael had been able to satisfy neither the puzzle of his mind nor the growing desire of his body's awareness.

The source of his befuddlement had risen before him and was already prepared for the day, her thick auburn braid once again tucked beneath her simple bonnet and threadbare gray shawl wrapped around her shoulders. She sat waiting in one of the chairs, her small bag of possessions at her side. He grunted an acknowledgement to her before making his way to the ewer and basin and splashing his face with water. He used the remainder in his hands to smooth down his untamed hair.

Despite the fact that she watched—or perhaps because she did—Michael tugged off the white shirt he'd worn through the night and walked, bare chested, to pull another from his bag. It was no less rumpled than the first, but it was clean and fresh. When he glanced in Miss Crawley's direction, he was further annoyed to discover that she had not moved and continued to face the smoldering remnants of the night's fire, her face turned downward under the brim of her bonnet. He didn't like it that she could so easily ignore him when he found it impossible to do the same.

He finished dressing, picked up his hat and bag and motioned toward the door to the hall, summoning both Gelert and the silent Miss Crawley.

She was paying enough attention, apparently, to be aware of his gesture, for she rose and walked silently into the hall, brushing past him without so much as a glance. He did not offer to carry Miss Crawley's bag along with his own, as he was not feeling particularly chivalrous.

When they reached the bottom of the steps, he sent both woman and dog out of the inn and lingered long enough himself to acquire a small bundle of food for their morning repast. He was feeling just surly enough to disregard his companion's possible hunger, but his own stomach grumbled, thus she benefited.

In all, less than a half hour passed between the time he awoke and the moment the carriage lurched into motion, finally making forward progress toward London, with Michael on the rear-facing bench, Miss Crawley on the opposite, and Gelert on the floor. Michael looked down at the dog, who slept, as all dogs seemed capable of doing at any given time—even after a full night of sleep. He untied the cloth bundle and took a crust of bread. Wordlessly, he handed the bundle to Miss Crawley. He was being rude, he knew, but she was being silent, so he supposed they were neither one of them made for pleasant company. She took the bag from him and set it on the seat, declining to take anything.

He didn't like being so surly. He wasn't used to it. Back home at Rose Hall, he could stay busy. The puzzles that challenged his intellect had rational solutions. When he was devising methods to brew larger batches of ale, or negotiating with tenant farmers to convert fields to hops, he did not find himself in a circular trap, chasing answers that eluded him because the questions kept changing.

Bread in hand, Michael rearranged himself on his seat, leaving one boot on the floor of the coach, while stretching the other leg across the bench. It was nearly long enough to lay the leg flat. Nearly. And then only if he sat fully erect. Sighing, he bent the leg and slouched into the cushions in an attempt to make himself comfortable. He was determined he should make it as far as he possibly could before stopping to walk and work the stiffness out of his leg. He ate his piece of bread and watched the trees pass by out the small window, but he was restless and too aware of the woman in the opposite seat.

With an inward sigh he glanced over to see what she was doing. She was reading, and apparently making herself quite comfortable for she had somewhat copied his posture and lounged against the side of the coach while holding her book. Both of her feet were still on the floor, at least, but it irked him that she was so relaxed and comfortably passing the time when he could not be. How was she to serve as a distraction if she was engaged in such a singular pastime? "What book are you reading?" he asked, addressing her for the first time that morning.

She lifted her eyes to his. "*Amelia*. It is a novel."

"Did you just begin it?"

"I did, but I have read it before."

"Good," he said sternly. "Then it will not disturb you to begin again. Aloud this time, please."

She sat upright and looked at him, then down at the book in her hands, and again at him. "You...you want me to read to you?"

He shrugged. "We have to pass the time somehow. Since I am providing you passage to London, without charge, you can at least help to distract me, can you not?" He caught her uncertain gaze and held it. It might have been the lack of sleep or only partially slated hunger that made him say, "Of course, if you prefer not to read aloud, we can always set the book aside and you can tell me the truth of your plans in London."

Her eyes fell to the book again. "I...I don't mind reading. I've just never read aloud to anyone before."

He shifted his weight again. "I'm sure you'll be quite competent. Have we an agreement, or should we begin with questions?"

Her eyes lifted to his and, for a brief moment, he thought he saw the slightest quirk of her lips—amusement perhaps—at his persistence. It was gone before he could be sure and she said, "I shall be delighted to read in exchange for my passage. It is the least I can do for your forbearance."

He nodded in approval and she reopened the book. She resumed her reclining posture, turned back to the beginning page, and began reading:

"*The various accidents which befell a very worthy couple after their uniting in the state of matrimony will be the subject of the following history. The distresses which they waded through were some of them so exquisite, and the incidents which produced these so extraordinary, that they seemed to require not only the utmost malice, but the utmost invention, which superstition hath ever attributed to Fortune: though whether any such being interfered in the case, or, indeed whether there be any such being in the universe, is a matter which I by no means presume to determine in the affirmative...*"

Michael settled himself more deeply into the cushioned seat and closed his eyes, willing himself to focus on the words and the story in the hopes of forgetting the tightening in his leg and the frustrations of his preoccupation. It helped that she had a very pleasant voice—a melodic one—that rose and fell in soothing rhythm as her inflection changed through the prose.

He let the sound of her wash over him, relaxing him, as though its effect was not isolated to his ears, but spreading to each limb, lightening it. He found he wasn't even paying attention to the story. He had wanted the distraction of the tale, but this was better yet. She could be reading in another language altogether. Her voice became fingers that soothed his ache and frustration better than any massage could.

Even as he thought it, he realized the absurdity of the idea. What sort of witchcraft was this? She was only reading, but the faraway, haunting quality to her voice, soothed him like a mother's song.

He opened his eyes to look at her, presented in profile, and found himself transfixed by watching her lips form the words from the book in her lap. He glanced down at it briefly, but then back up at her face. Her expression bore the same ethereal quality as her voice, her eyes gazing, unseeing, at some distant point through the carriage window.

He sat bolt upright. "What are you doing?"

She gasped, startled, and the book fell to the floor of the carriage with a thud. "What?" she asked, facing him with wide eyes. "What did I do?"

He peered at her. "What were you doing just there?"

"What do you mean? I...I was reading." She reached to retrieve the fallen book and clutched it in her lap, avoiding his eyes. She swallowed. "Was there something wrong?"

"How many times have you read that book?" he asked, curiosity consuming him.

She shook her head. "I don't know. Twice, perhaps three times."

"You're lying."

Her eyes flashed to his even as she recoiled from his suggestion, pressing herself back into her seat. "But I'm not. What a useless thing to lie about. Why would I?"

"I don't know, but you must be. You were not reading that book to me. You were reciting it. From memory. You weren't even looking at it." Her defiance fell away, and as he'd seen happen so many times before, her expression became a guarded mask of outward subservience. She wore it like defensive armor, but he was convinced it was as much a lie as so many other things she'd told him.

"I do not lie about the book, Mr. Rosevear. I possess an unaccountably strong memory."

"A strong memory?" He could hear his voice rising in frustration. "Strong enough to recite a novel?"

Silently she nodded, flush blooming on her porcelain cheeks.

"Have you always remembered things this way?" he asked.

"Certain things, yes."

"Which things?" he demanded.

She looked down at her fingers as the traced the edge of the seat cushion. "Things that I look at—like papers or paintings."

"What about things that you hear?"

"I remember things that I hear, depending on their importance, but not any differently from other people, I suppose. Not in the way I recall things I've seen. I can't really explain it other than to say it is a memory of my eyes as opposed to my ears."

"How did you learn to do it?" he asked.

"I didn't learn it. It simply happens."

Michael slowly shook his head, as though denying this thing that she was telling him, despite having witnessed it. He was unable to take his eyes from her. She was, without doubt, the most enigmatic person he had ever encountered. "I've never heard of such a thing."

She turned her head to one side and lifted one hand to tuck a nonexistent stray hair into the side of her bonnet. "It is unusual, I know. It has a way of making others uncomfortable, in particular my father, so I generally don't discuss it."

"There seem to be a lot of things you generally don't discuss, Miss Crawley."

She bit her lip.

"Is that even your name?" he asked. "Miss Crawley?"

She said nothing and did not lift her eyes to his. Michael took her silence as confirmation that her name had been another lie. He was annoyed with himself for even posing the question when he'd resolved to remain uninterested in her shrouded existence. Everything about her made no sense. He leaned forward, resting his elbows on his knees, and stared at her, unrelentingly, until she had no choice but to meet his eyes. "I've had nothing but mysteries and lies from you, Miss Enigma, so I think it is time that you have a bit of truth from me."

She swallowed and stared silently back at him, green eyes wide with alarm.

She should be alarmed. He was done with all of her stories and half-truths.

"You are, without doubt, the most mysterious woman I have ever met. Your stories are inconsistent and your lies are so outlandish as to have no chance of being believed. The few truths I have received from you—the very few—are incomplete and shed no further light on who you are or where you came from." He scooted forward in his seat as he continued. "What I do know is that you have thrown yourself on the mercy of a strange man and trusted him with none of your secrets but all of your safety, a choice which might have gotten you considerably worse than a stolen kiss in the middle of the night if you had happened upon someone other than me. You behave as though you are desperate and frightened to death of something, but the only rational explanation you have provided for your journey, Miss *Crawley*, is that you are burdened with the chore of keeping your father's house. Maybe your father does not treat you as gently as he should, but you are naïve to abandon that protection. You appear to me to be an unhappy and ungrateful daughter running away from home with the misguided notion that the world will be kinder than your present intolerable life. Let me save you a great deal of trouble. The world is not kinder. It will destroy you, then blame you for your own destruction. I've a mind to stop in the next town and have you kept there until your parents can collect you."

Having released his frustration on her in one lengthy outburst, Michael sat quietly, catching his breath and awaiting her response.

She gave none.

Some women might have cried. Others might have argued. She only looked. And then she blinked once. That was the entirety of her response.

He could have torn the hair right out of his head, he was so frustrated. Who the devil was this woman?

He was about to ask that very question when a loud snap startled him. The noise finally drew a reaction from her as well, her jade eyes going round. Almost immediately the carriage lurched, followed by the sound of more splintering wood. Fear filled Miss Crawley's face as her arms flung wide to brace herself on either wall of the carriage just as Michael did the same.

Their eyes met in silent question for the briefest of moments then Michael reached for her, pulling her from her seat and clutching her to him just as the carriage pitched violently to one side. She slid hard against his side with a startled "oof." As soon as Michael thought he could gain his bearing again, the carriage pitched the other way. A sharp curse came from outside and the entire seating compartment fell several feet from its perch. It stopped with a jarring thud, sending Michael and Miss Crawley careening from their place on the rear-facing seat and onto Gelert on the floor of the carriage. Michael threw his arm out to stop his full weight from crushing Miss Crawley's smaller form and heard the dog yelp as they fell into him. The passenger compartment bounced painfully along the ground as the vehicle was dragged forward for a minute or more. Outside, Albert cursed and called to stop the frightened horses.

With one final bump, the entire thing came to a stop.

Michael was draped over Miss Crawley, partially on top of the dog, with one hip pressing uncomfortably into the edge of the seating bench. "Are you hurt?" he asked.

Miss Crawley blew out a shaky breath. "No. I suppose not." She lifted her head as much as she was able, green eyes wide with question. "What has happened? Have we collided with something?"

He shook his head. "I don't know. We seem to have fallen into something."

With the entire seating compartment tilted backward, and the dog tangled at his feet, it was difficult for Michael to lift himself off of Miss Crawley, but he did so, cringing, as he had no alternative but to push himself up with his sore leg.

"Ho, there, are you all right?" Albert's call came a moment before the door was opened, spilling sunlight into the disordered interior of the coach. He peered in at them, whip in hand and hat askew.

Gelert somehow managed to squirm out from underneath both Michael and Miss Crawley and leapt toward the opening. Albert quickly darted out of the animal's way to avoid being trampled before returning to the door again. "Well?" he asked.

Michael grunted and pushed himself farther away from Miss Crawley. "I think we're fine." He slid toward the door and looked back at his passenger. "Miss Crawley, are sure you're all right?"

She turned awkwardly and sat on her rump on the spot recently vacated by the dog, a bewildered expression on her usually unreadable face. She looked around the interior of the coach, then looked down to assess herself more thoroughly. "Yes. Yes, I think I am."

As Michael was nearest the door, he took the hand Albert offered and allowed himself to be assisted from the tilted vehicle. He had to tug his frock coat back into place and felt a twinge where his hip had been jammed into the seat, but was otherwise unharmed. He watched as Albert handed Miss Crawley down. She shook her twisted skirt and then her head as though still righting herself from the jolt.

"You should step aside, miss," Albert said. "The carriage is not stable."

Michael watched as she nodded mutely, still looking rather shocked by the ordeal, and backed several paces away from the upset coach. Then he turned to Albert. "What the devil happened?"

Albert pulled the crooked hat from his head and wiped the back of his hand across his brow. "I've no bloody idea."

Gelert ran back toward the coach and barked at it, like some odd canine reprimand for behaving unexpectedly.

The thing was a shambles. As he'd felt from inside, the entire back end of the passenger compartment had come off its elevated perch above the rear axle and plunged to the ground. At first glance, it was impossible to tell which damage had caused the fall and which damage had been caused by it. Michael crouched slowly, not minding the pain of the stretch, and looked under the carriage. Albert did the same. Gelert barked again, running between the two men and the carriage, barring their view. He darted away just as quickly, excited and anxious from the incident.

"Gelert. Sit," Michael snapped. The dog sat. "Stay." The dog obeyed, firmly planted in his spot, but there was anxiety in his coal-colored eyes. He was as riled by the incident as the rest of them. Michael turned back to the coach and to Albert who reached in to feel along the broken structure.

"The axle's split in two," he said.

"Did we hit something?"

Albert shook his head. "Nothing. But look here." He crawled partway under the tilted carriage and indicated the point of break in the axle. "Half the break is clean," he said, still laying on his side.

"Clean?"

"It's not splintered like the other half is."

Michael looked. Albert was right. Someone had sawn partway through the main axle, knowing that it would only bear a certain distance of rough road before it would split. They had been the victim of sabotage.

He met Albert's grave expression. "Who would want to do this to us?"

"Us, sir?" Albert asked, "Or her?"

The question gave Michael pause. Could Albert be right? *He* had no enemies. If she was being chased by someone, it was past time to find out by whom.

Michael rose from his crouch and pivoted to face down Miss Crawley.

The visage he met was a far cry from the hauntingly familiar features of his recent companion. Instead he was met with a wide, square jaw, a crooked nose and the red eyes of a man who'd had more pints of drink than hours of sleep. Michael didn't hesitate. The moment he saw him, he ducked, anticipating the man's attempt at a meaty blow to his face. Instead, Michael drove his shoulder into the man's gut and used his legs to force him backward—not far, just enough to be unsteady on his legs.

"Albert." Using his moment of advantage to both alert the coachman and assess the threat, Michael quickly looked around and saw no other men. In fact, he saw no other person—man or woman.

*Miss Crawley.*

The man with the crooked nose gained his footing, forcing Michael's attention back to the immediate threat. Michael landed a blow quickly that turned the man's face, but didn't faze him as much as he would have liked. He followed up with a second, but his foe found contact with Michael's side, pushing a bit of the breath from him. Michael pulled back, intending to land a finishing punch that would end the fight and allow him to attend to the matter of the missing Miss Crawley, but a rope slipped over the man's head and he was jerked backward, away from Michael.

While Albert had him thus restrained, Michael found another piece of rope and tied the man's hands behind his back. When he was certain the man was bound sufficiently for Albert to control him despite the coachman's smaller size, Michael ran back to the coach. He quickly climbed into the tipped carriage and reached underneath the forward facing seat. His hand closed around the flintlock musket he kept stowed there and he pulled it from its place, handing it out to Albert. He reached again and recovered a smaller flintlock pistol, passing this to Albert as well. He then reached under the other seat and found the ammunition box, backing out of the carriage. As he was not hunting for sport, Michael loaded the muzzle with a musket ball rather than shot.

He looked to Gelert who watched him, dutifully sitting where he had been told to stay. The dog looked toward a spot in the woods and let out a plaintive whine.

*Damned obedient dog.*

"Where is she?" Michael asked.

Gelert whined again and looked into the woods.

"Go!" Michael shouted. Gelert darted off into the forest and Michael followed, unable to match Gelert, but keeping the quickest pace he could.

# Chapter Eight

The farther Juliana hurried into the woods, the more she doubted the sense of her decision to flee. She'd been struck with the thought rather suddenly and there had been no time to consider anything but the fact that Mr. Rosevear had very clearly threatened to return her to her father.

Surely the man would be happy to be rid of her and have no reason to give chase, but the trouble was she was now alone in the woods with no possessions or skills that would be of any use to her. She had no earthly idea how to survive in the forest. What did she know of tramping about in the woods? How would she even be sure she was walking in the correct direction?

Walking all the way to London could not be a possibility, but neither could she put herself at the mercy of another stranger. Relying upon the compassion of a kind traveler had been a miscalculation. She supposed if she came across a farm or village, she could steal a horse. She had never stolen anything before, save the few coins from her father, but as his daughter it seemed somewhat her due. She was certainly not due a stranger's horse, but she didn't see another way. Asking the help of a stranger had not so far gone well. Better to take it than to ask for it, she supposed.

Assuming she found one.

As she walked, Juliana was quickly learning one important fact of tramping through the woods—doing so required a specific type of sturdy shoe. Judging by the moisture already soaking her feet and the sharp jabs that penetrated the soles each time she trod upon a rock or twig, Juliana was not in possession of the desired type.

Under the canopy of the trees, everything was still wet from the prior day's storm. Every branch she brushed dampened her clothes and soon her hem was as soaked as her shoes. A breeze rustled the leaves all around her, turning the dampness to a chill. She shivered.

Still she did not turn back. She trudged on.

She was no longer likely to arrive in London before her birthday, but she would get there somehow. Mr. Rosevear had been right about one thing. The world was not kind. People were just as dangerous as the wilderness.

She walked, reciting her destination as a chant to keep her company. Hammersley, Brint & Peale. Number 48 Hardwick Street. She knew she could not fail to remember it, but reciting the information comforted her. When she was fairly certain she'd walked deep enough into the thick forest to be undetectable from the road, she pivoted and began walking in what she hoped was a parallel course.

Once sufficient time had passed, she would allow herself to walk more closely to the road so as to not find herself too far off course. If they were still several hours from London by coach, how long would it take her to walk there? Days? What would she eat?

She immediately felt hungry for no reason other than the uncertainty of her next meal. It was her own fault, of course. He had offered her something to eat and she had obstinately chosen to decline.

Sleeping would be another difficulty. She had never slept outdoors before. What of the wild animals? What if there was another storm such as the previous day's? She would have no shelter.

She stopped walking and looked to the patches of sky visible through the breaks in the trees. It was blue enough, but would that last until she reached London?

She looked behind her. Maybe she should go back. If they had been able to repair whatever was wrong with the carriage, she could be warm and dry and speeding toward London. Yes, he had threatened to return her to her father, but would he really do so? Now that she thought more clearly, he was as anxious to reach London as she. It would be irrational for him to further delay his arrival when he could be rid of her by simply proceeding directly to town and parting ways there.

Nearly as irrational as Juliana believing she could walk all the way.

She turned, pushing a thin, flexible branch out of her path, only to displace another that sprang back and struck her on the cheek, narrowly missing her eye.

"Ouch."

She nearly started at the sound of her own voice, so out of place among the sounds of the woods—the leaves and birds and falling droplets. Another breeze rose as though from the forest floor. This one shook the leaves above her so thoroughly, the rainwater they still held fell in a deluge, as though mother nature had thought it humorous to create a rain shower just for her.

"I am an idiot," she announced to whatever woodland creatures might be hiding nearby.

As though in agreement with her declaration, one more fat drop of rainwater fell, striking the brim of her bonnet before dropping onto her collarbone and sliding into the bodice of her dress.

*Lovely.*

She reached down with both hands, grabbed fistfuls of her skirt and pulled the hem clear to her calves, fully determined to march herself right back to Mr. Rosevear.

Only she didn't march. There was a new sound in the forest. She held her breath and listened.

*Snap.*

There it was again—the cracking sound of steps breaking twigs on the forest floor. She was not alone. Someone or something was walking nearby.

*Gelert.* Had he sent the dog after her? As she stood, frozen, her mind recalled the story of the original Gelert. He had savagely bested a wolf. If Mr. Rosevear instructed his dog to give chase, what would the beast do when he found her?

*Snap.*

She turned her head in the direction of the sound. She stared into the tangle of trees and brush, watching as the source of the noise emerged.

For a moment, she relaxed. It was not Gelert. It was a stranger. The moment was fleeting, however, for he stepped closer and she saw he was not unfamiliar to her. She had seen him in the common room at the inn, with another man. Looking for someone.

As she stared at him, he stopped walking, met her eyes, and grinned.

She hiked her skirts even higher and took off at a run, desperately hoping she was running in the direction of the road. Branches scraped her and she kept going. She nearly stumbled on a rock, but she righted herself.

Her efforts were futile. He caught her easily. He caught hold of her sleeve and yanked her back. She tried to pull back from his hold but only succeeded in causing a tear in the garment. She stumbled back toward him with a force that pulled her bonnet from her head and expelled her breath. "Just where do you think you're going?" he grumbled low at her ear. His breath was warm and rotten and he smelled of filth. She should have known her father would not lay out the coin for a kidnapper who bathed or washed his clothing. She wriggled in his arms in an attempt to work herself free. Her bonnet, still tied under her chin, was crushed between them.

He pinched her arm and she winced. "Be still girl," he hissed, "else I'll knock you dead out and carry you like a sack back to your father."

She had assumed that he had been sent by her father, but hearing the confirmation spoken by this awful man sent a spike of rage through her. The vision of her father meeting this miscreant face to face and willingly sending him after his only child steeled her resolve more than any of the blows he'd given her directly throughout her life.

She went limp in compliance with his reprimand. The sudden change in her posture gave her enough room within his hold to free her arms and pivot towards him. She lifted her hands and slapped, as hard as she could, with open palms against his ears. His grip immediately loosened and she twisted away.

She didn't wait to find out how quickly he would recover. She hiked her skirt and ran again, breathless with both panic and the victory that her attempt to free herself had worked.

Only it had not. Not really. He caught her quickly again, this time reaching up to yank her cruelly by her hair. She yelped, unable to stop it, and cursed her father again. Whenever he'd boxed her ears, she'd suffered dizziness for hours—sometimes her ears rang for days.

She scratched at his arm and he cursed.

"You little bitch." He yanked her hair again and tears stung her eyes from the pain of it. He pulled her up against him once more and hissed, "Your father promised me you'd be real meek and scared. He ain't paid me enough for this. I'll have to take payment from you for that scratch."

She squirmed in his hold and he pulled her more tightly. "Yes, I think I'll enjoy that very much. Maybe you should scratch me again, so's you'll 'ave to pay twice." His fist closed around her upper arm and squeezed, mercilessly. She tried very hard to stoically bear the pain, but she could not. She whimpered and hated that she did. She retaliated by kicking backward with her heel, hoping to find contact with his shin.

At first, she thought the low growl that followed her kick emanated from her captor, but she quickly realized it did not. It was from farther away and it was not human.

She wrenched herself in his hold and confirmed her suspicion.

*Gelert.*

The dog stared at both of them for a moment, teeth bared, the hair along his spine spiking upward. Then he charged.

Out of instinct, she turned away from the attack the best she could in the tight grip of her assailant. But she was not the intended victim. The man howled and she turned in time to see the dog lunge, clamping down on his leg. The force of the impact sent him tumbling to the ground, freeing his hold on her and she stumbled away.

Gelert lunged at the man again. Juliana watched in awe of the dog's ferocity, unable to feel remorse for the awful man. Despite Gelert's vicious hold, the man landed solid blows around the dogs head and onto the dog's back, but Gelert did not give any sign of pain and did not relent. He held the grip tightly and growled deeply. When the man continued to struggle, Gelert began to pull, thrashing his head back and forth with the man's arm in his jaws, drawing a wild howl from the criminal.

"Gelert. Enough."

Mr. Rosevear's firm call halted the dog immediately. The beast stood over his prey and stared at his master, awaiting further instruction.

Juliana lifted her eyes to Mr. Rosevear's as he emerged from the brush. He made a brief gesture with one hand and the dog sat back on his haunches, all signs of aggression gone, save the blood on his nose and the intermittent groans from the man on the ground.

Mr. Rosevear looked at Juliana then, and she back at him. It was only then she realized the item he carried along his side, the full length of his right leg, was not a cane this time. It was a long gun. They stared at each other across the small clearing. He had lived up to his word. He had protected her even after she had fled. She was certain she looked nearly feral with her dress torn, her bonnet gone, and her hair pulled in all directions. She was breathless from fear and the exertion of fighting off her attacker and couldn't imagine her heartbeat would ever be peaceful again.

The dog gave a brief whine and Michael nodded, releasing him from his hold command. The dog stood erect and looked between his master and Juliana. Then he lumbered away from his victim, slowly but directly, to Juliana's side. He turned and sat, shoulders tall, at her right elbow.

She stared down at him. She had never been this close to him before— close enough that she could hear his breath and feel his warmth. She lifted her hand and set it, gingerly, atop the dog's head. It was warm and solid underneath the wiry tangle of fur. He pressed upward into her touch with surprising gentleness. She crooked her fingers and scratched into the fur as she'd seen Mr. Rosevear do. He pressed his head more firmly into the scratch.

"Thank you," she whispered to the dog, her voice still unsteady.

# Chapter Nine

Michael walked to stand over the groaning man, surveying his condition. He'd seen Gelert attack a man only one other time. As that man had been preparing to beat the dog with a heavy club, Michael could not fault the dog's judgment. Unfortunately for Gelert, he'd been a mere pup the first time. He had required Michael's intervention and, that day, became Michael's companion.

This man was unlucky enough to meet Gelert full grown.

"Will he live?"

Michael looked over his shoulder to see Miss Crawley approach. She was in complete disarray—her dress torn, her hair falling about her shoulders in a riotous red tumble. Her hand rested on the mottled fur of Gelert, who stood sentry by her side, muzzle stained with blood. Her shoulders were straight and her chin was high. Her face bore the determination of a warrior goddess, as though she had come from the pages of a legendary tale as opposed to an inn in Peckingham.

She bit her lip and stared at the man, reminding Michael of her question. He wasn't certain which answer she might have preferred, but he looked back at Gelert's victim. He had large, ragged tears on both his right leg and his right forearm. Judging by the odd angle of the arm, it was broken as well. He was bleeding a fair bit.

"He may live," Michael said after completing his assessment. "That will depend upon him I suppose. His wounds are not fatal. He will either summon the determination to haul himself out of this forest, or he will not." He faced Miss Crawley. "Either way, he will no longer be a threat to us."

"Thank you," she said.

"You only have Gelert to thank," he answered, with a nod toward the dog. "He had your attacker well in hand without my help."

"You came after me."

Michael lowered his head. It was there again in her expression—that gratitude that made him feel as though he would battle anything for her. He tried to ignore it. "Of course I did. You may be the most maddening woman I've ever met, but no man would have simply ridden on to London after his passenger had been abducted from right under his nose."

She gave him an odd look, as though he'd said something that didn't make sense. He rather thought she was the nonsensical one. "What I don't understand," Michael continued, "is why you didn't make noise when you were taken—to gain our attention. When I realized you were gone, I thought perhaps you'd been knocked unconscious or taken at gunpoint, but neither seems to be the case. Why did you go quietly?"

"You came after me because you thought I was taken from the road?"

"Weren't you?"

"No."

"Explain."

She didn't cower or avert her eyes this time. She faced him defiantly, daring him to find fault with her words as she said, "You threatened to return me to my father. And then you and Mr. Finn were distracted by the carriage." She gave a small, one-shouldered shrug as though to suggest he could imagine the rest.

He could. "So you ran."

"It was a rash decision. I realize that now."

Michael looked at the man on the ground. "That is not the sort of man a concerned father hires to locate his missing daughter so that she may be safely returned home."

"No. It is not."

He looked at her again. She too, had turned her attention to the kidnapper. She was still, but with her riotous hair, torn dress, and wild eyes, she looked the way Michael felt inside. Disordered. Unsettled.

"I would have run," he said quietly. "Were I in your place."

She nodded at this acknowledgment then asked, "Why did you think I'd been taken?"

"Because Albert noticed that our carriage accident was not an accident, but sabotage. Well, that, and the other miscreant who is currently tied to the wreckage of my father's coach."

She inhaled a slow deep breath and released it. "I am to blame for the destruction of your father's beautiful coach. I have no way to make recompense."

Michael shook his head. She had just fought for her life and she apologized for a carriage. "My father has others. You have only the one neck. We should return to see what Albert has done with this man's associate."

She looked in the direction of the road but did not begin walking.

"I can promise you," Michael said, "I will never again threaten to return you to your father. Whatever awaits you in London, it must be better than this."

She nodded and they headed toward the road, Gelert trailing behind them. Michael didn't bother looking back at the man on the ground as they walked away. He noticed she did however—one quick backward glance followed by a shudder that rocked her entire being.

\* \* \* \*

Juliana emerged from the woods flanked by her protectors. As such, she was not frightened when she spied the other of the pair of men sent to fetch her. Also beneficial was the fact that he was already bound and lashed to the wreckage of the carriage. She recognized him as the darker man of the pair she'd feared at the inn. He didn't even glance at the group that came out of the woods. He was too occupied staring at the pistol held by Mr. Finn.

Mr. Finn, however, did glance quickly in their direction, assessing each of their party in turn—man, woman, and dog.

"Run into a spot of trouble?" he asked as one might inquire as to another's morning stroll.

"Nothing Gelert couldn't manage," Mr. Rosevear answered. He strode to the carriage but ignored the man on the ground, instead conducting a thorough examination of the vehicle. "The axle is broken in two," Mr. Finn offered. "One wheel is broken as well and the other is splintered, ready to break. The fittings are fair bent. 'Twill not be a simple matter to have it functional again."

Michael nodded his understanding. "I assumed as much. As this coach won't be carrying anyone anywhere, we will walk to the next town or village and ask after whatever we might buy or rent to convey us the rest of the way to London." He looked pointedly at Juliana. "We may end up on the mail coach yet."

The rebuke was deserved, but Juliana thought she noticed some humor in his tone. "Can we not ride the horses?" she asked, looking to the pair of chestnut brown horses that had been unhitched from the damaged vehicle and were now tied to a nearby tree.

Mr. Rosevear shook his head.

Mr. Finn offered the explanation. "Those horses have never been ridden in their lives, Miss. It's not what they're trained for, and they're still riled from the crash. The best horse trainer in the world isn't getting on either of their backs."

Juliana nodded. She was fine to walk, only she worried about Mr. Rosevear. He was very large next to his coachman—a head taller and a shoulder broader. He was the picture of strength, standing there in the sun, long gun at his side, glowering at her would-be kidnapper. But she'd noticed his limp as they'd walked out of the woods.

She nearly asked if he would be all right to make the walk, but didn't see the point. There was no avoiding it, whether he was capable of it or not. Besides, she would likely only offend his pride.

Her silence did not shield the course of her thoughts evidently, for Mr. Rosevear answered her unspoken question. "Walking is not my trouble, Miss Crawley. It is the lack of it that pains me. I shall likely be more comfortable after a long walk than I have been in days."

She nodded.

Mr. Finn sighed loudly and looked to the massive, useless coach. "Broken as it is, it's still a grand carriage. I can't see as how it won't be looted entirely by the time someone gets back to it, sir."

"There's no help for that, Albert. While I lament my father's loss of property, I've no intention of sitting out here for days standing guard over his velvet cushions and expensive fittings."

"What of him?" Mr. Finn asked with a nod toward the bound man.

Mr. Rosevear walked to the man in question, seated on the ground with his legs sprawled before him and arms bound to the carriage wheel behind him. He poked the man with the barrel end of his musket. "Your friend did not fare well. I suggest you consider whether the payment you've been promised is more valuable than your next breath."

The man's eyes moved rapidly, shifting from Mr. Rosevear to Mr. Finn, then to Juliana, and finally to the dog and his bloodied muzzle. When he finished his circuit, his attention returned the barrel end of the gun. He gave a single silent nod.

"If I allow you to leave this place with your life," Mr. Rosevear continued, "could you be sensible enough to scurry away and forget that you ever knew of any of us?"

The man licked his lips and nodded again, more vigorously this time. "I swear it," he said, his voice thick. "You'll never set sights on me again. You or the woman."

"Be sure that we do not," Mr. Rosevear said. "Or I shall let my dog do to you what he has done to your associate."

He nodded again.

Mr. Rosevear signaled to Mr. Finn who approached, once again raising the pistol to train it on the bound man. Abruptly, Mr. Rosevear walked to Juliana and handed her the long gun. Too startled to object, she took it, holding the barrel end in her hand and resting the butt on the ground. She had never touched a gun before. It was heavy. The metal was cold.

She held it away from her body and watched as Mr. Rosevear untied the man her father had sent to take her, wondering if the act became necessary, she could find the presence of mind to lift the weapon and point it at her attacker. She did not learn the answer, however, for once the man was free, he spared her not a glance but set off down the road, back in the direction from which they had come.

When Mr. Rosevear was done, he returned and stood directly in front of Juliana, staring solemnly down into her face. Her breath caught. She blinked up at him. He extended one hand and closed it over hers where she held the barrel of the gun. She relaxed her grip and slid her hand from under his.

"We had no choice but to let him go," Mr. Rosevear said, answering her unspoken question. "There will be no one to whom we could hand him over in the next town and we have no way holding him."

She nodded. He was probably right. They didn't even know how they would be getting to London at this point. Still, she didn't like knowing he was out there.

"He seemed suitably unsettled by the realization that his friend had been attacked by the dog. I don't think he will bother you again."

Juliana nodded again. She hoped so.

"I suppose we should take what we can carry," Mr. Finn said, pulling a few items from the coach. He walked over to hand Juliana her small bag of things. He looked steadily at her and she had no idea what he was thinking in that moment, but she suspected it was not particularly favorable and likely had to do with the fact that their predicament was her fault. She accepted this censure silently and couldn't disagree.

Once they had gathered what they believed were necessities from the coach, they left it—an ornate tragedy—on the side of the graveled road and walked in the opposite direction of her father's hired abductor, toward whatever village the London Road might pass next.

# Chapter Ten

What a sight they must have been when their little group finally walked into a small hamlet—a disheveled woman in a torn dress accompanied by two armed men leading horses and a menacingly large dog. They must have looked like criminals themselves. Juliana thought it was no surprise that no one ventured out to greet them. The village was quite small, just a few buildings clustered together. There was a public house at the center of it, and Mr. Rosevear indicated they should proceed there.

They had walked for two hours at least and she was relieved to have reached someplace—whatever place it was. The men had been mostly silent as they walked, leaving her to her thoughts. As such, her mind was as tired as her feet. She had tried not to dwell upon thoughts of what she might have endured had Gelert and Mr. Rosevear not arrived to rescue her, but her disobedient imagination had insisted upon providing disturbingly clear visions of the precise manner in which her attacker would have taken payment for the bit of damage she'd inflicted.

She could admit, now that she'd had time to contemplate, the acute betrayal she'd felt upon hearing confirmation of what her father had done and, worse, who he'd chosen to do it, meant she'd been holding at least a thread of hope that somewhere he possessed a fatherly feeling toward her.

Evidently not.

She had feared a beating, but now knew she would have endured far worse. As her father was even less concerned for her well-being than she realized, there could be no relaxation of her vigilance. Any last remnants of pity or loyalty she might have been able to muster for her father were gone forever.

As the two men discussed who should inquire as to the arrangements that could be made for the remainder of their journey, Juliana reached down and touched Gelert's fur, as she done a number of times during their long walk from the site of the accident. She was, as she'd been on all the prior times, surprised by the comfort she took from it. Gelert had saved her. Mr. Rosevear had saved her by sending Gelert to her aid. And he'd come with his gun, ready to fire it, if necessary, on her behalf. She seen that—the wildness, the ferocity in his eyes as he'd come upon them and she'd known the weapon was not merely a threat. She was frightened and thrilled at the same time to possess such a fierce duo of protectors, even if only for a short while.

She'd found herself watching Mr. Rosevear as they'd walked—noticing the breadth of his shoulders and the loosening of his gait—just as he'd predicted the walk would accomplish. He walked—did everything, really—with such self-possession. She was envious of it, but even more so, drawn to it, as though she could feed from his confidence to build her own.

She'd had the odd thought, as she'd watched him, that she wanted to touch his shoulders, his arms, to feel the strength from which he was built, so she could know it and somehow share in it. But then her imagination had gone off on its own accord again and thoughts of running her hands over Mr. Rosevear had her remembering his kiss. The memory had flushed her cheeks and she'd had to pretend to gaze into the field along which they'd been walking, so the men wouldn't notice. The kiss at the inn had taken her entirely by surprise. He'd not caught her unaware, as he'd approached slowly and she'd sensed he was going to do it. But kissing, as an experience, was completely unexpected. She'd felt it literally everywhere—in otherwise innocuous places like her fingertips. She'd felt light, as though she might have risen from her firm contact with the floor. And she'd felt restless, as though it had awakened an appetite she wasn't certain how to satisfy.

She could deduce, she supposed, what sort of activities were meant to satisfy such an appetite, but she understood those only generally. Mr. Rosevear, she imagined was likely familiar with the specifics. The thought made her blush again as he turned and handed his leading rope to Mr. Finn.

"The two of you can stay here," he said. "I will see what arrangements can be made." With a nod from the coachman, Mr. Rosevear disappeared into the small stone building with a worn wooden sign announcing its purpose.

Left alone, the two of them stood in silence for a long while, Juliana and Mr. Finn. Eventually, she spoke because it was too uncomfortable not to do so. "I am sorry, Mr. Finn, for the trouble I have brought on you both."

He accepted her apology with a dip of his chin. "I presume you know who sent the men after you."

"My father."

Her answer caught his attention and he slowly turned, both brows lifting at her admission. "Can't say as though that seems a fatherly thing to do."

She shook her head.

He pressed his lips together, gave another tight nod, and faced the public house again.

"Mr. Rosevear told me you fought together, that you saved him after he was shot. It's clear he thinks very highly of you."

Mr. Finn did not face her again, presenting his back as he answered. "Just the man who chanced to be there when it happened, is all."

"I'm very lucky that you and Mr. Rosevear were the men who chanced to be there when today's events happened, Mr. Finn. I know you don't trust me, but I hope you at least believe my gratitude is genuine."

He looked across at the small stone building when he answered her, as though he could see Mr. Rosevear inside. "If you want to show your gratitude, miss, you won't cause any trouble for him."

"I did not mean to. I hope there will be no more men between here and London."

He looked at her, gray eyes challenging. "I don't mean the kind of trouble that ruffians cause on the road. I mean the sort of trouble that unmarried girls cause by showing up on people's doorsteps and claiming they've been compromised."

Juliana swallowed. "I have no intention of that."

"Good. But in case you change your mind, let me tell you this: he's not a lord, he's a lord's bastard and that means he's entitled to nothing. He'll inherit nothing unless his father decides to be generous. Marrying this girl his father's picked for him may make the old man generous. Ruining his father's plans by showing up with some unknown, unconnected girl from who knows what family will not make the old man generous. Do you see my point?"

She did. Mr. Rosevear had already told her the same. "I told you before, Mr. Finn, once we are in London, he will never see me again."

She'd made the claim a number of times and had meant it sincerely in each case. This was the first time, however, when the statement caused a pang of something she couldn't quite identify. She decided to believe it was only unease at the thought of losing her protector.

\* \* \* \*

"Mail coach came through already, shortly before you arrived. Didn't you pass on the road?"

Michael's eyes closed briefly before he looked at the proprietor again and said, simply, "That's disappointing to hear."

The man lifted open palms, disclaiming responsibility for the schedule of the mail coach.

"I don't suppose there is anywhere nearby that I might be able to obtain horses so that we could ride to London? I have two carriage horses to offer as trade."

He shrugged. "Now you might talk Mr. Pince into renting you his horse, if you can bring it back." His head bobbed. "Then again, he might sell it. He's too old to get up on the thing anyhow. 'Course the horse is nearly as old as Mr. Pince, so keep that in mind. He'll ask too much for it as well."

"Does he have only the one horse?" Michael asked.

"Just the one."

"There is no one else?"

The proprietor shook his head.

Of course there was only the one. "And where would I find Mr. Pince?"

"Across the road and down a bit." He lifted his hand in the required direction. "There's a small house right before the smithy's. That'll be the one."

"Thank you," Michael said. "Since there is only the one horse available, I will have to send my man to London for help, and remain behind. Do you have rooms to let?" he asked, then thought to add, "for me and my wife?"

The older man clucked his lips. "I have one room, but it's let already."

*Blast.* One room and one horse in the entire village. After all of this trouble, his father had better sign over Rose Hall immediately upon Michael's arrival. "Have you absolutely nothing else, sir?" he asked.

The innkeeper expelled a heavy, reluctant sigh. "There's a cottage in the back, but it's not as nice as the room here. It's...primitive."

Michael looked around at the small room in which they stood. The public house was well-scrubbed, but the plaster between the timbers crumbled in spots. The creaky wooden floor was worn from at least a hundred years of boots and brooms. The sparse furniture was a hodge-podge of unmatched pieces, some of which were broken. If the cottage was primitive compared to this...well, it didn't matter. "If that's all there is, then I suppose we'll take it."

His host didn't seem entirely pleased at the decision. He squinted at Michael. "It will take my girl a bit to open it up and set it to rights for you."

"If she can get it done quickly, I'll make it worth her effort," Michael promised.

That seemed to improve the man's view of the matter—so much so that Michael wondered how much of the coin the girl would be allowed to keep. "If you don't mind setting her to the task, sir, I'll see about finding this Mr. Pince and return with my wife."

The idea to refer to Miss Crawley as his wife had occurred to Michael rather suddenly. He didn't give a damn about anyone's reputation at this point, but with there being only the one room in town, he could not risk some moral objection to their being allowed to use it.

He exited the public house and rejoined Albert and Miss Crawley where they waited outside.

"There is only one horse to be had, but I've not spied it yet. It is apparently as old as its owner."

Albert grunted. "It may be as broken as your father's coach."

Michael sighed. "If the horse is living, it will have to do. You will ride to London. Inform the marquess. I will wait here with Miss Crawley. My father will send another carriage to fetch us."

Albert looked at the sky. "I'm sure I can reach London by nightfall if that horse isn't half-dead, but no one will return for you until the morning."

Michael nodded. "I have arranged accommodation for the night."

"With Miss Crawley?"

"Do you have a better idea, Albert?" He glanced at the subject of their discussion. She was unaccountably interested in the ground. "Should I send her to London on our sole horse, while you and I wait?"

Albert shook his head, but looked none too pleased.

"I've told him you're my wife," Michael said to Miss Crawley, who looked up at this announcement. "We shouldn't allow them to learn otherwise unless we want to spend the night in the woods after all." He looked sternly at Albert to convey that the instruction applied to him as well. "Now. Let's find this old man and his horse so you can be on your way."

# Chapter Eleven

Juliana remained quiet as Mr. Rosevear and Mr. Finn went about the business of obtaining the sole available horse. The elderly man in possession of the animal began with a greedy gleam in his eye and seemed to anticipate a lengthy negotiation, but Mr. Rosevear simply agreed to the first exorbitant price. Mr. Finn was saddled and on his way to London in almost no time at all.

Mr. Rosevear and Juliana returned to the public house to learn they had been too quick about their business and the promised cottage was not yet prepared.

"Could we not go there now and you can send the girl around when she's available?" Michael asked. He held a hand toward Juliana. "As you can see, we've had a bit of an ordeal and I think my wife would like to sit and rest a while."

At Michael's invitation to do so, the proprietor looked Juliana up and down, taking in all aspects of her disheveled appearance. She lifted her hands to gather her loose hair and twist it over her shoulder.

"I suppose." The man clucked his tongue and wiped his hands on his apron. "Follow me." He led them out the back door and along a pebbled path to a smaller structure of the same stone as the main building. It had a thatched roof and a small door that required Mr. Rosevear to duck particularly low in order to enter. Inside was a simple square room with a dusty wooden floor. A large stone hearth dominated the space—so much so that Juliana guessed the building's original use was as a detached kitchen. Now the space looked mostly neglected, though there were two mismatched chairs facing the fire, a trestle table against the wall with a single bench on one side, and a small bed against the wall opposite the table. The room was dusty and dark, but Juliana examined the corners checking for signs of mice or rats. She didn't see evidence of unwanted residents. When she'd slept on the floor the previous night, their room had not been on the ground floor and was thankfully clean. She hoped for the same here, even if she had to clean it herself.

The introduction to their accommodation did not take long as there was not much to see. "Mary will be around as soon as she can," their host said, his wide smile only half-full with teeth. His enthusiasm had Juliana wondering just how much Mr. Rosevear had paid for their night's lodging.

"Thank you," Mr. Rosevear said. "And can you point me in the direction of where we might fetch bathing water?"

"There's a pail in the corner and a stream not too far behind the cottage. Mary'll fetch it for you if you'd like." Having delegated all of the work to Mary, their host left, pulling the door closed behind him.

"Well." Mr. Rosevear spun around. "I suppose we will survive. I can't say as though I'm looking forward to a frigid stream water bath."

Juliana spotted the promised metal pail in the corner and went to retrieve it. "There is a hook above the fire," she said, pointing out the charred metal hook extending from one side of the stone hearth. It was nearly identical to the one she used regularly back at home to heat water, soup, or nearly anything else in a pot. "Should I collect some water and heat it for you?"

Mr. Rosevear shook his head. "I will collect the water. Is there only one pail?"

It was her turn to spin, surveying the room. "Only the one, it seems."

"All right, then. One pail of water shall have to suffice." He extended his arm for the pail and she held it out to him, draping the handle over his open palm. "I shall return," he said, then glanced toward the chairs. "I suggest you brush those off before you sit."

Juliana looked down at her dirty and torn dress. She didn't imagine a little dust could make it much worse, but she smiled anyway and said, "Thank you. I'll be careful to do so."

When Mr. Rosevear was gone to find the stream, Juliana looked around again. There was a small pile of dust-covered firewood at the side of the hearth and flint and steel on the mantle, so she went about setting a fire by which to heat the water. The task was accomplished quickly, so she looked around to see what else could be done while she waited. She walked to a small, square window on the wall opposite the door and unlatched the shutters, letting in what light could shine through the narrow opening in the thick stone.

The evidence of dust and neglect in the cottage were only more evident with the better light. She spied a broom leaning in one corner, so she set her small bag on the trestle table and rolled up her sleeves. With no Mary in sight, there was no reason not to set the place to rights as best she could. The floor was filthy, but the chore helped her to recover her equilibrium. Focusing on something small and practical was easier than further contemplation of all that had transpired.

"You are not housekeeper here."

The words startled her from her task and she looked up. She had not heard Mr. Rosevear return, but he was back, standing just inside the doorway, filling the small place with his substantial presence. She wondered how long he had watched her sweep.

"I have offered good coin for the girl from the house to come set the place in order," he said, walking toward the fire. She envied his strength as he easily lifted the full pail of water to hang it on the hook.

He turned and she lowered her eyes, not wanting to be caught watching him. "It must be done," she said, returning to her broom.

He went to her and placed a staying hand on her arm. "You are robbing the poor maid of her wages and me the satisfaction of my chivalry."

She looked down at where his hand touched her bare arm where her sleeve was torn away. The contact was gentle, but in that moment, it was as though she could be aware of no other place on her body. She had such familiar contact with so few people, and mostly then as a child. He had touched her before though. He had held her when she was frightened.

He removed his hand from her arm and she wanted to object, to tell him that she wasn't upset by it, but she couldn't ask him to touch her again. What sort of request would that be? He would take it as either ridiculously odd or an indecent invitation.

He gently took the broom from her hand, swept the accumulated pile of debris out the door of the cottage, and replaced the broom in the corner.

"I don't mind finishing the task," she said. "I can't be certain we shall see the promised Mary."

"Perhaps not," he said, "but we shall wait a little while and see." He looked at the pail hanging over the fire. "It will take some time for that water to heat," he said, "and just as long again if we want to warm another pail. The stream is relatively private and not as cold as I expected. I will bathe there and you may have the pail of warm water."

"I don't…that is…" She considered offering the opposite, that she bathe in the stream and he use the warm water, but she couldn't suggest that she bathe outdoors. She had never done that before in her life and didn't think she was bold enough to do so now.

He smiled, sensing her quandary. "It is decided." He gathered a few of the things that he had carried from the damaged coach and walked toward the door of the cabin. "I will be curious to see if you have met this Mary by the time I return."

She returned his smile, feeling more warmed by it than she should.

Once he was gone again, she walked to the hearth and tested the temperature of the water. It was a very full pail and not even beginning to warm, but she could not risk waiting for the luxury of hot water, when he might return before she was finished. She removed her torn, dirty dress and took the pail from its hook, not even needing to protect her hand in doing so. She removed the chemise she'd been wearing and, because she had nothing else to use, applied it as a washing cloth. She took her only other chemise—that Mr. Rosevear had called a rag—out of her satchel and put it on, despite being still damp from her washing. She then set the bucket up on the trestle table and leaned over it to wash her hair the best she could. The cold water on her scalp was more chilling than it had been elsewhere on her body and she hurried through the task.

Once she was finished, she wrung the excess water from her hair over the pail, and donned her other dress. With her fingers, she did the best she could to shake out her wet tangle of hair. She considered taking the brush to it, but brushing her hair was usually a time-consuming task. Since Mr. Rosevear was not yet back and there was still no sign of the elusive Mary, she went to the bed instead. She lifted the blanket to find there were linens on the bed and no visible stains or holes. She took the blanket outside to shake it out and realized quickly it would have been a better task for before she had bathed herself.

"Miss Crawley," came the reprimand as she shook the blanket. "You had explicit instructions." He emerged from the path and strode toward her. The stern expression on his face was belied by softness in his eyes. "No Mary, I assume?"

She shook her head. His complexion was brightened by the cool dip in the stream and his hair was damp. His white lawn shirt clung in the places where it, too, was damp.

He sighed. "All right. Give it here." He took the blanket from her and she stepped back. He shook it hard three times, sending a cloud of dust into the air that even he had to step back from. He grimaced. He shook the blanket again. With each successive shake he sent less dust into the air, so he shook it until it seemed he could free nothing more from it. They went inside together.

He brushed off the chairs by the fire and motioned for her to sit. She did and Gelert took a spot at her feet. She reached down and touched his fur. She looked up to find Mr. Rosevear watching her. He leaned forward, looking steadily at her until she blushed and looked away.

"Now that I have seen the sort of men who are coming after you, I must insist you tell me more," he said. "Why won't you tell me exactly what sort of danger you are in? It's undeniable that you are, in fact, in danger."

How could she object? Surely he had earned the right to explanations. "I told you the truth when I said it was my father who sent the men. He doesn't want me to reach London on my own because he doesn't want me to claim my birthday present."

"Your birthday present?"

Her lips curved into a sad smile. "It's not really a present. It's an inheritance—from my mother's family. It's not much, not to a marquess anyway, but it's mine upon my twenty-fifth birthday. My father didn't know I knew of it, but he has obviously not missed the coincidence of my leaving so near the day."

He leaned forward. "He doesn't want you to claim it?"

"Not on my own. I believe he intended to claim it on my behalf."

He scoffed at this. "He wants to control your inheritance?"

She nodded. "It's not a large sum, but I don't think that is what's important. He is greedy enough to want it for himself, regardless of the amount. I imagine he also wouldn't want to grant me any measure of independence."

"There is a growing part of me that wishes your father had been man enough to come for you himself and that he had met Gelert in the woods instead of that filthy criminal he sent in his place." He said it with such ferocity that she believed it, and it warmed her better than the fire could have done.

"Thank you," she said, staring into the flames. "I do not want to think what would have happened if you had not come after me."

"Any man with a conscience would have done the same."

She didn't think so. Maybe in her imaginings people were regularly heroic—she had once convinced herself that her mother had left her behind to become a spy for the crown, after all—but maturity had cleared away her illusions. "I think people like the idea of being heroic," she said, "but rarely have the opportunity, and even more rarely take it when it comes." She turned away from the fire and looked up at where he stood instead. "Look at me," she continued. "I am not particularly courageous. I snuck away, relied upon a stranger to protect me, and will hide from my father the rest of my life."

"Given what I am able to understand of your father, I would say you have been very courageous. Many women would simply have accepted their fate."

"As would I, but for the letter."

"The letter?"

"When I was younger, just a few years after my mother left, on one occasion when my father sent me into his study to clean, I found a letter. There was a paper on his desk with my name on it and I read it. It was a letter from Mr. Peale of Hammersley, Brint and Peale, informing my father of the settlement from my mother's family that was to be mine on my twenty-fifth birthday."

He took the other seat near the fire and leaned forward, resting elbows on knees as he considered her revelation. "But I thought your mother left when you were very young? How old were you when you found the letter?"

She shook her head. "I'm not certain. Twelve, perhaps thirteen."

"You were a very clever child if you read the letter and understood the terms of the arrangement."

"I did not understand it. Not then. I knew somehow it was important, but I didn't understand until much later."

"You saved it."

"I never saw it again."

"Then how did you…" Understanding dawned in his dark eyes and he peered at her. "Your memory. Do I understand that you have left your father's house for London to meet a solicitor whose name, direction and purpose you've taken from your memory of a letter you saw once as a child, more than a decade ago?"

She nodded.

"What if your memory is incorrect?" he asked, though his tone was not unkind. "What if you misunderstood or misremembered the names?"

She looked down at her hands. "I haven't misremembered. It is an oddity, I know."

"I think it's brilliant."

She looked up.

He was smiling at her. "Brilliant."

The warm feeling suffused her again. She could not account for why his opinion of her was of such significance, but in that moment it seemed the most important thing. She'd been strange her entire life. Her father had told her daily how unnatural she was, but he was not the only one who believed her so. Sheltered though she may have been, she understood the looks she received from people when she ventured from home to attend services on Sunday, or the rare occasion when her father would send her on an errand. They thought she was odd—and different was always frightening to people.

But Mr. Rosevear thought she was courageous *and* brilliant. Her eyes traveled over his frame as he sat, hunched forward, strong forearms resting on trouser-clad knees. The strength of his frame lent the posture an expectant air, rather than a relaxed one. She could imagine him leaping to attention at the slightest provocation. His build gave truth to the claim that his leg was not usually so limiting.

She lifted her eyes to his face and saw that he watched her, watching him, yet still she looked. Even his face was powerful, determined—every expression borne confidently. And this man had declared her brilliant and courageous. Yes, she liked very much that he believed those things. How tempted she was to remain in his company until she, too, believed it.

If only she could.

She sighed.

"How long have you understood your inheritance?" he asked. "How long have you planned to leave?"

She shook her head. "I don't know if there was a moment in which I suddenly understood. I think it was more gradual than that. I would sit quietly in my room sometimes and wonder what the day might be like. I imagined Mr. Peale as a very magnanimous and exuberant fellow, as thrilled to finally meet me as I him, and ever so helpful." She gave a wan smile. "I have always had the company of my imagination."

He reached a hand up and brushed aside a wisp of hair from her forehead. "I think you are a clever and surprising woman."

She only grinned back at him, not wanting to say anything that might disturb how lovely this moment felt.

He spoke. "I would like to kiss you. I know that is a very unwise course in our present circumstance, but I thought I should caution you that the threat is there." His lips quirked into a crooked smile at this admission and she found it not at all threatening.

It felt thrilling. Her gaze fell to his mouth and the suggestion took hold of her imagination so completely she nearly felt the promised touch on her lips.

She imagined all sorts of reprimands from her father regarding her indecency and inheriting her mother's wantonness, and she smiled. Yes. She wanted him to kiss her very much. She had no wiles or experience with flirtation. She had no way of communicating indirectly but clearly that his kiss would be welcomed wholeheartedly.

She had only plain speaking, so she relied upon that. "I would very much like for you to kiss me," she breathed.

And he did. Her invitation had barely been delivered when he swept forward, his mouth meeting hers a full moment before his arms pulled her from her chair and into his lap.

Excitement shot through her and she knew she wanted that as much as the kiss—to be held by him, to feel his body as well as his mouth. She melted into his hold, her fingers spearing through his hair as she clung to him.

His mouth moved urgently over hers and his hands roved her form and she thought this was the most heavenly thing she'd ever experienced. She sighed and pressed herself further into him, feeling as though she could never press close enough to satisfy the need growing in her. It was so lovely. She could spend hours doing just this. It was everything, yet the longer it lasted, the more she wanted and somehow it became not enough.

Surely any more would be wrong. Even this was wrong. But it didn't feel wrong. His hand closed over her breast and she sighed into him. It felt like the best thing she'd ever done. She felt desirable and womanly and excited. She felt as though she was feeding from his confidence and power after all, or rather he was feeding it to her in the sweetest, most primitive way possible.

She was delirious, of course. Her thoughts were the cloudy revelations of an imbecile, but she knew it and didn't care. She only wanted it to keep happening.

*Rap. Rap. Rap.*

Three sharp knocks on the cottage door broke the kiss. Mr. Rosevear's lips were gone from hers with startling immediacy. Her own recovery was not so rapid. She blinked at first, then she looked at him, questioning. He had pulled away so suddenly. Was he ashamed? Did he regret the kiss? She made his eyes meet hers, needing to know what he was thinking, but there was only mystery there.

Gently, he moved her from his lap and rose. As he walked to answer the door, she turned to the fire, certain whomever had arrived would know from her face what they'd been doing. She heard the door open and felt the gentle rush of cooler air spill into the fire-warmed room.

"I've come to ready the place for you, sir," a feminine voice said.

"I believe the chore has been taken care of," Mr. Rosevear said.

"Oh." There was a world of disappointment in the one syllable, no doubt as the girl counted her lost earnings. "I brought a hamper for your dinner," she said, brightening again. Juliana heard the jingle of coins and the voice became more enthusiastic. "Thank you very much, sir. Will there be anything else you're needing?"

"No. Thank you," he said.

"Food in the morning, sir?" she pressed.

"Yes. Yes, that's fine. Thank you."

"My pleasure, sir. Happy to help."

Juliana heard Mr. Rosevear chuckle lightly as he closed the door behind the girl. She turned.

He looked at her and she looked back and she wasn't certain what to say. Should they talk about what they'd just shared? She didn't want to hear him tell her it had been a mistake, but what else would he say? If it had been a mistake, it was the loveliest mistake she'd ever made. She could not regret it, and she didn't think she could bear just then hearing that he did. Irrationally, she searched his features to find some hint of his thoughts, even as she willed him not to speak them directly.

"We should eat," he said, ending the expectant silence, and she was relieved. "There is no certainty Miss Mary will actually return with food in the morning." His tone was teasing but sounded strained to Juliana. She was desperate to know what he was thinking. He set the basket on the table and, with his back to her, began unpacking its contents—bread, cold meat, a wedge of cheese and a jar of jam. It was a simple task, but one that her father would not have done. He would have set the basket down and waited for her to be useful. After all that had happened, she owed this man a great deal—for the journey, for his protection—but he'd not asked for repayment in any form, save a bit of reading aloud.

She rather wished she had the distraction of a chore anyway. She wasn't quite certain what to do with herself. She turned back toward the fire. The wide log in the center was barely burned. It would last the whole night through. A night could be a very long time.

"Are you hungry?" he asked.

She faced him again. "A little."

He waved his hand to indicate the spread he had just unpacked. "Come and eat then."

She came to the table and sat, as he did, on the narrow bench. He cut a piece from the loaf of bread and handed it to her. She took it silently and ate, mostly looking down at her food as they sat, side by side.

He spoke into the awkwardness first. "I am sorry that I kissed you," he said. "I know that is not why you're here, and I should not have taken liberties."

"Please don't apologize." She hated that he was sorry for the kiss when she could still feel it on her lips. "You didn't take anything that wasn't given to you." She broke the bread in her hands, toyed with it, but did not eat.

"Still, it was not mine to take. You've endured a harrowing ordeal and I took advantage of your need for comfort."

A harrowing ordeal? Did he truly think she was simply overset? She set the bread down and stared at him. "Are you suggesting that I was too upset to know my own mind? That you, as a man I have known for a pair of days, are better equipped to decide what I want?"

He shook his head. "What? No. I only mean that I should not play the cad. Stealing kisses from an unmarried, unprotected woman mere hours after an attack seems rather selfish and insensitive in hindsight."

His words made her feel like a child, erasing everything he'd done to make her feel like a woman. "You cannot steal something that is freely given," she said, unable to keep the edge from her tone.

She had chosen the kiss. She. He couldn't take away that choice. He couldn't turn it into something that had simply happened to her, rather than something *she* had done. She'd lived her entire life unable to choose for herself. She stood, setting her hands on the tabletop as she rose and stepped over the bench. "If you imagine yourself a skilled Lothario who has led me astray because I am so foolish or naïve as to be manipulated, you are wrong."

He rose as well, pushing back the bench and turning to face her.

She stepped away. She didn't want to hear his explanations. She understood. He regretted the kiss. Worse, he believed she was too stupid to know she should regret the kiss.

He followed, unrelenting, reaching for her hand to halt her. "Miss Crawley. Ana. I only sought to apologize for any offense, not to offend you further."

She snatched her hand back and shut her eyes to the false name. She was so tired of hiding and being frightened—hiding in her room from her father, running from his kidnappers, and hiding her true self from this man. When would she be allowed to be herself? To speak when she wanted? To kiss when she wanted?

"No." She nearly shouted it, opening her eyes. "I am not Ana Crawley." She lifted her chin and leveled him with her most determined look. "My name is Juliana Crawford. I have waited twenty-five years for my life to be my own. Today is my birthday and if I want a kiss, I will have it."

# Chapter Twelve

Michael could only stare. She stood, proud and furious, facing him down as she had her attacker from that morning. Her unbound hair fell around her shoulders, looking like a continuation of the red-gold light from the flames in the hearth behind her. Her fists clenched at her sides and her breasts rose and fell with the exertion of her indignation.

He believed in that moment that she was a woman who would take what she wanted. God, she was beautiful. "Juliana," he said, giving her back the name she had given him—acknowledging it. He stepped closer to her, unable not to.

"I'm so tired of waiting and hiding."

"What do you want?" he asked, stepping closer still. God, he knew what he wanted. He'd known from moment he'd returned from the stream to find the cold water had done nothing to cool his ardor. He'd known before then—maybe from the moment she'd lifted her face to his outside the coaching inn at Peckingham, but he would honor her choice. Only please let her choose well.

Then she was in his arms, as though one moment she had been restrained and the next she was free. He was full of her, her scent, her feel, her taste. Ever a woman of contradictions, she smelled of freshness and flowers, but tasted like rich spice—clove and honey. He crushed her to him, felt her breasts pressed to his chest. He responded to her fervent kisses with equal hunger, running his hands along the length of her as their mouths melded. He kissed her with abandon, letting his passion rise until he was nearly drunk with it.

Then he slowed. He lifted his mouth from hers then returned, differently the second time—slower, lingering more carefully over her taste and feel. He didn't want to consume what she offered in haste, when he could savor it.

He liked this version of her—Juliana—not only because she was currently nipping at his lower lip, but because she was not meek or compliant at all. She was asking and taking and doing so in a way that he would have given just about anything she desired, good sense be damned.

"I'm going to do whatever I want from now on." She nearly growled the fierce declaration into his mouth as they kissed through the words.

Good. He pushed aside her thick hair and took his lips to her neck, below her ear, wanting to taste her there.

She sighed in pleasure at his kiss in this new place and he wanted to encourage the sound by kissing as many new places as he could. His hands explored her slender curves through the fabric of her dress and he felt her respond, reveling in the contact. "You are beautiful everywhere," he breathed against her neck, drawing a shudder from her body that passed through to his own everywhere that they were pressed together.

"Do you mean it?" she asked, tilting her head to provide him easier access to the place underneath her jaw where he pressed his mouth.

How could she question it? He had never been more on fire for a woman in his life. It was as though the truth of her was right there within reach, and if he could kiss her deeply enough—touch her everywhere—he would discover it. Yet the more he kissed, he found not answers but need. Merciless need.

"God, yes," he muttered into the soft skin on her neck. "I think you are the most bewitchingly beautiful creature I have ever known."

Bold hands splayed across the thin lawn of his shirt, their warmth searing him through the fabric. "I want you to make love to me."

His passion for her was so consuming, he was hearing her speak his fantasy aloud, when he knew she could not be. "What did you say, love?" he asked, between kisses on her throat.

"I want to do what couples do. Husbands and wives, men and mistresses. I want to do that. With you."

*Damn.* He pulled back and stared down at her.

What? No. He set her from him and stepped a safe pace away. Disappointment crushed him as he did so. Good sense, it seemed, would not be damned after all. "We cannot." He said it firmly, to convince himself as well as her.

"Why not?" Her question was insistent, but her eyes lowered to avoid his.

*Damn, again.* Guilt speared him. He felt the rejection as keenly as if he had received it rather than given it. He reached for Juliana and pulled her to him, only holding her this time. "It is not for lack of wanting, I promise." He laid his cheek on the top of her head and willed his heart beat to slow, his hunger to subside. "I cannot think of anything I want more in this moment." He couldn't think of anything else, full stop.

She was quiet in his arms, but both felt the quaking they shared, as it was no longer possible to determine from whom it originated. Their embrace, still as it was, was alive with it.

"Tell me why we cannot," she implored.

"Because you are…" He exhaled. "Because I am…" *Damn it.* There were reasons. Several reasons. Good reasons. Yet he couldn't seem to call upon them just then.

"Have you been with a woman before?" she asked.

He lifted his head from where it rested atop hers. "What?" If he had made a hundred guesses, he would not have guessed she would ask that.

"Have you made love to a woman before?"

It felt very odd to answer the question while holding her, but he did. "Yes. I have. I am a grown man."

"But you've never met this woman who will be your bride?"

"No. I have not."

"If you are not yet engaged and you've never met her, I don't think you dishonor her if you simply do again what you have already done before."

He pulled back enough to look down at her. He gently set his fingers beneath her chin and lifted it, forcing her eyes to meet his. "Juliana."

She blinked, sending dark lashes up and down over jade pools.

How could he explain? "It is not only my situation that makes this impossible. You will have enough trouble beginning your new life away from your father without being ruined as well. And I'm in no position to marry you to cure it."

She retreated. Brows furrowed she looked up at him, aghast. "But I don't want to marry you. I don't want to marry anyone. Ever."

He sighed. "You may. You should."

"No." She shook her head vehemently, sending a ripple through the cascade of auburn waves. "Not ever. I've already told you, I will live quietly as a widow someplace where no one knows me. What we do or do not do this night will bear no significance, save the memory that I shall have."

A selfish part of him felt a premature pride at the thought of being the memory that warmed her on future lonely nights. He liked it too much, the vision of her on some later eve, slowly reliving in her perfect memory their night of shared passion.

Only they'd not shared a night of passion—not yet. But damn his irresponsible soul, he was already experiencing it, planning it, ticking off in his mind the things that he would show her, the places he would touch her.

She moved forward again into his hold and laid her cheek on one side of his chest. She drew her hand up and, with her fingertips, began tracing light, teasing circles over his chest and his stomach, drawing tension and gooseflesh to each place she touched. "You think I don't understand," she said, softly, still tracing. "That I can't be allowed to decide for myself, but I do understand—fully—and I have already made my choice. It is only for you to make yours."

He stood stock still, but for the involuntary reaction of his skin tightening and his nerves pulsating where her circling fingers touched. He tried to tell himself that he had not yet chosen, that a chance still remained for him to be wise, cautious, sensible.

He was a liar.

He had chosen the moment she had stepped into his embrace. He caught her hand in his, halting the torturous circles. "I choose your pleasure," he said, unable to keep the words from coming out as a low growl.

She stared up at him, and he wondered for a moment if she regretted her bold request now that he had acquiesced to it.

Then her lips curved upward. The minute movement at the corners of her mouth altered her expression dramatically, from uncertainty to bold satisfaction. All hint of the meek, unsure maid was gone and remaining in her place was a beautiful woman who knew her mind and was courageous enough to give voice to her desires.

She had given them voice.

He would give them meaning and memory.

He lowered his lips to hers and tried to tell her with his kiss just how slow and thorough her pleasure would be. This time when he kissed her, there were no limitations to where he allowed his hands to roam. He lifted one hand to cup her chin as his lips toyed with hers, then her drew the hand down her throat and splayed it over the warm skin above the bodice of her dress. He dragged it even lower then, over the fabric that bridged the valley between her breasts, finally closing over one pert curve. She pressed herself into his hand and he squeezed gently, letting his palm tease the cloth-covered peak.

"Does that please you?" he asked, though his male pride already swelled at the knowledge that her body had answered the question. He moved his hand to her other breast, this time brushing his thumb across the tightened peak.

"Yes," she breathed.

He tucked two fingers over the top of the dress and underneath the fabric, grazing them across the bare peak of her breast and she shivered. He nearly did as well.

"I choose your pleasure," he repeated, turning her to unfasten the ties that closed the back of her simple day dress. The fabric loosened at her breasts. He untied the lower fastenings and the skirt loosened as well. He pushed the dress forward, over her shoulders, pressing a kiss to each one. He whispered in her ear as he pushed the garment down the length of her and let it fall away. "I am going to show you so much pleasure that you will want to call on the memory every night forever."

She shivered again and stepped from the circle of fabric at her feet. He clutched her to him again, in nothing but her worn-thin chemise, her back to his chest, and ran his hands over her front from breasts to hips, touching everywhere, lingering only long enough to awaken sensation in each place.

"Every time you call on the memory," he promised, "I want the thought to leave you flushed and breathless."

She sagged against him, making no effort to hide herself or her pleasure as she allowed his hands to roam where they might. "I…think I am breathless now."

He wanted her to be more than breathless. He wanted her to be insensate. Never before had he been so consumed with the need to bring a woman more pleasure than she could imagine—enough pleasure to replace a lifetime of experiences. He almost didn't want it to begin, because he didn't want it to end.

Almost.

He lowered his hands to the hem of her chemise and drew it upward. "Lift your arms," he whispered and she did, allowing him to pull the garment over her head and toss it aside. "Face me," he asked and she turned, bared completely before him, her fair skin touched only by firelight and a fall of flame-colored hair. "You are more than beautiful. You are a fairy tale or a legend, full of fantasies and secrets and too perfect to be real."

"I know that I am real," she said, her lips curving into a teasing smile, "because I am cold."

He laughed and swept her up in his arms, hating that he had to test his leg before he carried her to the bed and laid her gently atop the bed linens.

She sat on the edge of the mattress, swinging her knees. "I think this is not the way it's done," she said with a shy smile, "where I have none of my clothes, but you have all of yours."

He grinned. How could he deny such a request? He pulled his shirt over his head and stepped from his boots. He unbuttoned his trousers and they sagged low over his hips, but he did not remove them yet. He stepped forward within her reach and she took advantage, placing her hands on his chest. They searched him, smoothing across the hair on his chest and down the length of his arms. They played over scar and muscle and skin teased into gooseflesh, and he waited, allowing her to explore as long as she wished. She leaned forward and placed a searing kiss on his stomach. When she looked up at him again, eyes searching, he swept his arm beneath her knees, sliding her into the center of the bed where he could stretch himself out beside her.

This time when he pressed his lips to hers, he felt the kiss everywhere that their bare skin touched. He loved the feel of her soft breasts pressed to him, and the round of her backside, now free to his touch. He wanted to roll her onto her back and bury himself inside her, but that was not the promise he'd made.

It was not his pleasure he sought, but hers.

He gentled the insistence of his kiss and smoothed her hair from her face. Lifting away from their touch he gazed at her wide, green eyes— watching and waiting for him to fulfill his promise. He kissed the tip of her nose and rose again from the bed. He sat on the edge to remove his trousers, not trusting his leg to support the task standing. When he was as bare as she, he slid between the covers and stretched out again beside her.

She lay on her back, very still.

"Are you sure?" he asked, willing his hands not to roam again until she'd given her answer.

Her eyes held his in the dim firelight that reached their shadowed corner. "Yes," she whispered. "I am sure. Only I,"—pink stained her cheeks, "—I don't know what to do."

His passion leapt in anticipation of how he might show her, but he willed himself to be unhurried. "I'm going to kiss you and touch you and you may do whatever that inspires you to do in return." To give truth to his words, he reached for her running his hand over her breasts, closing briefly over each one as he grazed them. "You may find," he continued, "that you would like nothing but to lie back and feel. You can tell me what feels best to you," he said, splaying his hand across her smooth stomach, "and I shall endeavor to exceed it."

He slid his hand over her waist to her back, drawing her against him and she came eagerly, anticipating his kiss and meeting it. He drank her in, deeply and thoroughly, letting the heat between them build until he ached with it. If he had awakened half as much desire in her as she'd aroused in him, they would consume each other. And still he kissed and clutched at her, and she at him. He was determined that she would be drunk with her need before he answered it, so long as he could keep hold of his own. She squirmed in his embrace, pressed herself against him, and he knew she was near to the point he wanted her to reach. He cupped her backside and pressed her heat against him. She released a pleading whimper into his kiss. He slid his hand between them then, rolling her gently from her side to her back as his touch moved lower, grazing down the outer curve of her hip, across her knee, drawing slowly back upward along the inside of her leg. She shivered has his fingers neared the apex of her thighs.

He cupped her there and then began to tease her, drawing from her a sharp intake of breath. He watched her a moment, drinking in her reaction to his touch, then lowered his head to take the tip of one breast in his mouth. "So beautiful," he whispered against her. She may not have heard his voice, but her skin reacted to his breath as it skimmed across her.

He continued to touch and kiss her, drawing out mewling sounds and breathy moans that each felt like a prize for his efforts, until she clutched at the bed linens and he knew she was close to the edge. Then he slid lower on the bed and teased her with his mouth the way he had with his hand, drawing her sighs and moans with his caresses until she called out and her hips lifted from the bed.

He stroked his hands up and down the length of her smooth, pale thighs as she slowly recovered herself. She opened her eyes and looked at him. He thought that look—the passion-sated gaze of longing, gratitude and wonderment—was the most arousing expression he'd ever seen, and he'd found her arousing from the moment he'd looked at her.

Confusion mingled with her expression. "That's not..." She was still breathless. "We haven't..."

"No," he said softly. "We don't have to. Your pleasure doesn't require it."

"But what of yours?" she asked, concern drawing the tiniest line between her brows. "I thought we would do what couples do."

"We don't need to," he said, though his body defined need quite differently than this mind.

"But I would like to," she said. Her eyes were pleading. God, how could he deny her when she asked for *his* pleasure?

"It may not be comfortable for you," he warned.

"How shall we know unless we try?"

He could not fault such sound logic. He rose over her then used one hand to guide himself slowly inside her, in small increments so as to ease any possible discomfort. He knew the point at which she was no longer comfortable, for he felt her twitch. "Are you all right? I don't want to hurt you."

"It doesn't hurt," she said. "Not exactly. It's only...tight."

Michael held himself there, torturous as it was, until he felt her begin to relax around him. Her hips squirmed, drawing him deeper and he continued, slowly, until he was fully inside her. He waited, running one hand along the curve of her hip and touching kisses along her neck until she again relaxed around him. Slowly, he withdrew then ever more carefully advanced.

She closed her eyes, but this time from pleasure. He withdrew and entered her again, more quickly, and she gasped her surprise. The sound was followed by a smile and he knew the pain had passed. He pulled back and advanced again, more quickly each time, letting his need and hers build with his quickening pace. He clutched her and continued until he had no sense of pace or control at all, but was himself swept into a sea of feeling and sensation. When he made the final thrust, he had just enough presence of mind to fully withdraw, spilling himself onto her smooth stomach, instead of inside her where all of her plans and his could be incurably altered.

He collapsed at her side and lay there a moment, sated and weak, before he pushed himself up on his hand and then left the bed to retrieve a cloth to wipe away the results of their act. She watched, curious, as he wiped her stomach, but did not ask why. She must have understood why he had done it.

When he was finished with the task, he stretched out alongside her again and pulled her against his length, loving the feel of it—loving the freedom he had to do it, for this night at least.

"Are you comfortable?" he asked.

She nodded against his chest. "Does this mean I may call you Michael now?" She asked it with a smile.

"I suppose I shall allow it," he said, very much liking the way her voice made his name somehow better, more important. He rubbed his hand along her back, in part because he wanted it to be soothing for her, but also because he found it soothing himself. Her soft, smooth skin was a treat to touch. "Tell me something more about you, Juliana," he whispered. "Take something else that you're hiding and share it with me."

"I don't think there is anything else," she said.

"That can't be true, when I know so little," he coaxed.

"There is very little about me to know," she said. Her hand traced up and down his arm as they lay and he wondered if she had the same need to be touching him the way he wanted to be simply touching her. "I have experienced more with you in the past days that I have in the first twenty-five years of my life. Beyond living with my father and imagining my mother, my life was simple and, I suppose, rather empty."

"What did you imagine," he asked, "about your mother?"

She sighed in that wistful way that was not a laugh because the thing she was talking about wasn't humorous, but rather she wished it could be merely a funny memory. He wanted to take the sorrow away from her. "I recall at one point hearing my mother speak French," she said. "I don't know how much or how little French she knew, but a common daydream as a child was that she was an agent of the crown and had been sent to France to spy for England."

"That seems particularly imaginative for a young child. How did you even know such spies existed?"

She smiled and shook her head. "I don't know. I also imagined she had been mistaken for another and taken away for a crime she had never committed. I daydreamed fantasies of finding and rescuing her." She pulled herself more tightly against him. "And sometimes I dreamt that she had only meant to go away for a visit, not forever, but something had gone wrong, or she had gotten lost and she was trying to find her way back to me."

"They seem like comforting dreams," he whispered, noting each one explained why the mother was unable to return to her child.

"They were, for a time. Once I began to gradually understand the letter I had seen about my small inheritance, I think I realized that she must be truly gone—not just away for a time, but truly gone for good. Why else would her family leave funds for me, instead of her?"

"Do you think she is alive?" he asked, not certain what Juliana had meant 'gone' to include.

"I don't know. I suppose she could be. She would not be so old. But she is gone because she chose to be. Once I accepted that my mother was not a spy and left of her own accord, there were no explanations left as to why she chose not to take me."

Except, of course, Michael thought, that she was a selfish, horrible woman who left her defenseless daughter in a situation that she herself found intolerable enough to flee.

"It doesn't matter where my mother is, or what she has done. I am grateful that her family has remembered my existence and provided a means for my independence."

Provided she could keep it from her father, Michael appended silently. "Do you know them? Do they visit you?"

"No. I have never met them," she said. "Perhaps they choose not to know me. Or perhaps my father would never allow it. I will likely never know which it was."

Michael regretted that he would not meet her father. He would have relished the opportunity to give the man what he deserved. He understood now the desperation that led her to lie to him. Given the harm her father was willing to cause her, he could imagine the sort of father he was when she was in his clutches. He was only glad for her sake that she'd happened upon him rather than someone who might have been less able to protect her, or taken advantage of her innocence.

Of course, isn't that what he'd done after all? They were shut up here in this cottage, and he'd done precisely what they should not be doing. He was so tempted by her. He could still recall the vision of her as they walked out of the forest together—she was quiet and mystical, like Joan of Arc, battered but triumphant, with Gelert at her side.

"Are you really going to marry a woman you've never met?" she asked and he stiffened. The question struck him as odd at first, but perhaps it was not so strange that her thoughts might linger on the fact that he would soon be married.

"I will meet my intended bride first," he said, deliberately misinterpreting her question. "I imagine there will be some time for arrangements before there is a wedding."

"All for your Rose Hall." She lifted herself on her elbow to regard him curiously.

He nodded. "Yes."

"Tell me about it."

He lifted a brow.

"It is just that...well, it must be very important if you are willing to marry a stranger to have it."

"It is very important," he assured her quietly.

She leaned her chin on her hand and waited to hear more, so he tried to explain. "To my father, Rose Hall was just some property too far north for him to bother about. When I returned from the war, I suppose that made it an ideal place to send the bastard son he no longer wished to bother about."

"Yet you want it to be yours."

"It is already mine, except legally," he told her. It was the way that seemed least significant each day while he was running the estate on his own, but the most critical when he considered his future. "When I arrived, the place was neglected. The manor needed repairs, the tenant farms were failing, the village was poor."

"What did you do?" she asked.

"For a while, I moped around the place as though I and my injured leg were a match for our pathetic surroundings. But eventually, I became bored and my leg became mostly better. Then I needed something to do."

"You made improvements."

"I built a brewery."

She laughed her surprise. "You built what?"

He rolled onto his back, pulled her to his shoulder and decided he was quite comfortable with her there, fingers tracing over his chest. It had been painfully arousing before, but was soothing now. "The estate needed more than just improvements," he told her. "It was slowly dying. A few repairs here and there were not going to change anything. Something had to happen that was vastly different, that had a chance of bringing real prosperity."

"How did you decide on a brewery?" she asked, her hands still moving. He liked knowing that she continued to want to touch him this way now, even if they couldn't after this night.

"War is not all marching and battles," he said. "There is a lot of waiting in between—long hours spent passing the time doing anything but contemplating the last battle or the next one. There was a soldier in my regiment who was a brewer. We spoke at length about it."

"And your brewery, it was a success?"

"It is, I am happy to say, though I had a few missteps in the process." He did not tell her of the long hours that he labored away alongside the first handful of tenant farmers who had agreed to plant hops, the repairs he'd made himself because there were no funds to hire additional laborers, nor how he'd had to negotiate with his father's steward for the additional funds to complete the brewhouse when it cost more than he'd anticipated. "I don't want to be away too long, though. I am anxious to return."

She lifted her head again and, sadly, stopped the soothing movement of her hand. "If the property is not part of the entail and your father doesn't care about it anyway, why doesn't he simply give it to you? Or if not now, will it to you? Even if you are not legitimate, you are his acknowledged son."

Michael sighed. "I am acknowledged, yes. I have been well fed, well educated—provided for in every respect, but that does not make me a son. I am not family. I am merely a matter to be dealt with."

"Has he said as much to you?"

"Not in words, but consider—my father has countless properties throughout England. Don't you imagine there is a reason why I am tucked away in Yorkshire, as far as possible from London?" He didn't intend for her to answer the question. Instead he continued. "He will not simply gift

Rose Hall to me, but as he wants something only I can provide, I intend to barter for it."

She watched him closely, likely finding the traces of bitterness in his carefully guarded expression. She reached her hand out to lay on his and spoke softly. "I am sorry. I know what it is to be unwanted, except when I prove useful. I have been housekeeper, cook and general servant to my father for all of my life. It would have been different, serving those roles if we were a family in any sense, but we were not. He hates the very sight of me. I remind him of my mother."

"Your father is an ass and an idiot." Michael declared. "I should ride to Peckingham and sic Gelert on him right now."

"I am not from Peckingham," she told him softly. "I am from Beadwell. I took the mail coach to the first stop. I couldn't very well wait for you where my father might simply walk down to collect me."

*Wait for you.* She said it as though they now knew it was supposed to have been him. He looked at her. He could become dangerously accustomed to this sort of comfort and understanding. Michael had friends—a few in whom he'd even confided now and then—and there had been lovers. But the two categories in his life had never intersected, until now. He didn't just want this woman, he wanted her to know everything about him and he about her. He wanted to offer comforting words to her as she did to him. Every instinct in him wanted to tell her that she never had to worry about her father again, but how could he make that promise when less than a day remained before they would part ways and not see each other again?

# Chapter Thirteen

Juliana awoke to the foreign sensation of sleeping next to another person. A very large, warm, solid person. She wanted to roll toward him and appease her curiosity, but she did not know if he slept still and did not want to be caught staring at him.

She gave in to temptation just enough to turn her head slowly. The blanket crossed low over his abdomen and his chest was uncovered. She wanted to reach out and touch it. She had touched it the night before, but that had been…then. She didn't know what to expect now, or what he expected.

And if she touched him, she would surely wake him.

She considered the light filtering in through thin, ineffective curtains and wondered at the time. They would be back on the road to London very soon. Juliana knew she should feel more relief and excitement at the prospect than she did. She would collect her funds and be on her way— away from her father.

Away from Michael.

It was a silly thought. Of course she would part ways with Michael. They were only travelers on the same road. Beyond that, their lives held no connection.

Except that she had asked him to make love to her and he had obliged her request—most devastatingly. Her cheeks heated at the thought of all that they had done—and the realization that she was stretched alongside him, still as bare as she'd been the night before. She clutched the covers to her chin and scooted away from the sleeping stranger who'd seen more of her than anyone else ever had—or ever would.

"Good morning."

She started and turned her head to look at him. He was smiling at her, unburdened by the same uncertainty. He pressed a kiss to her forehead before rolling to his side and rising from the bed, pausing briefly before standing to test the weight on his leg. She looked her fill of him as he crossed the small room, unabashed in his nakedness.

She held the blanket tightly and considered how silly she was. Of course he shouldn't be bothered with modesty. They had passed that point, had they not? She should feel no hesitation in rising herself to collect her clothing on the other side of the room.

And yet she couldn't.

He dressed efficiently and she knew she was wasting time. She spied her shift and dress draped over the chair by the fireplace. Where was her bold courage now? Where was her determination to be surprising and independent?

Apparently her determination was now cold and frightened and no longer comfortable without its clothes on.

Michael returned to the bedside. "If Albert has kept his promise, a carriage departed London at first light and will collect us by midday."

He was implying it was time for her to be out of bed, but she didn't rise. She only nodded.

He must have sensed her quandary, for he retrieved the dress and shift from the fireside chair and brought them to her, laying them on the quilt. "Would you like my help?"

*No. Yes. No.* She didn't know.

"I can manage on my own." She always managed on her own. She could do so again if he would only give her some privacy. He did seem awfully relaxed about the whole thing. And positively gleeful about the prospect of continuing on to London.

To be rid of her.

But that was what she had promised him.

"Well," Michael said, allowing his hands to fall against his thighs as he looked about the room, "apparently my coins were not enough to ensure a morning meal delivered after all. I am off to the public house to see what fare I might find there. I will return."

With a nod, he was off, taking Gelert with him, and she was grateful. She rose quickly and dressed even more quickly, unsure of how long the errand would take. Once fully dressed, she took her hairbrush from her satchel and began the task of taming the tangles she should not have neglected the night before. She was only halfway through the chore when Michael returned with the promised meal. She knew it for an unnecessary errand, for the bread and meat from the night before was still largely untouched on the table. She thanked him and they ate. He commented on the clear weather and the certainty of passable roads and the cheerier he seemed, the more melancholy she felt.

* * * *

True to his word, Mr. Finn must have left London at the very break of dawn or even earlier, for he arrived before midday and they were soon ensconced in a very comfortable, if slightly smaller, coach—finally on their way to London. Juliana was quiet, contemplative, and unreasonably bothered by Michael's lack of torn feelings about their separation. He was at least quiet while she wrestled with her thoughts. The quiet did not last however.

"You should marry," Michael blurted, not ten minutes into the ride.

She looked up at him. "I beg your pardon?"

"I have been considering your situation, and you should marry."

She had been avoiding looking at him, but she looked now, needing to confirm with her eyes as well as her ears that after their evening together he had spent the morning considering plans for her to marry another. And apparently he had, for his expression was earnest and determined as he leaned toward her with this suggestion.

"No," she said. "I've explained I will not marry."

"What do you intend to do next, once you've seen these solicitors and gained access to your funds?" She opened her mouth to speak but he cut her off her response with a warning. "And do not tell me you shall sail the ocean with your friend the sea captain. No more fantasies, Juliana. We speak only the truth."

She had spoken the truth, but he didn't want to hear it. Now she didn't particularly care to clear it up. "I shall go...far away...and tell people that I am a widow. I shall live quietly and give them no cause to question my history."

"You said that before, but what of the fresh evidence that your father will continue to want to control both you and your inheritance? You will live in fear of discovery by him. He could find you and return you to the state of veritable prisoner in his home."

Juliana nodded gravely. She knew all of this, which was why she had fled. It annoyed her considerably that he felt he should have an opinion on the matter when they would know each other for only a few more hours. "I intend to go farther than he would expect," she assured him, unable to provide further explanations he would not dismiss as lies.

"You can't go far enough on your own. You should consider marrying."

She only stared in response.

"To protect yourself," he explained. "If you are married your husband will have control of your funds and there will be no further purpose to your father's pursuit."

She shook her head. If she married, her husband would have control of *her.* "I am not bound for the altar. I have already explained that. I am five and twenty. I am old enough that I might have been married and widowed, but young enough that I had not yet borne children."

"You miss the point," Michael insisted. "Can't you see you are better protected by a marriage? You will benefit from the protection and you have the funds to offer."

"As I assured you before, I have no intention of marrying," she said, her jaw tightening. Couldn't he see how cruel it was, to discuss her marriage in such a cavalier manner after what they had shared?

"You must reconsider your intentions. For your own security."

"You suggest that I shield my inheritance from my father by gifting it to another man? You propose that I become another man's prisoner."

"A good man would not make you prisoner."

She was just offended enough to say, "You forget, I am no longer pure."

"A virginal bride is the ideal, but reality is more practical."

His pragmatism stung. "Perhaps I am the practical one and you are spinning fantasies, Michael. Where is this savior of a man who shall marry me, become my protector, and treat me like a treasured wife? The funds I go to claim will allow me to live modestly, but I am by no means an heiress. I am no longer young and no longer virginal. Beyond that, I know that I am awkward and strange. People find it no easier to converse with me than I with them. I will not inherit an amount sufficient to tempt a man into marriage with me."

"You do not require a fortune, Juliana, to tempt a man."

She didn't particularly want him to say such things, when he did not seem to dread their parting. "Let me be clear. I am not an heiress, but if I live quietly and modestly, as I am well used to doing, there may be enough to keep me. If there is not, I shall take in mending or apply for service."

He pressed his lips together in consideration of her statement.

"I am grateful for all of your help, Mr. Rosevear," she said, making a point of using his surname, "but the fact that you have given it does not entitle you to direct my life going forward. When we are in London, you will proceed to your future and I to mine. Those paths could not be more divergent. And once our lives are again separate, I am certain we shall fade quickly to the recesses of each other's memories."

*Liar.* For the rest of her life she would be able to close her eyes and not only see him, but feel him. Smell him. She would recall forever—not from her aberrant picture-book memory, but from her body and her soul—the particular sense of being in his presence. He had promised that she would call on the memory each night and she believed him. She simply couldn't decide if the fulfillment of the promise was a gift or a curse.

She prayed to reach London quickly.

Thankfully, her words quieted him. When the pastoral views of the countryside gave way to ever more concentrated clusters of buildings and people, her heart slowed and she dreaded the moment of their arrival.

She looked at Michael, resting with his eyes closed, hand resting lightly atop Gelert's fur, undisturbed by their imminent goodbyes. How silly she had been to believe she could run off on her own with no help. She hadn't been on her own at all thus far, but she would be shortly. As soon as she'd collected her funds from the solicitors.

On her own.

The thought did not carry the same appeal as it had a few days earlier. A few years earlier. She had been yearning to be on her own for as long as she could remember and had never doubted that she would be perfectly fine.

But now...

It didn't matter, she reminded herself. Doubt was only a feeling and feelings passed. She did not doubt herself enough to return to life with her father. She would never doubt enough for that.

\* \* \* \*

The carriage rolled to a stop and Michael's stomach lurched. Already? Had they already arrived?

He looked through the window and spied a simple, three-story red brick building outside the carriage. There were numbers on the building. Number forty-eight. It seemed rather unremarkable, this place that had been the focus of so much planning and difficulty for her. He looked at her and found her staring, likely as uncertain as he just how they parted company. Should he hold and kiss her as lovers did when they said goodbye for now? Only it was not goodbye for now.

He waited too long and she turned away from him. Albert was at the door and helping her down. Michael felt a moment of panic as the last moments in which he might speak to her swiftly passed. He wanted to caution her to be safe, convince her again of the security of marriage, to tell her how much it mattered to him that she be safe and happy.

She looked back at him and said, "Goodbye, Michael. Thank you."

"Goodbye, Juliana." There had been too much and all he'd been able to say was that before she walked away toward the entrance of number forty-eight. He watched as she disappeared inside.

He had wondered if she might ask him to accompany her inside, but that had not been the arrangement, had it? She had made it very clear on their drive that, although she appreciated his help thus far, she no longer required it. She never had told him the amount of the settlement. He sincerely hoped it was large enough that she could do all she planned.

Michael lifted his arm, preparing to rap on the roof of the carriage to let Albert know he was ready, but he lowered it again without signaling. For a moment, he considered the possibility that the story of the letter and the funds that awaited her were just as much a fabrication as the duchess and the sea captain. What if nothing awaited her and she would be alone, friendless and penniless, in London? Even women familiar with the city would be in danger under those circumstances. Juliana was not familiar with any place but her little village.

He strained to recall the name. Blackwell? No. Beadwell. He had never been to Beadwell, but he knew whatever it was, it had not prepared her for London on her own.

Indecision tortured him. If she were without a place to go, what could he offer her? He could not appear on his father's doorstep with a young woman. He could find her lodging, perhaps, a place to stay for a night or two.

But what then? What of the third night and the fourth?

He watched the entrance of number forty-eight. If she had no legitimate business there, he reasoned, they would turn her quickly away. She would not be inside for long.

On the other hand, if she were expected, there might be papers to sign or transfers to effect. Michael looked at his pocket watch and immediately realized the futility of the effort. Consulting his watch would only allow him to calculate the passage of time if he had checked the time upon their arrival, which he had not. He resolved to wait a few minutes longer.

Albert descended from the box and opened the door. "Is there a problem, sir?"

He shook his head, ignoring Albert's curious assessment. "There is no problem. We shall depart soon."

"Very good, sir," Albert said with a nod and returned to the box.

Michael stared at the wide black door for several minutes longer. In all the time that he watched, no one entered and, more significantly, no one exited. Uncertain if he was relieved or disappointed, Michael lifted his right arm and rapped on the roof of the carriage.

# Chapter Fourteen

"I must say, Miss Crawford, that I was not expecting you here, in London," Mr. Peale said, after she'd been shown into his office, introduced, and offered a seat across from his desk. He was not as she had expected. He was small and thin, with a long narrow nose and an equally long and narrow beard. He regarded her as though she was also not as expected.

"No?" she asked.

He gave a discreet cough and continued. "Your father wrote to me of your desire to begin receiving your allowance immediately, but his instructions were that I should forward said funds to him on your behalf, as you are unmarried and still reside with him."

He had already written. She had considered that he might.

She gave what she hoped was a calm and reassuring smile. "Yes," she agreed, "but there has been a change in my situation. I have decided, now that I have reached my majority, that I will be arranging my own financial affairs and will not rely upon my father for such things."

His wrinkle-framed eyes widened. "And your father is aware of this intended change?"

As she had reached the stipulated age, Juliana did not believe she needed her father's permission to manage her own inheritance. Whether the aging Mr. Peale approved of her decision was clearly another matter. Still, she preferred not to upset the man. She attempted a smile. "I am five and twenty, Mr. Peale. My father understands that I am capable of handling this detail on my own." Certainly he understood that. He would object—strenuously—but he knew she was capable, otherwise he would not have worked so hard to prevent it from occurring.

Mr. Peale narrowed his gaze at her and pressed his lips together in annoyance at this irregularity. "Then it is not your wish that your allowance be forwarded to the address in Beadwell?"

"It is not." She paused, leaning forward to inquire, "Did you say 'allowance', sir?"

"I did."

She cleared her throat. "It is my understanding that my settlement was to be a fixed sum."

He leaned back in his chair and stroked his beard. "As I would expect your father could have apprised you," he said, communicating his disapproval, "your settlement was two thousand pounds at age twelve, to be invested in the funds on your behalf, earning interest at four percent per annum. Interest accruing through your birthday was to be reinvested. Now that you are five and twenty, you may withdraw the annual income. The settlement must remain intact."

Juliana was suddenly rather warm. She reread the letter in her mind. It had made no mention of how her settlement would be handled—only the amount and that she could access it upon reaching the age of twenty-five.

"These matters are complicated," Mr. Peale said, taking the tone of a stern lecturer. "I strongly suggest that you reconsider your father's assistance, at least until you are married and your husband can guide you."

Juliana inhaled slowly and exhaled ever more so. "I appreciate your patience given my limited experience with financial dealings, Mr. Peale, but as I am here now, without my father, perhaps you would be willing to answer just a few clarifying questions."

"I suppose I could," he said, clearly unhappy with the prospect. "Though I should point out this is precisely the reason that women find it more appropriate to rely upon their fathers and husbands in their financial dealings, Miss Crawford."

Mr. Peale's loyalty to fathers and husbands did nothing to alleviate Juliana's growing concern. "Am I to understand that I may not withdraw the original two thousand pounds, but instead am entitled to the income of four percent per annum, or eighty pounds per year?"

He interlaced his fingers atop his desk. "As your income has compounded from age twelve, the settlement is presently worth,"—he examined the ledger in front of him—"three thousand three hundred thirty-one pounds."

"Each year?"

"Yes." He gave a clipped nod. "Each year."

The room had become stifling and somehow she shivered. "And how shall I receive said allowance?" she asked, willing the rising panic out of her voice.

"However you so choose, Miss Crawford. I can prepare a bank draft for you today and next year you may write to me with instructions as to how I should arrange to forward you the funds. Or, you may withdraw the funds in smaller increments—monthly if you prefer."

"What if I am not in England next year?"

Her question gave him pause and he considered her with squinting eyes, as though she'd said something incriminating. "I suppose it would depend upon how exotic you chose to be in your travels. You should have no difficulties receiving your allowance on the continent, Miss Crawford. Again, simply write to me with your location and we will make arrangements."

"Just write to you with my direction?"

"Yes." He made no effort to veil his exasperation with her repetitive questions.

"Every year? In perpetuity?"

"Yes," he said impatiently.

"And I may not simply withdraw the entire balance?"

"No. You are fortunate to have family who thought to secure your future in this highly responsible manner." He emphasized the word responsible as though to imply she should be grateful that the structure of the inheritance protected her from her own irresponsibility.

She didn't care. What did it matter whether this man thought she would be sensible? Of course she could not be sensible now. Everything was ruined.

He rose from his desk and said, "We weren't anticipating you, Miss Crawford, so I shall see that your bank draft is prepared, if you would please wait here."

He left her then, to consider her disappointment. She couldn't take her settlement and run away, never to be seen again. In order to receive the money she intended to live on, she would have to provide her location, once per year, every year, to the solicitor who so clearly believed she should be allowing her father manage her affairs. She may as well send her father a postmarked letter once per year.

Her plans were fatally flawed. She could take the settlement, or she could run away, but she could not have both together. Yet neither was possible without the other. How could she disappear if once every year, she had to provide her location? If she collected her funds, her father would find her, but how could she leave with no money? Where would she go? How would she live?

How naïve she had been. She had considered a thousand times what Mr. Peale might look like, but had never considered what he might have to say. Had she really thought he would reach into his desk and hand her a purse with two thousand pounds in it?

Even the one hundred thirty-three pounds he would give her was to be in the form of a bank draft. It was already four o'clock in the afternoon. What good would a bank draft be in finding food and lodging in London that night?

She'd been stupid. She needed help.

She wanted Michael. No.

She could not seek out Michael. She had promised him that he would be rid of her as soon as they reached London. She had promised she would not interfere with his plans—his bride and his hope for Rose Hall.

Mr. Peale returned with the bank draft and handed the paper to her. She looked down at it. She cleared her throat, anticipating the growth of the solicitor's already considerable frustration. She hated admitting that she had been foolish in this way, but there was no help for it.

"Mr. Peale, sir, perhaps you could assist me with one more slight difficulty."

He glared.

"I did not anticipate the lateness of the hour and as I must obtain a room for the night, and you see, well…" She waved the bank draft limply. "I'm afraid I haven't any coin for the night's lodging."

# Chapter Fifteen

The carriage halted in front of Willow House. Michael had never spent long at his father's London home, but long enough to know its name was a mystery, as there was not a single willow tree in the vicinity of the house.

Albert opened the door and lowered the step for Michael. He climbed from the carriage, leaning onto his cane as he did, as the day's incarceration had brought a return of the stiffness in his leg. His arrival was anticipated, for the door to the house opened before he reached it.

"Good afternoon, sir." His father's butler looked as though two decades had passed since they had last met, rather than a handful of years.

"Good afternoon, Bernard."

Just as Bernard nodded in sober acknowledgement of Michael's greeting, a great howl emanated from inside the house, bringing a low rumbling growl from Gelert at Michael's side.

Bernard, who in all of Michael's memory had never possessed a human emotion, looked to Michael with a most exhausted expression and released a beleaguered sigh.

Michael's curiosity was piqued.

"I will vanquish you!"

This time the shout was recognizable as a boy's. The boy in question darted past the entryway, brandishing a sword of some sort, from what Michael could see in his brief opportunity. He looked to Bernard and lifted his brow in question.

"Lord Brinley, sir." Bernard stepped to the side, allowing Michael and Gelert into the front hall. Gelert, hair on his back still standing, surveyed the space, seeking out the noisy creature.

He appeared on the second floor landing next, though how he got there Michael couldn't say. "Die, Traitor!" he shouted, stabbing forward with the sword in the mimic of a death blow. Thankfully, he impaled only empty space.

Bernard cleared his throat loudly, drawing the boy's attention to the hall below. He came to the bannister, staring at Michael. Now that he was still, Michael could see that he was tall for his age, with a mop of unkempt, pale blond hair and large brown eyes widened by curiosity.

"Are you my brother?" he asked. Before Michael could respond, the boy dropped his sword and ran to the staircase. Halfway down he halted, wide brown eyes resting on Gelert. "Is that your dog?" He stared a moment then continued again, more slowly, walking to stand directly in front of the dog.

Gelert, now aware of the source of the wild noises, no longer stood at alert, but sat calmly, watching the boy as Michael did.

"I say, she's very large," he said, walking around to take in the view of the dog's profile from either side.

"He," Michael stressed, "is a wolfhound. His name is Gelert."

"Hello, Gelert," the boy said, addressing the dog. "I'm Alexander. I'm very pleased to meet you." He then brought his heels together, lifted his chin and bent forward in a courtly bow."

Gelert turned his head, looking to Michael. Michael shrugged.

Alexander looked to Michael next. "My mother said you were coming. She said you live in Yorkshire. What's it like in Yorkshire?"

Michael blinked. "Far." His answer was not sufficient to clear the expectant look from the boy's face. "Perhaps I could tell you about it later, after I have had a chance to rest from my travels."

Alexander nodded gravely, in support of Michael's suggestion. "Should we discuss it at dinner, then? I'm to eat in the dining room this evening, on account of your visit." He turned to Gelert again. "Where will your dog sleep? Can he sleep in my room?"

"Alexander, that is enough." A feminine voice entered the hall a moment before its owner did. The marchioness was a handsome woman, closer in age to Michael than his father, with the same blond hair as her son. She sent a warning glance to the boy before smiling widely at Michael. "Welcome," she said. "Please forgive Alexander's exuberance. The weather has been dreadful this week and I fear he's been trapped indoors far too long."

"There is nothing to forgive," Michael said, surprised at the warm welcome from his father's wife. They'd been introduced before, but only interacted briefly. She placed her hands on her son's shoulders and turned him toward the staircase. "Run along, Alexander, and leave your brother be."

With one final grin over his shoulder at both Michael and Gelert, the boy ran off. Michael considered the marchioness. Both she and her son had referred to him as brother. It was odd to hear it. Michael had been raised by his mother, as the only child of a woman who had never married because of her predicament. It tested the truth, he thought, to think of the young Alexander as his brother. Their lives were so separate and distinctly different, but he appreciated the gesture nonetheless.

"You must be exhausted. Your room has been readied for you. Shall I take you there?" she asked. Unlike her son, the marchioness was more subtle in her assessment of Gelert, but her anxious glances at the dog were not completely hidden.

"He's no threat to you," Michael assured her.

She nodded, but her expression remained doubtful.

"And there is no need to show me to my room. If it is the same, I know the way."

"It is the same," she said. "Perhaps once you are settled, you can visit your father in his study. You recall your way there, as well?"

He did. Michael had learned of all the significant changes in his life after being summoned to this house and, specifically, to his father's study—that he would be sent away to school, that his mother had succumbed to illness, that he was to take an officer's commission, and the last time—that he was to be sent off to Yorkshire. This time they would discuss his marriage, and that discussion would be different. He would not simply listen and obey. He fully intended to negotiate.

"Yes. I can find my way," he said. "I am expected, I presume."

"You are. Your father is quite anxious to speak with you. But he can be patient if you need to rest awhile first." Her eyes fell to his cane and he bristled at the pity in them.

"I am not in need of rest," he said, for once as impatient for the conversation as his father was, "only a few moments to refresh myself after my journey."

"Very well." She stepped aside, clearing his path to the stairwell. "I look forward to your company at dinner."

Michael nodded and proceeded to the stairs, obstinately refusing to rely on the cane he held in his hand. He did not want to be these people's poor lame relation any more than he wanted to be their problem to solve. He climbed the stairs slowly, refusing to wince each time he put weight on his right leg. When he reached the landing, he looked back, but she was gone. He signaled to Gelert, and the dog followed him to his room.

\* \* \* \*

Mr. Peale, though not at all the magnanimous gentleman of her imaginings, did aid Juliana with the direction to a boarding house appropriate for ladies and a brief note of introduction, for he had explained to Juliana that the proprietress did not accept anyone who had not been referred. He also begrudgingly provided her with a few pounds and, collecting back the bank draft he'd given her, reissued it for the net amount. Juliana knew she would have to find her own lodging elsewhere soon. Judging by Mr. Peale's distaste for women who managed their own affairs, he would happily provide her father with the address of her location if he arrived in London to inquire.

As absolutely nothing in her journey thus far had proceeded in accordance with her imagination, Juliana was careful to have no preconceptions of the conditions of the lodging house that was, thankfully, only a short walk from the offices of Hammersley, Brint & Peale. Her brief, unchaperoned walk through the streets of London was thankfully uneventful, but still, she was relieved to arrive at a tidy row house on a respectable-looking street. Her knock was answered by a young maid who took Juliana's note and bid her wait while she carried it to her mistress.

The mistress returned in the maid's stead—a tall, severe-looking woman who pursed her lips as she made a thorough evaluation of Juliana's appearance. Juliana was keenly conscious of her worn day dress and slippers still filthy from her tramp in the woods. Most women would consider the dress only suitable for chores, but as her other dress was as dirty as her shoes and torn as well, she'd had no other choice.

"I am Mrs. Stone," the woman said. "We are a quiet house and I will not tolerate trouble of any kind."

Juliana nodded, relieved that she had apparently been approved to stay.

"You may not receive callers, in particular gentlemen callers. Dinner is prompt at six and you shall not leave the house after dinner. We are respectable women here and if you do not fit, you may not stay."

"I believe I shall fit quite well, Mrs. Stone," Juliana assured her. "I have no callers to receive and I much prefer quiet."

Mrs. Stone's mouth pinched skeptically at this declaration, but she nodded. "Very well. Come with me."

Juliana followed her up the first and second staircase to an upstairs room. It was small and plain but tidy and much better than she had expected. There was a small writing desk and a narrow bed atop which sat a square pile of neatly folded linens.

"Thank you, Mrs. Stone."

"You have only a half hour until dinner," the woman said, ignoring her gratitude. "Follow the others and you shall find it." At Juliana's nod of acknowledgement, Mrs. Stone left, shutting the door, leaving her alone in the unfamiliar room.

Juliana could not recall the last time she cried. Her father wouldn't tolerate it, even when he'd punished her, brandishing the long wooden spoon like it was a whip—across her knuckles if he was mildly annoyed, everywhere if he was truly angry. Even in those moments when she'd sat on the floor, covering her head with her arms while he smacked at her with the spoon, she'd not cried.

But tears came then because there was no one to see them. And because she possessed the wooden spoon now, anyway. She didn't know if they were tears of relief or disappointment, of fear or exhaustion—only that she couldn't stop them. She slumped onto the bed and tried not to sob aloud, not wanting anyone to hear. She needed to think. She needed to consider her circumstances and decide what to do next, but she couldn't seem to do that just then. Just then, she cried.

# Chapter Sixteen

Michael saw no reason to delay his conversation with his father. He took a brief respite to wash his face and change his clothes, but then proceeded to his father's study. The sooner they could have the matter of Rose Hall settled the better, as far as he was concerned.

The door was closed when he arrived, so he knocked.

"Come."

Michael turned the handle and went inside. After years away, everything about the room was startlingly familiar. The pulled-back drapes on the far wall of windows could not sufficiently brighten the dark space and candles burned in the sconces even in the day. The room smelled of vellum and whatever oil was used to maintain the woodwork. The wall to the left was lined with bookcases. The opposite wall was dominated by a large sideboard topped with a collection of decanters and glasses that bore the telltale disarray of regular use. At the center of the room sat a large wooden desk and behind that desk, in a tall leather chair sat the Marquess of Rosevear.

He stood and Michael noted that he kept a steadying hand on the desk as he did so. That was unfamiliar. His father was a large man—as large as Michael—and had always appeared youthful and robust despite the graying at his temples. But several years had passed since they'd last laid eyes upon each other. Michael saw as he approached the desk that the gray was no longer isolated to small patches. The lines around his broad mouth and bark-colored eyes seemed to have webbed outward. The skin on his face sagged in the manner of one who had recently lost a fair amount of flesh.

"Michael," the marquess said, "You have finally arrived."

"I have."

"You encountered trouble on the road, I understand?"

"A bit," Michael answered. He wondered, as he had every hour since his arrival, how Juliana had fared. He reminded himself, as he had every hour since his arrival, that her future plans were none of his concern. Because his father seemed unsteady standing, Michael sat, encouraging the older man to do the same. "It is done and I am here now, if a bit later than I should be."

"You are not as late as I," the marquess said obliquely. He reclined in his chair and lifted a glass filled with three fingers of amber liquid. Scotch, Michael knew. It had always been scotch.

"I am not certain what you mean," Michael prompted.

His father sighed heavily. "I mean that I waited too long to succumb to the truth of my responsibilities. I should have been married and producing heirs long before you were born, Michael. Instead I wasted another score of years afterward and was married for too long before Alexander arrived. Now I am a man approaching the end of his life with a young wife and an infant heir." As though to illustrate his point more eloquently, the marquess released a ragged cough then took another long draught of the whiskey.

End of his life? Michael considered the man across from him. The thought had never crossed his mind that his father would not always be a force in his life, like the sun around which he was bound to orbit, whether he wanted to live in its light or not. He had never seen his father so frail either. He looked several stone lighter than the last time they sat in this room together. Michael had been the weak one that day, limping in on his still healing leg, accepting his banishment to Yorkshire. His father had not known then that it wouldn't prove a punishment, sending his son to a neglected estate at the end of the world. He could not have known it would prove Michael's salvation.

Today, Michael felt strong and he wanted nothing more than to return to Rose Hall. He did not intend to announce that desire. One of the many lessons Michael had learned in the successful management of the estate at Rose Hall was that the first to name their price was the first lose the advantage in any negotiation. Michael could be patient and wait for his father to introduce his own request before making a request in return.

He did not have to wait long.

"There is a need now—an urgent one—to have matters resolved." Michael was mildly surprised at his father's words. While he knew every aristocratic family required an infusion of wealth now and again to maintain their way of life, he hadn't expected his father to announce that it was pressing. Life certainly seemed to be continuing in the normal grand style at Willow House. "My days are running low and I must see my family settled."

Michael stilled. The urgency was not a need for funds but his father's failing health? His family settled? The idea that his father considered him family was enough of a surprise, but to think that he cared whether or not Michael was settled in a marriage was entirely unexpected.

"I have failed, Michael, in my duty as a father." He shook his head with the admission.

Michael was struck dumb. Of all the conversations he had expected to have with the Marquess of Rosevear in this chair, he would never have guessed the man would have lamented shirking his duty to his bastard son.

The marquess leaned forward and laid both palms flat onto the desk. "I have failed Alexander, Michael, and I need your help to set it right."

Michael exhaled. All was as it always had been. His father was not concerned with Michael's welfare. He was concerned with Michael's ability to help him see to the welfare of his legitimate family. Of course. He leaned back in his chair. Death did not change life. His father's illness did not make him a legitimate son.

"You need my help in the form of a wedding," Michael prompted.

"That is only part of it," the marquess said. "I need much more from you."

Michael was immediately suspicious. "More in what way?"

The older man drove a hand through his thick gray locks, leaving them uncharacteristically disordered. "The proper way of things is for a man to learn the duties of his father so that he may one day fill his role. My dawdling in getting an heir means that I will not live to see Alexander reach his manhood. He will have to learn from someone else. I would like him to learn from you."

Michael stared at him. What illness had hatched this plan? "You expect me, a bastard by-blow, to mentor your son in the ways of a nobleman?"

"I want you, my son, to aid in the education of your brother."

*Now* he was a son? "You forget that *I* have not been mentored in the ways of a marquess."

The marquess cleared Michael's objection with a wave of his hand. "Nonsense. You've been educated right alongside aristocrats and your performance at school was exemplary. I purchased you an officer's commission so that you might add that distinction to your record, but you far exceeded expectations. You've had a commendation from Wellington himself."

"And a daily reminder of my military service," Michael added, knowing full well it was a churlish reaction to the praise.

"I can't do it, damn it," his father bellowed, bringing a hand down to slam it on the desk. The force of the action drew a hacking cough from him, weakening the drama of the moment. "I can't do it," he said, less vehemently.

"How, precisely, do you imagine me teaching Alexander the duties of a marquess?"

"First you shall marry Miss Thatcher. She will bring a significant marriage settlement. I will name you as trustee for Alexander. You will take over management of the family estate at Brinn Abbey. The funds from Miss Thatcher will be sufficient for you to make necessary improvements. You shall run the estate and teach Alexander to do it as he grows, so that he can take it over when he reaches his majority."

"So I shall manage Alexander's estate for him until such time as he is able to displace me?" This was preposterous. No. He didn't want to go to Brinn Abbey. He wanted to go back to Rose Hall. "No. The boy is only twelve. It will be a decade or longer until he is able to manage the estate on his own."

The marquess's expression was grave. "There is no one else I trust."

Michael nearly laughed. Should he feel complimented? His father trusted him enough to see to protection of the worthwhile son? Why not, when he was the expendable son? Where was the grave remorse for the next ten years of Michael's life that would be sacrificed on the altar of familial duty?

He spoke slowly and clearly. "I will marry Miss Thatcher, and you may keep the marriage settlement, provided I am given Rose Hall. Then you can find another steward to manage your estate."

"I've already told you—I want you. That is the point. I want you to run it."

"You want me to run your estate—Alexander's estate—until I am no longer needed, then you would like me to go away again."

"What are you getting at?"

Michael shook his head. "I have served your convenience enough. Either I am an asset to to the marquessate or a liability. Which is it?"

"Liability? What are you blathering on about? You should have been a damned marquess instead of me. You've become a better lord of the manor than I've ever been. That's why you must be the trustee. Don't you think I receive the reports? Why do you think I put you at Rose Hall after the war? Second to Brinn Abbey, it's the largest and most complicated of my properties."

"You sent me to Rose Hall to teach me to run an estate?"

"Of course. Why else would I send you?"

"To have me out of the way."

The marquess scoffed. "Nonsense. If I wanted to forget about you, I'd have settled a sum on your mother thirty years ago and sent her off to find her own way, posing as a widow or some such thing."

The suggestion brought forth a thought of Juliana, for that had been her plan precisely—posing as a widow. Of course, Juliana was not the mother of a bastard child. He had made certain of that.

"Or I would have sent you somewhere insignificant to live," his father continued. "There's a cottage in Scotland I've only seen once. Maybe I should have sent you there instead," he mused, his lips curving at the thought. "I would like to have seen what you would have made of it." He laughed fully then, the vision taking hold. "You would have set yourself up like some clan chieftain up there, I'm sure of it."

"What would make you think that?" Michael asked, not in the least amused by his father's imaginings.

His father laughed again. "Don't pretend I don't know what's going on up there in Yorkshire. All the women are in love with you and half the men owe their livelihoods to you directly. The other half have you to thank indirectly. My secretary keeps me informed. You are like some benevolent version of a feudal lord who has brought prosperity to all your subjects with your hops growing and your brewery."

His expression sobered as rested his forearms on the desk. "I've no right to ask more of you Michael, but I want to learn from my mistakes and do better for Alexander than I have done for my first son. This arrangement shall see you both settled."

"Impossible. I belong at Rose Hall."

"Do this," the marquess said, leaning forward in his chair and tapping a finger on his desktop. "Do this and I shall give you Rose Hall. You can go there now and then, keep things running smoothly. And when Alexander is ready, you can return there permanently. Do this and Rose Hall will be yours."

Michael did not respond. Taking a wife he'd never met and had not chosen had seemed a high price for Rose Hall, but a worthwhile bargain in the end.

He'd underestimated his father's price. His father wanted the marriage and a decade of Michael's life. The entire reason Michael wanted Rose Hall was so that his life would be his own, his efforts toward his own gain. But it would not be—not for years—if he agreed to this.

He hated it. He hated the entire idea. He looked around the room. Perhaps he had considered too soon, and the power between father and son was not so reversed after all. Here he sat considering another banishment, another direction for his life that was not piloted by him.

The cut crystal of his father's glass glinted in the candlelight as he lifted it to his lips, awaiting Michael's response.

Damn him, Michael thought. He hadn't even offered Michael a drink.

\* \* \* \*

Dinner at the boarding house was subdued. Mrs. Stone presided over the long table with a pinched expression and ate little, seemingly more interested in supervising the behaviors of her diners. Conversation was allowed, but kept in hushed tones and thus limited to those in one's immediate proximity. Juliana sat between a thin, quiet girl in the starched gray uniform of a housemaid, and a buxom girl with sly eyes and a wide mouth who looked exceedingly disappointed to find her herself seated next to the newcomer. She spent most of her time quietly gossiping with the girl at her other side.

In all, there were eleven women at the table including Juliana and Mrs. Stone. She tried to smile at a few of the unfamiliar faces, but she had no idea how to go about beginning a conversation and assumed they were likely to be more comfortable if she did not. She mostly kept her head down and attended to her meal. Because of her quiet, however, she did overhear a number of the conversations. Most of the women, she learned, were employed and discussed the happenings of the day at the house or shop in which they worked. Others discussed wages. She learned a few of their names. The dark-haired girl to her right who liked to gossip was named Kat. She seemed to be an authority on everyone and Juliana wondered how long she had stayed with Mrs. Stone.

When the meal was finished, several of the girls made their way to sit together in the front parlor. As no one invited Juliana and she would not want to simply tag along, she followed the others who chose to retire to their rooms. She lay on the narrow bed and considered her housemates. Most seemed younger than she was. Although some were just as quiet as she'd been, none seemed particularly anxious or frightened. They were all women living independently in the city, supporting themselves and managing their own lives—under the watchful eye of Mrs. Stone of course. She wondered what some of the young women below would do if faced with her particular quandary.

Based on the wages over which one woman had complained at dinner, she thought they would be shocked at the prospect of her two-thousand-pound inheritance—or three thousand now, she amended. The amount was likely more than would cross their palms throughout their entire lives. Even her bank draft for one hundred thirty pounds would seem like a fortune. Surely, if one of these women meant to set sail for a new life, one hundred thirty pounds would seem like a vast amount with which to depart. It would support her modestly in England for an entire year. Surely, it would be enough to find a start in America.

But only a start. In order to be truly safe from her father, she could never contact Mr. Peale again, never notify him of her whereabouts. She would have to find a position and support herself. She wouldn't mind the work. She was used to hard work. But she would have to find the work first.

She would make do.

Because she would not go back.

And maybe someday, when it was likely that her father was gone, she would return to England, collect her years of unpaid allowance, and settle into a quiet cottage. If she returned from abroad, no one would question her widow story then. She could live out the rest of her days as she had always intended.

She felt relief to have decided. She lay back on the pillow and granted herself permission to rest easy, now that her decision had been made.

Only she didn't rest—not right away. Michael had been right. As the sounds of the house quieted around her and other thoughts cleared away, she was confronted with the memories of their night together. He was even right about the blushes and the breathlessness. She wondered where he was this night? It was not likely that he was somewhere in the city, lying abed, thinking of the same thing as she. Had he met his bride-to-be already? Had he obtained his father's commitment to give him Rose Hall?

She hoped he had. She hoped he was pleased with his bargain and would be content in his changed life, with a wife by his side, as true owner of Rose Hall. She even wished Gelert well.

* * * *

Alexander plopped onto the sofa next to Michael and looked at him with that scrutiny of a child that would be impolite if practiced by an adult. "My mother says your leg was hurt in the war," he announced. "Did you fall on it?"

Michael set the newspaper aside. It was not as though he'd been concentrating enough to actually read it anyway—he'd merely been passing the time until dinner and it had been ineffective in distracting him from his thoughts. He turned and looked at the boy. "Yes. After I was shot."

New interest lit in the boy's eyes. "You were shot?"

"Yes."

"Did it hurt?"

"Yes. It was quite painful."

"Did you scream?"

"No. I don't believe I did."

Alexander nodded in approval at this fact. "Is there shot in your leg, still? Is that why it pains you?"

"Soldiers don't use shot," Michael explained. "The musket ball was removed by a surgeon."

"How did he take it out?"

Michael paused. "How?"

"Did you see him do it?" Alexander pressed.

"I did not, actually." Michael had no recollection of the surgeon removing the musket ball. He distinctly recalled being shot. He had vague recollections of Albert calling to him. He also clearly remembered awakening later, with his leg wrapped, and receiving an account from Albert. He was either drugged or unconscious when the surgeon tended him. "I was not awake, or at least not aware when the surgeon removed it," he told Alexander. "If you would like to hear all the vile details you shall have to ask Albert, the coachman. He was there."

Alexander nodded and Michael felt quite certain Albert would be receiving a visit before the day was out. The boy—his brother—seemed very young. Was Michael so bloodthirsty at twelve? He could not recall. At that age, he was already away at school.

"Do you not attend school?" Michael asked him.

"Not yet. I have a tutor. Father says I need to go away to school, but mother says it is not time yet. Father tells her she is being silly and only wants to keep me here because she will be sad when I am gone."

That seemed a very probable story to Michael. "Do you want to go to school?" he asked.

Alexander stopped and gave a full moment of consideration to Michael's question. "Yes. I think I should like to go to school. There will be other boys there."

Michael nodded. It was sound logic.

"But it doesn't matter, really," Alexander continued. "If father decides I will go, then I will go."

Michael understood that aspect very well. In some ways, it seemed, life was not so different for Alexander than it was for him.

"Alexander," the gentle reprimand of the marchioness floated into the room as she did. "Are you pestering your brother again?"

"We were talking," Michael said. "It's no bother." It wasn't.

"He's always so full of questions," his mother said.

He didn't mind Alexander's questions. But he couldn't help noticing how very young they made him seem. Perhaps not sending him to school had stifled his maturity. Alexander had a very long way to go before he was capable of managing his own affairs as a peer of the realm.

The marquess joined the group then, smiling indulgently at his wife and son then turning last to Michael. Michael received a nod and significant narrowing of the eyes that were meant to communicate the need for his timely decision. His response was a bland smile that offered no comprehension or commitment. He could not respond, as he had not yet decided.

A brief flash of frustration crossed his father's face, but it passed quickly and the group went in to dinner.

* * * *

Juliana fell asleep thinking of Michael and Gelert, but woke up determined to leave them behind. She would leave everything behind in England—her father, her mother, and Michael too. The farther she traveled from these ghosts the more difficult it would be for them to haunt her.

She donned her lone wearable dress and went downstairs. She was not surprised to discover breakfast was very simple at Mrs. Stone's boarding house. While she took her tea and toast, she listened to the chatter of the other residents, envious of their easy ability to exchange pleasantries and converse on idle topics. When she was finished, she sought out Mrs. Stone.

She found her seated at a small writing desk in the corner of the front parlor.

"Yes?" she asked when Juliana entered the room, not lifting her head or halting her hand as she wrote.

"I have a dress I need to mend. I was wondering if you might be able to direct me to where I could buy a needle and thread to do so."

"There is a kit on the third shelf," Mrs. Stone said, still writing but lifting her unoccupied hand to wave toward the bookcase on the other side of the room. "You may borrow it, provided you return it to me before dinner. If you require anything special, it will not be in the kit and you shall have to visit the haberdasher."

Juliana found the referenced kit, a small metal box resting, as promised, on the third shelf. She unlatched it and looked inside. It contained needles, threads, miscellaneous buttons, a few scraps of fabric and crude lace, and a number of other items one might need in mending various garments.

"Thank you," she said, closing the box and lifting it from the shelf. "I shouldn't require anything beyond this."

Mrs. Stone, back straight and tall in her chair, continued writing.

Juliana stood in the center of the room and held the box. She bit her lip, tapped the box with her finger, and finally spoke again. "I am very sorry to bother you further," she said, "but could I ask your assistance in another matter?"

"You may ask," Mrs. Stone clipped. "I cannot promise that I will be able to assist."

"This is my first time in London and I have a friend I should like to visit," Juliana said. Lucy Brantwood may not consider Juliana a friend, precisely, but the exaggeration was a harmless one.

"You may go visiting provided you do not receive callers here and return by supper."

"The trouble is ma'am," Juliana said, "I don't know how to go about finding her, but it's rather important that I do."

This drew Mrs. Stone's attention. She finally halted in her task, pivoted in her chair, and peered suspiciously at Juliana "What is it that you are up to?"

Juliana quickly shook her head. "Nothing untoward, I assure you. A friend from home is recently married and living in London. I don't have her direction, but I have…messages. From home. To deliver to her."

Mrs. Stone's eyes narrowed.

"She is the vicar's daughter," Juliana added, in the hopes that fact might make the entire situation appear more wholesome, but it did not appear to help.

Mrs. Stone pressed her lips into a thin line and Juliana wondered for a moment if this was precisely the sort of 'trouble' Mrs. Stone had meant when she had given Juliana the rules for residing here and if she was about to be turned out.

"What do you know of her?" the older woman asked sharply.

It took a moment for Juliana to register that she was not, in fact, being turned out and that Mrs. Stone was going to help. "Oh. Um. She is Mrs. Brantwood now. I know that she is living in London with her husband, and that he has started a shipping company called Brantwood Trading Company. He owns a ship."

"London is a large city, Miss Crawford. Do you not know the general area in which she may live? Anything else that would help you to locate her?"

"I do not."

She released a disapproving huff. "Well then, you are on a scavenger hunt, and I have no way to help you."

Juliana's heart sunk as Mrs. Stone turned back to the task at her desk. She turned and started toward the door with the mending kit when Mrs. Stone spoke again.

"You are under no circumstances to visit the docks to find this shipping company, is that understood?"

Juliana swallowed. "Yes, ma'am. Quite clearly."

She dipped her pen in her ink pot and tapped the excess. "Return the mending kit before dinner."

"Yes, ma'am. Thank you."

As no further response came from Mrs. Stone, Juliana took the box and left the study.

# Chapter Seventeen

The boarding house, Juliana discovered, was very quiet during the day as most of the girls were employed. Those who remained were allowed use of the front parlor—not in the mornings, but in the afternoons, after Mrs. Stone had completed her tasks for the day. Though Juliana would have strongly preferred to remain in her room as opposed to congregating in the parlor, she forced herself to attend, if not participate, so that she might speak to one of her housemates. She had considered during the prior evening's meal, which of the residents might be most qualified to assist her and had one in particular in mind. Besides, she told herself, she had completed her mending and needed to return the kit.

There were four girls in the parlor when she entered. One was reading, one was sewing and the other two were huddled together whispering in the corner. The latter two looked up when she entered and she forced a hesitant smile. She recognized one of the two whisperers as girl with the raven hair and the sly manner from the evening before. She was called Kat. Of all the women in residence, she was the most intimidating to Juliana, but she also seemed the most likely to know the answers to her questions.

Juliana exhaled to calm her anxiety and made her way to the bookshelf, placing the mending kit on the shelf in the spot from which Mrs. Stone had collected it. She found an unoccupied chair and sat, glad that she had thought to bring her book with her. She opened it and it gave her something to look at, so she didn't seem out of place. Mostly, she was waiting. She waited for the two women in the corner to finish their conversation. As the dinner hour neared, both women rose to return to their rooms before dinner and Juliana followed, keeping watch on Kat.

"Excuse me," she said, after maneuvering to walk up the stairs nearest her. "Could I speak with you a moment?"

The girl looked back at Juliana and shrugged. She kept climbing the stairs. Juliana wasn't certain if the shrug had been an agreement or not, so she followed. At the top of the stairs Kat turned and said, "Depends about what, I suppose."

Juliana looked down the stairwell to make sure no one else was nearby, then returned her attention to Kat. "Would you have a moment to speak in my room?"

Kat looked over her shoulder as Juliana had done, then eyed Juliana curiously. "I suppose I do, as long as I'm not late for dinner," she said and Juliana knew it was curiosity rather than helpfulness that had lured her in.

"I would like to ask you a question," Juliana said once they were inside her room with the door partially shut, "but I am hoping that you will keep our conversation confidential."

Kat shrugged again and Juliana decided it was likely not a promise of silence, but more likely meant that whether or not she would tell the others depended upon how interesting the secret turned out to be. With no other way to get the help she needed, Juliana accepted the risk.

"I need to get to the London docks," she said, "but I don't know how. And I can't ask Mrs. Stone, because she wouldn't like my going there." She did not share that, in fact, Mrs. Stone had expressly forbid it.

Kat smiled knowingly. "The docks? Well, aren't you a surprise."

"I promise it's nothing improper. I need to find a friend and my only way of doing so is through her husband's shipping company."

"Mmm hmm. There's nothing proper about you going to the docks by yourself. There's only one sort of lady down there, and she's not the sort Mrs. Stone will be allowing here."

"I just don't know how to get there," Juliana insisted, ignoring Kat's opinions regarding the types of ladies at the docks.

Kat looked around the room. She spied Juliana's mended day dress draped over the chair in the corner, then her eyes fell on the book on the bedside table, and the small satchel with the rest of her things. "I think you should find another way to locate your friend."

"There is no other way," Juliana insisted. She felt certain any help she gained from Mr. Peale would be a direct communication to her father and she hadn't time to waste. "And it is terribly important that I speak to her."

Kat put one hand on her hip and leaned her entire frame to that side. "If you have the blunt to spare, safest way is a hackney cab. But, in my opinion, if you don't know enough to know how to get there, you don't know enough to be going there at all."

"I have to go." Juliana was firm.

"Whatever for?"

"I have to find…"

She rolled her eyes. "I know, your *friend*." She said it as though she knew it was false. Her eyes narrowed and she stepped toward Juliana. "You don't seem the type to have friends what spend their time at the docks."

"I don't," Juliana agreed. "I only hope to find my friend's husband so that he can direct me to her." It was actually the husband that mattered to Juliana, but if she clarified that now, Kat would believe something scandalous, she was sure.

Kat stood straight and again smoothed her skirts. Tongue tucked into the side of her cheek, she considered Juliana for a long moment. When she finally spoke, her tone was sharp. "Walk round the corner before you hail a hackney cab, otherwise Mrs. Stone will see you. Go in the morning. The drunks and whores will sleep late. When you get there, go directly to where you are headed. Don't talk to anyone. Never look lost." She crossed her arms and added, "And put your money in more than one place. That way, if someone picks your pocket, you'll still have the coins to get home."

Juliana listened carefully, nodding her understanding with each bit of sage advice. "I do have one question," she said after Kat had finished. Kat tilted her head to one side, waiting, so Juliana continued. "The bit about hailing a hackney cab," she said. "I don't really know…that is, I've never…"

Kat leveled Juliana with a disapproving expression that would have done Mrs. Stone credit. "I don't think this is a very wise idea."

Juliana didn't think it sounded like a very wise idea either, now that she'd received all of Kat's cautions, but she didn't see any alternative. "It's the only way," she told Kat emphatically.

Kat sighed again. "When do you plan to go?

"Tomorrow morning."

"I will put you in a cab. You can see how it's done. You'll be on your own to get back, though."

Juliana nodded. "I understand. I am very grateful for your help."

"Hmmm." She turned and placed her hand on the door, the turned back. "Don't tell anyone I've helped you. If you end up dead or missing, I don't want to be blamed for sending you there."

With that, she left. Juliana sat on the bed, anxiety building. Was it really as bad as all that, or was Kat just trying to scare her? If it was the latter, it worked. She had to go, but she wished she had Michael and Gelert to go with her.

It was a silly thought. Of course they could not. She had promised to leave them alone. Besides, she wouldn't even know where to find them.

As she thought on it, she decided that was for the best. If she did know how to find them, she might be tempted to do so.

Scared or not, she needed to do this on her own. Independence, she decided, was considerably more dangerous than she had anticipated.

# Chapter Eighteen

The announcement that Mr. Thatcher and his daughter, Miss Lydia Thatcher, would be their guests for dinner that evening was a surprise to Michael. He had not communicated to his father any decision regarding the proposed arrangements for Alexander's future—and by default, his own. He had not communicated a decision, because he had not yet made one.

There was risk involved, Michael thought with some detachment, in bringing Miss Thatcher to meet him before he had agreed to the bargain. Though she might prove perfectly lovely and thus aid the marquess in his cause, she might just as likely prove a disappointment and ruin his plans.

Nonetheless, the marquess, the marchioness, and Michael were assembled in the drawing room, awaiting the arrival of the Thatchers. Alexander was not yet old enough to dine with the family when there were guests. Michael churlishly wished he could be allowed to take a tray in the nursery as well, but that would thwart his father's purpose and they couldn't have that, now could they?

Bernard entered the room to announce the guests' arrival. "Mr. Thatcher and Miss Lydia Thatcher," he called to the room at large.

They walked into the parlor, he as large as she was small, and the marchioness floated over to greet them.

"Mr. Thatcher, how kind of you to come," she effused. "And Miss Thatcher. How lovely to see you again. We are so glad to have you here. I am only sorry that your mother was not able to join us."

"My wife is unfortunately ill," Mr. Thatcher responded, "but we are glad for the invitation, Lydia and I." When he spoke, each word thrust forth as its own separate burst of speech, giving the impression of shouting even though he was not being overly loud.

The marchioness took a small step backward. "Well, we are sorry to hear of it," she said. "I hope that it is not too serious or long of duration." He harrumphed. "Knowing my wife it is not too serious, but it will most assuredly be long of duration." The marchioness coughed quietly. "Yes, well, some of us are more delicate than others." "I believe my wife endeavors to be as delicate as possible, Lady Rosevear." Michael waited, but apparently even the marchioness could not produce the appropriately diplomatic reply to this latest comment, so she simply smiled and turned to Miss Thatcher, who had stood quietly by through this exchange. "Won't you come and meet my husband. And Mr. Rosevear," she said, taking the lady by the arm and leading her into the room.

The pair of ladies, with Mr. Thatcher in their wake, stopped in front of his father and the marchioness made a show of introductions, as Michael watched. Miss Thatcher was petite, with blond hair, brown eyes, and a perpetually placid expression. She was trim and dressed to the height of fashion. He wondered if she would like hiding away in Yorkshire.

Once everyone had been properly introduced to the marquess, they turned their collective attention to Michael. "And this is Mr. Rosevear," the marchioness said.

Michael stepped forward. He always found introductions to be awkward. He found his made-up surname rather silly, given everyone knew the family name was Brinley. Still he smiled graciously and pretended not to notice that the marchioness carefully avoided referring to his family position. "Good evening, Mr. Thatcher, Miss Thatcher. I am happy to make your acquaintance."

"Very good to meet you as well," Mr. Thatcher said with a wide grin.

His daughter smiled blandly. It was not a particularly sparkling beginning.

Thankfully they were called into dinner rather quickly. In Michael's experience, a lack in topics of conversation could always be resolved during a dinner by commenting on the food, and he expected no shortage of culinary appraisal in this meal.

They were not yet halfway through supper when the matchmaking began in earnest by both fathers.

"Lydia is an accomplished rider," Mr. Thatcher announced in his forceful brand of speech.

"Is that so?" The marquess took the bait, looking disproportionately eager at this bit of information.

"I'm not certain my accomplishments warrant comment, my lord," Miss Thatcher responded, "but I do very much enjoy riding."

The marquess grinned as though this was the best news he'd received in months. "Have you been riding in our parks, Miss Thatcher? London has so much parkland in which for you to ride."

"A little, my lord, but not everyone in my family is such an enthusiast."

"Well," the marquess drawled, "I think we can remedy that, can't we Michael?"

This unsubtle instruction to Michael as to the invitation he should be extending was sufficient to bring a tinge of pink to Miss Thatcher's unruffled expression.

"Miss Thatcher," Michael said, once again playing the obedient son, "I would be delighted to accompany you for a ride in the park this week, should you have the time and inclination."

"Of course she should have the time," Mr. Thatcher blustered. "What else would she do?"

This deepened the color on Miss Thatcher's cheeks to apple red. She gave a delicate cough and directed her response to Michael, eyes full of apology. "I am certain I could make the time for a ride in the park."

"Tomorrow morning," the marquess proposed.

"Tomorrow morning?" Michael asked Miss Thatcher, as though the idea of this particular timing had only just occurred to him.

"Tomorrow morning would be fine," she said, "but are you sure you would like to ride, Mr. Rosevear? There is no need. I think a drive should be just as pleasant."

Michael required a moment before he realized she was making a concession to his injured leg. How the hell would she have known? He hadn't used the cane that evening. Now that he was no longer trapped in a carriage for hours a day, he was barely even limping. What a callous negotiation his father must have had with Mr. Thatcher. He could only imagine.

*Yes, the connection to the Rosevear name is quiet valuable, but it is on the wrong side of the blanket and the leg is lame as well.*

*What shall we deduct from the settlement, then?*

And then, of course, Mr. Thatcher had broken the bad news to his daughter.

*There's an injury, dear, but remember you'll be connected to a marquess.*

To her credit, at least Miss Thatcher looked sincere in her desire to make an accommodation.

"I would much prefer to ride rather than drive, Miss Thatcher," Michael said, "So if you would prefer to ride as well, we are in accord."

She smiled widely for the first time that evening. "That sounds lovely."

"Very good," Mr. Thatcher said, beaming at his daughter.

"Excellent," the marquess announced. Then he waved at his empty glass and a footman swept forward to fill it with wine.

Michael didn't mind the prospect of a morning ride, but he thought the optimism of both fathers to be a bit premature. Additional time spent in the company of Miss Thatcher was not likely to change Michael's mind when his primary objection was not the woman but his inability to return to Rose Hall. No outing with Miss Thatcher would change his views on that.

He conceded she seemed perfectly nice, if a bit tepid. To be fair, he'd not been particularly enthusiastic himself. She simply didn't intrigue him.

He wouldn't have thought he possessed a particular taste in women, but if he did, this woman didn't seem to be it. She was pretty, he supposed, in the common way, with golden blond hair and large dark brown eyes. Her figure was perfectly formed, her smile pleasant. Her voice was even nice— lilting and soft. She just didn't seem to strike him in any particular way.

*She didn't have auburn hair and jade green eyes.*

No. No she did not. Neither did she tease him with an air of mystery that begged to be solved.

Then again, that wasn't entirely true. He knew nothing about her other than her love for riding. To be fair, she was more of a mystery to him than Juliana, but not a mystery that pulled at him, that demanded his preoccupation.

"I hope the weather will cooperate for your ride," the marchioness said. "We've had so much rain in the past week, surely the skies must be empty of it."

Michael rather doubted that was the case. And mention of the weather only reminded him of Juliana again. He could admit then that he deeply regretted not learning enough of her plans to at least contact her—to ensure that she was well and well taken care of.

And safe from her father.

Once he had broken down and freely allowed his mind to linger on Juliana, he was completely preoccupied with her safety. He barely paid attention to the conversation through the rest of dinner and he could tell his father was annoyed with him for not being more attentive to Miss Thatcher when she left with her father. The fact was, Miss Thatcher was clearly not in danger. He couldn't think of her when he was worried for Juliana's well-being. Why had he not considered that more seriously? They had discussed how she might preclude her father from accessing her funds in the future, but what if her father was en route to London even now? Where was she staying? Could her father find her there? The more he considered it, the more he felt a damned fool for ever allowing her to set foot out of his carriage without him.

He spent a second night thinking of Juliana. This time his thoughts were not pleasant memories but a burgeoning fear that she may already be in danger.

# Chapter Nineteen

Juliana did not approach Kat before breakfast, but made a point to catch her eye during the meal. The other woman met her gaze blankly, with no meaning or recognition, and Juliana panicked. She had no inkling of how one went about hailing a hackney cab, or even how much it should cost. She would very likely be cheated.

She supposed overpaying was the least of her worries. That would at least mean she had gotten one to take her somewhere. She supposed she could watch the street for a while. Perhaps someone else would come along to hail a hackney cab and she could watch how they went about it. It was not a perfect plan, but it was the best she had under the circumstances. She just hoped Kat would not tell Mrs. Stone the details of her outing. She did very much like to whisper with the others and tell secrets. It had been a mistake to trust her.

Juliana tried not to look at Kat anymore during breakfast. She went back to her room after the meal and gathered all of her things into her small satchel in case she did not return to the boarding house. She wasn't certain what she would learn once she found the Brantwood Trading Company or how soon the ship might depart. She had paid Mrs. Stone in advance for the week, so she would not be running out on an unpaid debt.

It had occurred to Juliana over the course of the night, when she sat in her bed reliving all of Kat's dire warnings and thinking of every other thing that might go wrong, that the ship may have recently departed for America. If that was the case, she would have a very, very long time to wait. She didn't know how long it took a ship to sail to America and back to Britain. Weeks? Months? Perhaps if that were the case, she could ask Mr. Brantwood to assist her in arranging passage on a different ship. She recalled her bravado in claiming to Michael that she would be perfectly fine on her own in London. She felt none of that bravado now. She was clever enough to realize how little she knew and how right he'd been to caution her. She did need help and she could only see one couple remaining who might be willing to provide it. If she could have devised any other way of locating Mr. and Mrs. Brantwood in this vast city, she would have pursued it instead of venturing to the docks.

When her room was tidy and she was as ready as she could be in her mended and washed dress, Juliana descended the stairs. She expelled a great breath of air and mustered her determination as she walked toward the front door. She opened it and peered outside, half expecting to see her father waiting there.

There was nothing but a normal, quiet street. The few people who walked nearby paid no attention whatsoever to the girl who peeked out from the tidy house with the black door. She stepped outside and considered which way to turn. In the end, she decided to turn left, but only because the street corner was closer in that direction.

"You took long enough up there."

She turned and there was Kat, in bonnet and shawl, falling in step with her as she walked away from the house

"I wasn't sure if you were coming."

She shrugged. "I told you I didn't want anyone to know."

Juliana was relieved she'd come. "Thank you for helping me."

Another shrug. Juliana was beginning to notice it was the way Kat responded to nearly everything. "I've nothing else to do most days."

Juliana was curious to know more of Kat, of where her home was, why she was at Mrs. Stone's, but they had reached the corner. Kat took a few minutes to explain the process of hiring a hackney cab and pointed one out as it drove by. "We'll watch for the next one," she said. "Did you separate your money, like I told you?"

Juliana nodded.

"Good. The more you show the driver, the more he'll charge you." Kat looked her over. "You don't look well off, so that's good."

Juliana looked down at her dress. Though it was the best she had, it would be a rag for most. She was not offended by Kat's observation.

"It's the fancy-dressed ones that always get cheated. And you won't draw so much attention at the docks, either." She gave Juliana another critical look. "Your dress is old and torn, but you're a bit too clean to belong there." She looked up at the street. "Here we are then."

She stepped toward the edge of the walk and signaled the driver. He slowed quickly, darting to their side of the street and coming perilously close to a collision with another carriage. He ignored the shout and the waving fist from the liveried coachman.

"Up you go, quickly," Kat said, helping Juliana into the vehicle as soon as it lurched to a stop.

Their driver had her destination and was moving again before Juliana even knew what was happening. "Thank you," she called, but Kat had already turned and was walking away.

She settled into the seat, anxiety building, and tried to notice the views of the city as they drove by. It all seemed a bit of a blur, but she couldn't say whether that was on account of the driver's speed or her own apprehension. She couldn't even say for certain how much time had passed when the driver slowed and then stopped. She paid him what he asked, for she had forgotten to ask Kat how much he should charge. Then he raced away and she was alone at the docks. She spun in a small circle. She could smell the Thames. She could see the masts of tall ships. There were rows of buildings down the quay, ramshackle huts alongside imposing brick structures and whitewashed fish houses. She smelled the fish, or the filth, or perhaps both. Everything was dusty, as well, kicked up from the bustle of activity from horses, carts, and dock hands.

The Docks, she realized belatedly, was a vast area along the river, many times the size of the village of Beadwell. She had no idea where to go next. She was keenly aware, however, that the more she looked around to evaluate her surroundings, the more she appeared lost, as Kat had cautioned her never to do. But she needed to get her bearings. She needed to determine where the shipping offices might be.

\* \* \* \*

Morning did not bring relief from Michael's growing concern for the fate of Miss Juliana Crawford. The longer he thought on it, the more he felt personally responsible. What brand of gentleman delivers a lone girl to London and leaves her to fend for herself? He couldn't imagine how he might go about finding her now, but he decided honor demanded that he try. He realized, of course, that if he could locate her, so could her father, so even as he determined to search for her, a part of him hoped that he would fail.

He felt some measure of peace once he'd made the decision. He would enlist Albert's help and they would begin that day—after he had participated in his obligatory ride through the park with Miss Thatcher. Thankfully, they had agreed upon an early outing.

She was prompt and, as before, outfitted with no expense spared in a jade green riding habit and jaunty hat. It was a smart ensemble and would have been stunning on Juliana as a perfect match for her eyes.

Michael shook his head. Miss Thatcher was quite handsome as well. Although Michael was not particularly captivated by her, he thought she could marry better than a nobleman's bastard, quite frankly, given her looks and fortune. Wisely keeping that opinion to himself, Michael kept the conversation to easy topics. Since they were not dining, food would be out of place, so he relied upon the obvious alternative. Horses.

"So you ride a great deal?" he asked while they waited for their mounts to be brought around to the front of the house.

"Oh, yes. My father complains that I am always on a horse," she said. "His business office is in Liverpool, so we have a house there, but we also have a house in the country and that is where I prefer to be."

"Do you?" He had assumed she preferred the city, as all young girls seemed to—the parties, shopping and theaters.

"Oh, I like the city as well," she rushed to add. "London has so much to offer."

Michael looked out onto the what could be seen of the city from the front steps of Willow House. "I do not fit well in city life," he said, feeling she may as well understand him now.

She laughed then. "I don't think London agrees with me either. I was only worried about offending you. Most of the people that I meet are vehement advocates of life in town."

The stable hand arrived with their horses then, leading them around from the mews. He helped Miss Thatcher onto her mount and looked to Michael, waiting to see if he required help.

The leg was sore, damn it, not cut off. He had only arrived with a cane because of the damned carriage. He put one foot in the stirrup and swung himself onto the horse. He looked pointedly at the stable hand to dismiss him and signaled to Gelert who waited by the door.

"Is your dog going to follow us to the park?" she asked.

"He needs the walk as much as I do," Michael said in Gelert's defense.

"And he'll stay by your side without a lead?" To her credit, she appeared impressed, rather than doubtful.

"He will," Michael assured her. "Shall we be off, Miss Thatcher?"

She nodded and they set off at an easy pace toward the park. It was not far from Willow House and they found the unfortunate consequence of the fair weather was the great number of people who'd decided to do exactly as they had.

"I was looking forward to an exhilarating ride, but I don't think I shall be stretching this horse's legs much today," Miss Thatcher observed.

"It appears not. Perhaps once we ride a bit farther, the crowd will have thinned."

"Perhaps." She didn't sound convinced, but as Michael didn't much believe it either, he couldn't blame her.

They walked in silence for a few uncomfortably lengthy moments. In an effort to break the silence, Michael asked, "Is this your first time in London, Miss Thatcher?"

"It is, yes."

As conversation topics went, Michael had chosen poorly. They'd already discussed that she didn't particularly enjoy London and neither did he. He felt guilty for being a poor companion, but he was too preoccupied with his task for the rest of the day. His thoughts were with a different woman.

"Your dog really is quite remarkable," Miss Thatcher commented. "I've seen the best-trained dogs tested beyond their abilities with all the noise and other animals on Rotten Row."

Michael glanced down at Gelert. In truth, he had forgotten the dog was there. He *was* being very well behaved, but Michael had expected no less. "Thank you," he said, accepting her compliment on Gelert's behalf.

They walked their horses for another few minutes in strained silence after that. Most who rode or drove by looked their way, but as neither of them seemed to have many acquaintances in London, there were few nods or waves to accompany the glances.

"Oh, look," Miss Thatcher called, pulling her reins as she broke the silence. "She's dropped something." Miss Thatcher deftly turned her horse and backtracked to a spot along the edge of the path where a bit of lilac-covered cloth was visible in the grass.

Michael followed. He quickly dismounted, retrieved the lost item, and swung back into has saddle. "Who has lost it?" he asked, turning to his sharp-eyed companion.

"She's just ahead," Miss Thatcher said, and spurred her horse into a trot. Michael followed as she expertly maneuvered around riders to reach her quarry.

"My lady," she called, when she neared a tall woman, also on horseback, dressed in a suspiciously familiar shade of lilac.

The woman turned in her saddle and watched Miss Thatcher as she closed the distance between them, bringing her horse to a halt.

"My lady, you dropped something," she said. "We retrieved it for you."

"Have I?" The woman looked around in an effort to determine what she may have dropped.

Michael reached the women, bringing his horse to a halt beside Miss Thatcher's. "I believe this may be yours," he said to the stranger, extending the lost item to her.

"Oh, that is my scarf," she said, looking behind her as though the path may provide some clue as to how she'd managed to lose it. "Thank you," she said, turning back to Michael and Miss Thatcher. "It was very kind of you to return it."

"Oh, it was no trouble at all," Miss Thatcher insisted.

*Particularly as the distraction rescued us from a painful attempt at conversation,* Michael added mentally.

"May I know the name of my heroes?" the woman in lilac asked.

"I am Mr. Rosevear," Michael said, "and this is Miss Thatcher."

"Well, Mr. Rosevear and Miss Thatcher, I am thrilled to make your acquaintance. I am Emmaline, Duchess of Worley."

"Your Grace," Miss Thatcher breathed, bowing her head and shoulders in what appeared to be her best horseback version of a curtsy. "We are so sorry for intruding upon your outing."

"Don't be silly. It is I who have intruded upon your outing by losing my scarf and obligating you to return it."

Miss Thatcher smiled nervously. "That's very kind of you to say, Your Grace."

"Nonsense. It is simply the truth." She gazed out on the crowded park and sighed. "I know London can be full to overflowing with self-important aristocrats, dear, but believe me when I tell you, I do my very best not to be one of them."

Michael found himself laughing at her frank assessment. "And you succeed, Your Grace. If only London were full of individuals such as yourself."

The duchess laughed. "And you are a flatterer, Mr. Rosevear."

"Not at all, Your Grace," Miss Thatcher insisted. "Mr. Rosevear and I were just discussing that we prefer the country to town, but perhaps we wouldn't if everyone were as pleasant as you."

"That's very kind of you," the duchess said. "Truth is, I very much agree with you. I have always preferred my little cottage and garden in Beadwell to the balls and parties in town."

Before Michael could think to stop it, his hand reached out to grip the duchess's arm. "Did you say Beadwell?" he asked.

She glanced down at the place where his hand clutched her arm and graced him with a bemused smile. "I did. Do you know it?"

Michael gently withdrew his hand. "I do not, Your Grace, but I recently met someone who hails from there."

The duchess laughed. "That seems very unlikely. It is quite a small place." Then her face brightened. "Unless you have met my dear friend, Mrs. Lucy Brantwood? She is here in London and recently married to my cousin."

"What an odd coincidence," Miss Thatcher said, smiling, "for I, too, have met your friend, Your Grace. My father had some business with her husband and they dined at our house last week. She was lovely. She was very animated in discussing her husband's shipping business. I recall so well because I was surprised. Most wives are not so knowledgeable of their husband's business affairs."

"Oh, she is quite," the duchess began.

But Michael stopped her. "I am sorry, Your Grace, but did I just hear you say that your friend is also from Beadwell, and her husband is a shipping merchant?" Was it possible that he was hearing correctly?

The duchess laughed again and placed her hand on his arm, much more gently than he had done. "I'm sorry, Mr. Rosevear. Have we rambled on and lost you? How insensitive. Miss Thatcher has had the happy fortune, yes, of meeting my lifelong friend Mrs. Brantwood, who is lately married to my cousin. He is the proprietor of Brantwood Trading Company."

"I see," Michael said, for he did. He now saw so much more clearly. "May I ask where his ships sail, Your Grace?"

"He has only one ship currently, Mr. Rosevear. It sails to Boston."

"Of course it does."

Both ladies stared at him.

"Whatever does that mean?" Miss Thatcher asked.

"It means I am a fool, Miss Thatcher." He turned to the duchess. "Do you know a Crawford, Your Grace?"

The duchess's well-practiced social graces were not strong enough to hide the shift in her expression at the mention of the name.

"A Miss Juliana Crawford," he clarified.

He had her curiosity now, he could tell, but she was measured in her reply. "She is a neighbor of sorts, why do you ask?"

"Your Grace," he said gravely, "I am in urgent need of your assistance. I must contact your cousin immediately."

# Chapter Twenty

Juliana knew for certain that she had stood in one place too long when people started paying her more attention. She could see them casting furtive glances her way. Asking directions from one of them was a risk, but the alternative was to wander aimlessly.

She chose a man who looked busy and rationalized that made him less likely to be up to no good. "Excuse me sir," she said, doing her best to sound sharp and intentional, rather than uncertain.

He looked up from the tower of wooden crates he was moving. His eyes traveled from her head to her toes and back again.

"Which way to the shipping offices?" she asked, not waiting for him to invite the question.

He wiped his brow and pointed down the row of buildings. "Down there," he said, and put his back to her again, returning to the task of stacking crates.

She didn't bother thanking him. She didn't think he was expecting it anyway. She walked briskly in the direction he had pointed, looking around occasionally to confirm she hadn't drawn unwanted interest. Just as she was beginning to wonder if the dock hand had led her astray, she passed a painted sign on one of the buildings that said Clarke Shipping Office. It was a good indication she was headed in the right direction.

There were fewer people down along this row of buildings and the isolation made her uncomfortable. She clutched her satchel more closely. She looked at the signs as she walked and her heart leapt when she read the name Brantwood carved into a hanging wooden sign just up ahead. She had found it. She hastened her pace.

A man darted in front of her and she nearly barreled into him.

"Where are you headed, luv?"

She tried to ignore him, to step around and be on her way, but he sidled in the same direction, preventing her progress. She tried the other way, but he anticipated her, blocking that path as well. Her heart began to pump more quickly. She was so close to the office. She could see the sign.

She had few weapons in her arsenal. She tried confidence. "Get out of my way," she spat, forcing herself to look directly at him.

*Oh God.*

She had seen him before. He was the man from the road, the one who'd been tied to the broken coach when she'd come out of the woods. He hadn't left them alone as he'd promised. He'd followed her.

"I don't think I will get out of your way," he said, sneering victoriously. "Where's your fancy gent and his big dog now?"

"Not far behind," she lied. "They'll be here any moment."

"Well, then," he said, grabbing her arm roughly, just below her shoulder, "I guess we'd better hurry."

She pulled against his hold. It hurt. "Let me be," she said, knowing it was futile. She needed an actual weapon. She'd wasted her time with the hackney demonstration when what she'd needed was a gun. Even if she couldn't shoot. She could still threaten with it, point it at him. Something. She yanked against his hold.

He only squeezed her arm more tightly. It pinched dreadfully.

"Stop wriggling, girl."

"How did you find me here?" she asked. "Did you follow me?" She wouldn't have thought it possible to follow that hackney driver, the way he darted through the streets.

He sneered again, showing a miscellaneous collection of rotting teeth and empty spaces. "I didn't have to follow you. I've been right here, waiting for you."

Waiting for her? How could that be? Why would he have ever heard of Lucy or the Brantwood Trading Company?

She stopped struggling. There was only one way he could have known. Oh God. Tears stung her eyes. No. He couldn't be there. She had gotten so far away. She didn't want to see him.

"Good morning, Juliana."

Hearing his voice again after believing she was free of it made her skin twitch. He was there. She didn't even look at him. She just closed her eyes and wept.

She felt him come closer. He was not much taller than she and his breath was at her ear when he hissed, "I hope for your sake you've gotten this little adventure out of your system."

She hated him. She hated that she stood there, helpless, crying in defeat instead of facing him down, telling him what she thought of him, and refusing to be cowed. But the years had taught her that would only lead to a harsher punishment. She was caught. What resistance could she bring? She had no way to overpower both her father and his lackey.

But still, she could not reconcile with the defeat. And so she wept.

Her lack of struggle built her father's confidence. "Did you really think you could go off on your own? You can't even take care of yourself, you stupid girl. What do you know of the world?"

She opened her eyes then. She wanted to scream it was his fault—*his*—that she knew nothing of the world. She looked at him with his pointed nose, dark, squinting eyes, and always scowling mouth. She was grateful that she looked nothing like him. She hated him. She regretted looking. She put her head down and vowed she would never look directly at him again.

He reached for her, displacing the larger man's hold and taking her arm in his own cruel grasp. "You've wasted a lot of my time and trouble," he growled. "You're going to pay for that." He pulled at her and she stumbled forward. "Walk, girl," he barked. "We're getting out of this place."

She pulled back half-heartedly, but it was a pointless resistance. Even if she could free herself from her father, the toothless one would intervene.

"I said walk," he hissed. "And you'd better do it."

She walked, stumbling forward, not seeing through her tears. She felt them reach her chin and fall to her dress.

"I always knew you weren't worth the trouble," he said continuing his tirade while she prayed for silence, prayed for a miracle. "You ran right to a man. A whore like your mother." It wasn't the first time he'd levied such insults at her. She was conditioned to hearing what a wanton her mother was and how grateful she should be for his firm hand in restraining her own wayward tendencies. "You thought you were clever, just like her. That you could run away from me. But you were wrong. Just like her."

She stumbled again. Wrong? Just like her? She let these words roll around in her mind. Her entire life, her father had told her she was a whore like her mother, because her mother had run away. After her child's imagination had cleared, she'd believed—as everyone else did—that her mother had selfishly run off, leaving her daughter in the very situation she found intolerable. And she'd never come back for her.

"You've behaved stupidly because you've always been stupid." He stopped walking and yanked her around to face him. "Look at me," he barked, shaking her until her eyes opened.

He was blurry, but she looked, already breaking her vow.

"If you try a stunt like this again, you will end up just like your mother. She was not half a clever as she thought, and neither are you."

He turned and pulled on her to begin walking again.

No.

Her feet refused to move.

He had killed her.

He yanked again. She yanked back.

For years, she had wondered why she'd been abandoned. Why her mother didn't care, didn't come, didn't try to find out about her at all. All that time, she'd been gone. Truly gone.

Dead.

He squeezed her arm impatiently and pulled her again.

No.

She twisted quickly and the unexpected movement allowed her to break from his hold.

"Grab her," he barked to the other man.

The burly man easily captured her, closing his arms around her like a vise. Still she struggled. When that didn't work, she kicked. He yelped and it spurred her on. She turned in his hold, clawing and scratching at his face and kicking with her feet. She drew her knee up to kick him again and made contact with his groin instead. He howled and his hold loosened.

She spun outward, then was yanked sharply backward by her hair. "Stop wasting my time," her father hissed. He waved a short, club-like stick in her face. She hadn't even noticed before that he had it. "You'll get worse than a spoon, I promise you."

She didn't care.

The realization stunned her. She didn't care how much he threatened or how badly he meant to hurt her. She wasn't going to stop fighting him off and she was not going back to Beadwell with him. He could beat her with his club a thousand times. She would not stop fighting. She punched blindly with her fists, twisting and kicking, ignoring the stinging pull as he kept his hold on her hair.

"Let her go."

*Michael.* Juliana stopped struggling. She tried to turn and look at him, but her father's grip on her hair kept her from seeing him.

"This is none of your concern," her father bit out.

She heard Gelert's low rumbling growl and felt more affection for him in that moment than she'd ever believed possible for an animal. Her father waved at his associate and the burly man took hold of Juliana again. Her father let go and she righted herself, finally looking at Michael.

He stood tall and menacing, furious eyes trained on her father. One hand held a gun—a pistol this time—leveled at her father's chest. The other hand was at his side, palm downward, signaling Gelert to hold. The dog stood fiercely at his side, teeth bared, hair standing on end.

It was, to Juliana, the most beautiful sight she had ever beheld.

"Let her go," Michael repeated.

She saw her father look at the dog and the gun and sensed his indecision. He swallowed, but spoke with bravado. "I said before. This is not your concern. This is my daughter. She's my responsibility. You and your dog can run along and trouble someone else."

"Let her go," Michael repeated, this time cocking the pistol.

Juliana tugged against the hold of the burly man, kicking him again. He smacked her face in response and Michael released Gelert.

Juliana watched as Gelert lunged forward toward the man who held her. But she saw her father step forward as well, raising the club.

"No!" she shouted. She rushed forward, placing herself between them, turning.

The blow came down on her back instead of Gelert's and she bucked with it, then crumpled forward in pain. She heard Gelert's growl and the burly man yelp.

She heard a gunshot.

# Chapter Twenty-One

Michael saw the moment she decided. He shouted to her, but she didn't hear and he couldn't get to her in time. He could only watch, helplessly, as the weapon came down forcefully on her back in a wicked blow. She arched back as it struck her, then doubled forward, crumpling to the ground. When her father raised the stick a second time, Michael didn't hesitate.

He shot.

Crawford fell.

"Gelert. Enough," he called, as he rushed to where Juliana lay curled on her side, frighteningly still. He crouched down and laid a hand on her shoulder. Indecision crippled him. If the blow had injured her, moving her incorrectly could make the injury worse.

She opened her eyes and spoke to him. "Michael. You came."

"My God, Juliana." Of course he had come. Thank God he had. She began to move on her own.

"Don't," he cautioned. "Not if you're hurt."

"I can move," she whispered and stubbornly tried to push herself up, cringing as she did.

He slid his arms beneath her and slowly lifted her from the ground. The relief he felt at finally holding her in his arms was overwhelming, even if she was hurt. She slid her arms around his neck and laid her cheek against his chest as he cradled her, shielding her from the image of the two men on the ground. He touched his lips to her forehead.

"What the devil is going on here?" a new voice asked.

Michael heard the click of another cocked pistol and he froze, lips still pressed to Juliana's brow. Calmly and slowly, he lifted his head. A man he had never seen before trained a pistol at them both, while keeping a wary eye on Gelert. He was well-dressed and neatly-groomed, so Michael surmised he was not an associate of Crawford, who seemed to only employ the dregs of society.

"She's hurt," Michael called to the man. "She needs to be examined by a physician."

"How did she get hurt?" the new man asked, pistol still raised. "And what of those two?"

Keeping Juliana's face turned away, Michael looked down at Crawford, face down on the quay, a growing red splotch on his back. Then he looked to check the other. He lay face upward, still groaning. Michael turned back to the newcomer. "Those two are beyond a physician's help," he said. He looked down at Juliana to see her reaction to this news. She met his gaze, gave the slightest nod, then closed her eyes.

"I see that," the man said. "I'm wondering how they got that way."

Michael met his stare unflinchingly. He should think it was obvious. "They tried to hurt her."

The man with the gun looked back at him and, for a long moment, the two men said nothing.

Michael spoke first. "My name is Michael Rosevear. My father is the Marquess of Rosevear. This woman is under my protection and I assure you, the threat is over as it did not originate from either of us. You may put your weapon away. Mine is there." Michael nodded toward the place on the ground where he'd dropped his pistol before rushing to Juliana's aid.

The man considered this. He expelled a deep breath and lowered his weapon. "Bring her to my office," he said. "I will send for a physician."

Michael looked down at Juliana.

Her eyes were open again and staring up at him, wide and green. "I'm all right," she said. "I don't need a physician." As she spoke, she tightened her hold, as though she feared this declaration might prompt him to set her down.

It was just as well that she preferred her present position, for he had no intention of altering it. "We shall let the physician decide if you are all right," he told her.

Michael placed another kiss on her forehead and followed the newcomer through the doorway of the nearest in the row of whitewashed buildings. They entered into a large square room with a staircase along the back wall. The room smelled of new wood and was sparsely furnished with two desks and a few chairs. There was a long table along one wall. The desks were generally tidy. The table was covered in papers—ledgers, drawings, letters.

"There is an apartment upstairs," the stranger said. "You can take her there."

Michael nodded. "Thank you, Mr.—" He waited for the man to introduce himself.

"Brantwood," the man said. "Bexley Brantwood."

"Of course." He looked down at Juliana and smiled at her surprise.

Mr. Brantwood eyed them curiously. "I beg your pardon?"

Michael stopped at the bottom of the stairs. "It is not a coincidence this altercation happened in front of your office, Mr. Brantwood. Miss Crawford was here looking for you."

This declaration drew him closer to take a better look at Juliana. "I don't recall ever meeting you, miss."

"We haven't met, Mr. Brantwood," Juliana explained from her place in Michael's arms. She looked up at Michael, blushing. "Perhaps you should put me down now," she whispered.

As he didn't agree, he said, "Not until I can assess your injury."

Juliana coughed and continued her explanation. "I know your wife, Mr. Brantwood. I had hoped you would consider helping me because I am an acquaintance of Lucy's."

"What sort of help do you require, Miss—Crawford, was it?" He lifted a hand toward the door, indicating the quay outside. "Other than the obvious, of course."

Michael watched the flush color her face again and answered for her. "Miss Crawford was hoping you might provide passage away from England and, more importantly, her father, but,"—he looked to the door—"that need has recently been resolved."

Mr. Brantwood nodded as understanding dawned. "I see." He indicated the staircase. "She can lie down upstairs. I will return after I find someone to send after a doctor."

Michael sent him a grateful look. "Thank you." He carried Juliana up the staircase, carefully adjusting his hold to bring her through the narrow doorway at the top. The upstairs room was as sparsely furnished as the lower, but with a bed and a chair, instead of desks. Gelert followed them into the room, investigating the corners and the smells before seating himself in the center.

Michael gently eased Juliana onto the narrow bed and let his eyes wander the length of her in a thorough examination. He untied her bonnet from beneath her chin and gently removed it.

She reached up and her hand closed around his wrist. "Michael, I don't know how I will ever thank you. You saved me." Her mouth tilted up at one corner in a wan half-smile. "Twice."

Without thinking Michael leaned down and kissed that tilted corner. "I was almost too late," he said, when he'd lifted his mouth from hers. His voice was thick. He took both of her hands in his then and held them. "Your father is dead, Juliana."

"I know," she said gravely. Her eyes closed and she said it again. "I know."

Michael held her hand in the quiet and wished desperately to know her thoughts. He had not killed a man in a very long time and only ever before on the battlefield. He could not regret the choice—he would not go back to that moment and allow her to be beaten. The decision he regretted was leaving her alone in the first place. He knew she was in danger. She never should have been on her own. He was to blame for the fact that she had been.

# Chapter Twenty-Two

The physician came and declared Juliana bruised, but otherwise unharmed, just as she had insisted. The authorities came as well and took the story from all involved. Juliana thought they must have been satisfied with the retelling of the morning's events, for they eventually left. Though she knew Michael tried to keep her from overhearing, she understood arrangements had been made for the removal of the fallen men. She wondered briefly where her father would be taken and buried, but she determined to set the thought from her mind. She would not mourn him

After the officials were gone, Michael came back upstairs to sit with Juliana, insistent that she rest despite clearance from the physician that she was not going to injure herself by getting out of the bed.

She was content to let him sit with her, as she took comfort in his presence. She didn't know what more to say to him, but she knew she liked it better when he was there. He held her hand and it felt reassuring, but woefully insufficient. She wanted him to hold her tightly. She knew if he did, she would abandon her calm façade, cling to him desperately, and weep for her freedom. He didn't, so for a time she lay quietly, just gazing into his eyes, wondering if he felt the same need as she to have him near. She reached up and brushed a fallen hair from his forehead and it felt perfectly right when he leaned down and kissed her.

"Oh."

He lifted his mouth from hers and they turned in unison to see the owner of the new voice..

Lucy Betancourt. Or, she supposed, Brantwood now. The smartly dressed woman had halted in the doorway, looking anxious and uncertain as to whether she should enter.

Michael pulled away, but continued to hold Juliana's hand. She was glad that he did.

"Hello Lucy," Juliana said.

"Juliana," she exclaimed and rushed forward. "Bex has told me everything. You were absolutely right to believe that we would help you. How are you feeling? Are you all right? What did the physician say?" Lucy's eyes darted everywhere, conducting their own examination of Juliana's state. They settled on the place where Juliana's hand rested in Michael's. She looked up at Michael. "Hello," she said. "I am Lucy Brantwood."

"Very good to meet you, Mrs. Brantwood. I am Michael Rosevear."

Lucy's eyes settled on their joined hands again. "Perhaps Juliana has told you that we grew up in the same village. I have known Juliana since we were children." Her voice lilted higher. "Have you known Juliana long?"

Juliana could not blame Lucy for her questions. She realized, with great disappointment, that none of the answers to those questions justified her allowing Michael to hold her hand. She slowly slid her hand away.

"I have not." Michael gave the honest answer. "But she is under my protection, nonetheless."

"Is she?" Lucy asked. She looked back and forth at both of them, considered a moment, and nodded. "Very well. I am pleased to meet you, Mr. Rosevear."

Judging by Lucy's satisfied expression, she assumed considerably more significance to Michael's declaration of protection than was accurate. Juliana sat up because she felt silly continuing to lie down when there was really no reason for her to do so. "I am so sorry, Lucy, to have involved you and your husband in all of my troubles." She hadn't said the same to Michael, because she was not sorry. She was grateful beyond reckoning for his involvement and she would not wish it away.

"Nonsense," Lucy said forcefully, waving her hand to brush the idea aside. "I am sorry that we weren't able to prevent this. I wish you had come to me sooner. I would have helped you in any way I could."

Juliana believed that was true. Perhaps, if she had left before, she could have relied upon Lucy's help until she became entitled to her allowance, but then she would have put Lucy and her husband at the risk of whatever her father might have done. And she would not have met Michael.

She sighed. Perhaps it would have been better for Michael, however, if they had not met. He was supposed to be at his father's house, arranging for his future. She knew she could not continue to cling to his protection and support, even if the thought of separating again tightened her chest with feelings of near-panic. She had her place at the boarding house and now that she could stay in England, she could begin to look for a more permanent arrangement.

"What time is it?" she asked, willing her eyes not to tear.

"I'm not certain," Lucy said, "Four o'clock perhaps?"

"I think I have sufficiently recovered," Juliana said, sitting on the edge of the bed. "I think it is time for me to go." The physician had cleared her hours ago. She was only sore and sorry to leave Michael. Those were not reasons to become a permanent convalescent above Brantwood Trading Company. She couldn't go with Michael, so she had to go back to Mrs. Stone's. If she didn't return soon, she would be late for dinner and lose her place there. She didn't want Kat to be blamed for helping her either.

"Are you sure you should be standing?" Michael asked, rising to her aid. She smiled. "I am not going to swoon. I am only a little sore. I promise." She looked between Lucy and Michael. She was very tempted to ask Michael to take her back to Mrs. Stone's, even if just to spend another half hour in his company. But she could not return with a gentleman. Besides, Michael may already be engaged for all she knew. "There is one thing I might ask of you, Lucy," Juliana said.

"Anything," Lucy answered without hesitation.

"Would you be able to return me to the boarding house where I am staying?"

"What?" Michael demanded.

"Boarding house?" Lucy laughed. "Of course you will not remain at a boarding house. You will be my guest, Juliana. You will stay with me until,"—she glanced at Michael—"until you make other arrangements."

"No." Michael's objection was swift and clear. "You will stay at my father's house. I insist that you do, at least until I am assured that you have suffered no injuries. Then you may stay with Mrs. Brantwood, if that is your choice."

Juliana stared at him. "I really don't think it appropriate for me to stay with you, Michael."

"I don't see why not," he clipped. "The marchioness is there."

A chaperone was not at all what she meant. He was supposed to be courting the merchant's daughter, wasn't he? How else was he to win Rose Hall for himself?

"Well," Lucy contributed. "If the marchioness is there, I don't see how there should be any trouble."

Juliana stared at Lucy this time. Lucy winked at her. *Winked.*

*Sara Portman*

Did she think she was matchmaking? She began to shake her head. No, Lucy had it all wrong.

"It's decided," Michael said. "You will return to Willow House with me."

Juliana didn't object. She told herself it was because she was tired and the day had been traumatic. She knew that was not the truth.

# Chapter Twenty-Three

Once Michael had assisted Juliana into his carriage and seen her comfortably seated, he climbed in as well. As a gentleman, he would usually have taken the rear-facing seat and allowed her the forward-facing seat. Instead, he gave Gelert the rear-facing seat to himself and sat next to Juliana, for no more thoroughly-examined reason than he wanted to sit next to her.

He was still reeling from the rage and panic he'd felt seeing her attacked by her father, much of which hadn't even taken hold and truly shaken him until after she was safe. He was unsettled from it even now. The feeling made him want to forbid her from ever being out of his sight again, irrational as that was.

"Thank you," she said once they were moving toward his father's house, "for protecting me, for comforting me. I don't want to think what would have happened today if you had not come."

Neither did he. "You are safe now," he said, as much to still his own heartbeat as hers. "That's all that matters."

"Thanks to you I am safe," she said. She gazed up at him adoringly and, damn him, he basked in it. He looked down at her, fire lighting inside of him, and wished they were speeding toward a one-room cottage in a tiny village instead of his father's house. His attention fell to her mouth.

She turned away. "I think Lucy...Mrs. Brantwood...may have misunderstood our relationship."

"How so?"

The color rose in her cheeks and her voice wavered as she answered. "I think she believes we are,"—she hesitated and spoke again in a whisper—"involved."

"Aren't we?"

Her eyes flashed to his.

He laughed. "You may call it something different, Juliana, but over the past week, you and I have been very involved."

Her color deepened.

"In fact," he said, reaching around to place his hand at the nape of her neck, "your friend may have been perceptive enough to realize that I rather like being involved with you. And I think you rather like being involved with me." He lowered his voice to a whisper as he neared her mouth. "Or whatever you would like to call it."

He touched his mouth to hers and immediately lost control of the kiss. Without conscious decision by either of them, all the fear, anxiety, and adrenaline of the day burst forth in a rush when they came together.

"Michael," she breathed, in between his plundering kisses. "I thought I would never see you again."

He lifted his mouth from hers and moved to her throat. "You were wrong," he said against the skin there. That either one of them thought they wouldn't meet again seemed ridiculous now. He couldn't feel enough of her. His hands couldn't move fast enough to touch every part of her.

And hers did the same. Their kisses were desperate and hurried like they had met in secret and had only a short while before being caught.

He supposed that was true. They would arrive at Willow House soon. If it was clear then what they were doing now, Juliana's arrival would be more uncomfortable for everyone—particularly Juliana. So Michael gave her one more lingering kiss, then released her.

"We will arrive soon," he said.

He saw the moment reality registered and the cloud of passion gave way to panic in her eyes as she smoothed her dress and checked her bonnet, which was definitely askew.

"Let me help." He untied, removed, and replaced the bonnet, making sure her hair was tucked up inside. "Just don't remove it until you are alone," he said with a wink.

Her eyes widened in momentary alarm, then she surrendered to mirth at the thought of her truly unkempt state being discovered.

He helped her retie the bow under her chin. "Lovely," he said, and dropped a quick kiss to her lips because they tempted him.

The carriage began to slow and Michael looked to see they were approaching the house. He felt a hand on his knee and faced Juliana again. The laughter over the bonnet had faded from her expression. Her round green eyes filled with emotion. "Thank you, Michael," she said emphatically. "My life will never be the same, because of you."

His instinct at hearing her words was to pull her into his arms and hold her there, but the carriage had stopped so he only lifted one hand and brushed a finger along the side of her serious expression. His heart swelled and, though he didn't speak the words, he believed in that moment that he could say the same to her.

* * * *

Michael had called it Willow House. In Juliana's memory, willow trees were drooping and sad. The London home of the Marquess of Rosevear in no way resembled the mourning willow. The house consisted of two stories of faded red brick topped by a third story of cheery white dormers. As though the builder had intentionally snubbed his nose at the window tax, the façade was a sea of tall, transomed windows bordered in white that beautified the exterior and must certainly have flooded the interior with sunlight on pleasant days.

It was a grand house and as Juliana ascended the front steps at Michael's side, she was very conscious of her appearance. Though they may have succeeded in tidying her hair, nothing could be done for the poor condition of her attire. She looked lowlier than a poor relation.

The painted white door was opened at their approach by an old and graying butler in surprisingly bright blue livery that managed to make her dress feel even more dingy in comparison.

"Good afternoon, sir," the butler said to Michael with a short bow of his head. He turned to Juliana and gave the same short bow in her direction, only with no greeting as he would have had no way of knowing how to address her. She saw the flicker of curiosity in his aged face, but it was gone by the time he turned back to Michael.

"This is Miss Crawford," Michael said, removing his hat and handing it to the butler. "She will be our guest for a time. Please see to it that a room is readied for her and ask the marchioness if she would please join us in the drawing room."

The butler nodded and waited until Michael began to lead her away before departing the front hall to accomplish these tasks.

The interior of the house was even more intimidating to Juliana than the exterior. She knew of grand houses, but she'd never seen one. She'd barely seen any houses other than her own. The drawing room into which Michael led her must surely have been larger than the entire first floor of the house in Beadwell. She was afraid to sit on the pale fabrics covering the furniture. She was covered in the dust and possibly the smell of the London docks.

As it happened, Michael did not invite her to sit before they heard the approach of footsteps. Juliana knew Michael could not hold her hand now, or place his hand at the small of her back as he'd done while they walked to the waiting coach after leaving Brantwood Trading Company, but she blessed him for sidling closer to her and straightening his shoulders. She did the same and took courage from his proximity.

A boy hurried into the room and smiled broadly as he spied Michael. "You're back. We all wondered where you've been all day. Mum asked everyone, but no one knew." He looked to Juliana, examining her thoroughly before asking, "Has he been with you?"

This, she assumed, was Michael's half-brother. His blunt questions and quick change of attention startled her and she hesitated to respond.

"Where is your mother, Alexander?" Michael asked.

"She's coming. Mrs. Kenton wanted to know which room to have made up." He looked at Juliana then. "But Mother told her she couldn't know where to put you until she knew who you were and why you were here."

A smiled tugged at Juliana's lips. She supposed that would be the sort of conversation the lady of a house such as this might have with her housekeeper, but not one she expected repeated to her guest. Better rooms were reserved for better guests, she supposed.

"I shall solve that trouble, Alexander. Go and tell Mrs. Kenton she's Miss Crawford, she's here because I've brought her, and she's to have a room in the family wing."

The boy ran off quickly, no doubt excited to be the first in the household to possess such important information.

"Please excuse Alexander," Michael said. "He's…"

"He seems very likeable," Juliana said.

Michael looked at her quizzically, though she didn't believe her comment to be so odd. "Yes," he said. "I suppose I do like him. Even if his questions are incessant."

Juliana thought a boy who asked so many questions at twelve years of age was surely a boy who'd received answers as opposed to punishments for his previous questions. For that reason alone, she was predisposed to like the marchioness.

At that moment, a beautiful woman, perhaps ten years her senior, sailed into the room, managing to hurry and appear graceful at all once, and Juliana wondered if she hadn't summoned the marchioness with her very thoughts.

"Michael," she exclaimed. "We've been wondering about you. I was told you returned early from your morning ride and left again immediately.

I hope there hasn't been any trouble." She spoke to Michael, but her attention was fixed on Juliana, who tried not to feel anxious. She waited for Michael to introduce her, belatedly wondering what explanation he might give to his family.

"I'm afraid there was trouble, ma'am."

Concern engulfed her features.

"Trouble? What trouble?" A man appeared in the doorway. He bore no resemblance to Michael but his fine clothes and authoritative manner identified him unquestioningly as Michael's father, the marquess. He walked into the room at an unhurried pace and settled his attention, as his wife had, directly upon Juliana. He looked up and down the length of her for an uncomfortable moment then peered directly into her face as though trying to place her. He spoke bluntly. "Who is this?"

The marchioness laid a hand on her husband's arm. "I believe Michael was about to explain, dear."

"This is Miss Juliana Crawford." Michael looked directly at her as he made the introduction and she met his eyes, letting their hold steady her the way his touch might have. "Miss Crawford," he said in a gentled voice, then lifted a hand in the direction of the older couple. "The Marquess and Marchioness of Rosevear."

Juliana forced her eyes from Michael's and faced Lord and Lady Rosevear.

"Welcome, Miss Crawford," Lady Rosevear said with a gracious smile.

The marquess only nodded. They both faced Michael again, awaiting further explanation.

"I am sorry to say Miss Crawford has had a traumatic event today. She was attacked and nearly abducted. The threat has been resolved, but I have offered that she shall stay here while she recovers from the incident."

The effect of Michael's blunt words was immediate.

"Oh my heavens! You poor thing," the marchioness gasped. She immediately reached for Juliana, draping an arm around her shoulders. "Are you hurt?"

Juliana was surprised by the unexpected rush of attention and hesitated to respond. "I...no, I am not hurt, ma'am."

"She is lying," Michael said flatly. He looked pointedly her way. "She may not be permanently injured, but she suffered a blow to her back and is most definitely hurt."

"Oh, no," the marchioness said, her shocked expression settling again on Juliana. "Shall I call the physician?"

Juliana hesitated. She didn't know how much to share, when clearly most of Michael's involvement painted their acquaintance in an inappropriate light.

"She's already been examined by a physician," Michael responded when Juliana did not.

"How did that come about?" the marquess asked.

"What did the doctor say?" his wife asked instead, casting him a warning look.

The marquess appeared unhappy with the rebuke, but remained silent for the moment. Juliana had lived in the quiet of no one's company but her own—or her father's when she was unlucky—for so long that she was overwhelmed to be the subject of their collective attention. She was relieved to let Michael answer their questions and decide how much of the truth they should know.

"The physician said she was lucky enough to be bruised but not severely injured, from what he could tell."

The marquess looked skeptical. "Who attacked her? Where did this happen? You're going to have to tell us more than this," he said, waving his hand toward Juliana. He earned another quelling look from his wife and Juliana wasn't certain how to respond. She should not have come. Her presence was already causing trouble.

"You will need to rest, dear," the marchioness said, both she and Michael pointedly ignoring the marquess and his insistent questions. "I'll have a room made for you right away."

"I've already sent a message to Mrs. Kenton that she's to make up a room in the family wing."

This announcement earned Michael a surprised look from Lady Rosevear and Juliana a closer assessment from Lord Rosevear.

She sensed Michael stiffen. "The doctor believed Miss Crawford was not severely hurt, but if she does suffer an ill effect of the incident, I don't want her to be in some remote part of the house."

"A thoughtful consideration," the marchioness said, and with her arm still around Juliana's shoulder, began to lead her from the room—to Juliana's great trepidation. "We shall find Mrs. Kenton," the lady said, "and see what has been done."

Juliana cast one quick, backward glance at Michael, wishing, like a child, that she could rush back and cling to his hand. But she could not, so she allowed herself to be ushered from the room, through the front hall and up the grand staircase.

\* \* \* \*

The marquess ran his tongue across his teeth and looked at Michael unhappily. "Who is she?"

The look Michael returned was equally unhospitable. "Currently, she is a woman who needs our help."

The marquess glowered impatiently at the uninformative answer. "Where did she come from?"

"Beadwell."

"Don't play games," he barked, stepping forward. "This is my house, you are my son, and you're supposed to be courting Miss Thatcher. So tell me who the hell she is and where she came from."

"I have not yet agreed to the proposed arrangement concerning Miss Thatcher," Michael said.

"That was not my question. What is your relationship to that girl?"

"We met a few days ago on the road from Yorkshire. She was in danger and required help. I provided it."

The marquess sighed unhappily, but Michael didn't particularly care if his father's curiosity remained unappeased. "I have asked very little from you, Father," he said, "when compared with how much you have asked of me. I would ask now that you find it in your heart to tolerate Miss Crawford's presence until other arrangements are made for her."

The marquess squinted suspiciously at him. "Is she married?"

"No."

"Is she your mistress?"

"No."

"Will she have parents arriving on my doorstep, demanding a wedding?"

"No."

The marquess was silent for a moment, his face pinched as though digesting this information wasn't agreeing with him. When finally he spoke, he said, "Tread carefully, Michael. Take care you don't ruin things for everyone, including yourself."

Michael said nothing in response, only watched him go. His father wasn't concerned about where Juliana had come from. He only cared how her presence affected his grand plan for his true son, Alexander.

* * * *

Lady Rosevear and Juliana encountered the housekeeper on the landing. She answered the question as to the prepared room and left them, without a second glance for Juliana. Lady Rosevear led Juliana around the corner and down a long hall until they reached a room at the far end. The door stood open.

"Here you are, Miss Crawford. I hope that you will be comfortable here."

She stood aside and allowed Juliana to precede her into the room. Juliana could not imagine anyone would not be comfortable in the cheery bedchamber with soft yellow paper on the walls and matching flowers embroidered into the coverlet. There was a low fire in the grate and heavy gold drapes were pulled back from the windows, letting late afternoon sun into the room.

"I am going to send my maid up to you, dear," Lady Rosevear said. "I think a soothing bath may be just the thing you need. The family will dine in a few hours, but please don't feel that you should try to join us if you are overset from your ordeal."

Juliana looked around the room and at the pretty marchioness in her elegant, rose-colored dress and knew, overset or not, she could not possibly appear in the dining room of Willow House. Even if she bathed, she had only her mended dress to wear and though she'd washed it the day before, it was once again filthy from her visit to the docks. "I...um, thank you, Lady Rosevear, but I am quite...tired, actually."

"That's understandable, dear." She went to the bed, turned back the covers, and fluffed the pillows. Then she stood and pivoted, taking the time to survey the rest of the room.

Juliana stood quietly while the marchioness satisfied herself that the room had been readied to her standard. While she appreciated the care, she found the silence uncomfortable. She did not speak easily with strangers, even kind ones.

Lady Rosevear's view landed on Juliana's small satchel, dirtier from the scuffle on the quay, and looked back at Juliana with mild alarm. "Are those your things?"

"Yes, ma'am," Juliana answered, aware she was not alone in understanding she did not belong in a place such as this.

"Well," Lady Rosevear said, her warm smile feeling surprisingly absent of the judgment Juliana had expected. "I imagine with your unexpected ordeal today you are missing a great number of necessary items. When my maid comes for your bath, I will send some things to,"—she tilted her head and considered—"fill in the holes, I suppose"

"I'm sure I can manage, my lady. There is no need."

Lady Rosevear stepped forward. She spoke firmly. "My dear, I don't fully understand what you've endured today or the events that brought you here, but it seems they were harrowing indeed. So often in these times, those who wish to help are unfortunately helpless. Please allow me to do this little thing so that I can feel I have aided your cause, however minimally."

Lady Rosevear, Juliana realized, possessed a graciousness and conversational ability beyond anything Juliana could ever have achieved. She had managed to very sweetly, but nonetheless absolutely, deny Juliana the ability to politely decline her offer. After such a speech, she had no alternative but to say, "Of course. Thank you."

"It's practically nothing, dear," she insisted, and with a final check of the room, she moved toward the door. She paused before leaving and said, "I will send a dress appropriate for dinner and I hope you will join us if you are well enough. My maid will show you the way."

* * * *

Despite the generosity of the marchioness, Juliana had determined that she would not appear at dinner. Her arrival had been too disruptive to the family and she could only imagine their reactions to her when she appeared at their dinner table looking like a poor beggar from the streets. The day had already seen enough discord and drama for a lifetime.

The promised maid arrived and introduced herself as Mary. Juliana couldn't help but notice that this Mary seemed considerably more efficient than the last she'd encountered. She brought an armful of towels and other garments and she was closely followed by two footmen, one carrying the largest metal tub Juliana had ever seen and the other carrying two large pails of steaming water. Mary directed the footman carrying the tub through a door at the far side of the room and Juliana peeked through to realize it was a small square dressing room that she had not even realized was there. After the first man delivered the tub, the second was directed in to empty his pails of water. Mary then hurried them out the door and turned to Juliana.

"Now, shall we be about your bath, then?"

Juliana had never been assisted in her bath before. She wasn't sure which portion really required assisting, as she was perfectly capable of washing herself, but she didn't want to appear ignorant of the way that highborn ladies were supposed to behave. Better, she thought, to allow herself to be directed.

She followed the maid's instructions, allowing Mary to assist in removing her dress and worn chemise and avoided looking to see whatever judgment the maid might be holding. Juliana realized this woman's garments were likely richer and in better condition than her own. When Mary gasped, she realized she had forgotten her back. She was sore and, she supposed from Mary's reaction, fairly bruised from the blow she'd taken.

Juliana wasn't sure how to explain the injury, so she said nothing. She stepped into the tub and sunk down into the water, gritting her teeth for a moment against the sting when the hot water touched her back. Fortunately, the pain was only sharp for a moment and then the warm water was soothing to the ache.

When Mary let down the remains of Juliana's braided knot and began to wash her thick length of hair, she realized precisely why those who could afford to keep servants might want to have their hair washed by someone else. The feel of having one's hair washed, she now understood, was absolutely lovely.

When Juliana was clean and likely smelling more like flowers than ever before due to the scented soap she'd used, she let Mary wrap her in clean linen to dry her and felt a little like a child. Again to avoid seeming out of place, she said only, "Thank you," and allowed herself to be led to a chair where Mary began the task of combing through her long hair.

The feel of having one's hair combed was almost as nice as having it washed and Juliana relaxed into Mary's ministrations. When Mary finished combing out the tangles, she used the cloth to dry it further then began to arrange it. Because she had complied all along, Juliana presumed an objection at this point would appear ungrateful or confirm her lack of familiarity with the ways of lords and ladies. Still, the effort was wasted when she would not be going down to dinner.

Arrangement of hair, it seemed, was not a simple matter for the aristocracy, for she had not anticipated when Mary began just how long she would be sitting before the task was completed. Mary, however, seemed quite satisfied with the results. "There," she said. "That's nice. You've very pretty hair, miss."

"Thank you," Juliana said.

"Shall we see how the dress fits?" Mary asked. "I've brought a few tricks in case we need to make some adjustments."

"Oh, I know the marchioness offered, but I don't think I should. I couldn't wear one of her gowns. It's not necessary. Really, it's too generous. I don't think the family expect me at dinner anyway."

Mary patiently waited, her expression placid, while Juliana rattled off every general refusal she could think to say. Then she went to where a green dress lay draped across the bed, picked it up by the shoulders and said, "This was always a bit snug for her ladyship. It may be a nice fit for you, miss. Let's try and see, shall we?"

More than a little tempted to at least try the dress, Juliana allowed Mary to help her into it. They discovered the dress fit surprisingly well with the aid of an extra sash under her bust to tighten the bodice. Mary brought a looking glass and Juliana was stunned at the transformation. She immediately imagined the cutting remark her father would make about her vanity and wantonness. Had her mother made such efforts with her appearance? She didn't remember, but she found it unlikely her father would have spent the funds for anything half so nice.

She wondered then at the cost of the garment she wore and decided it was probably better she didn't know. She could imagine what the women at Mrs. Stone's would think of the opportunity to don such a dress.

And she wondered, inevitably, what Michael would think to see her this way. That was the thought that caught her imagination and held it captive. That was the thought that tempted her to say, "When is dinner served, Mary?"

* * * *

Michael had received word that Juliana would be joining the family for dinner, so he was waiting in the drawing room well before the appointed time, careful not to leave her to his father's questions without his protection. As it happened, she was the last of the four to arrive for the meal. When she appeared in the doorway, she was utterly changed.

He crossed the room toward her and scrutinized her changed appearance, deciding on closer examination that she was not so changed after all. Her face was perfectly familiar, the same jewel-green eyes and dark lashes against smooth, pale skin. She was perhaps a bit more pale than usual, which worried him. Her auburn hair was piled atop her head in a fashionable arrangement of twists and curls that would have been common and, thus, unremarkable on any young lady in a London drawing room. He hated the style on Juliana. The wisps around her face curled like corkscrews. He had seen her hair unbound and knew it did not curl that way on its own. He liked it unbound. This style seemed all artifice and didn't fit Juliana at all.

The dress, however—he was fully in support of the dress. Any dress would have been an improvement upon the simple and worn garments she possessed, but she was lovely in this one. The color made her eyes brighter and the bodice dropped lower than the severely modest dresses she owned. The moss-colored fabric skimmed her figure in a way that made him want to run his hands over it.

He went to her, forcing himself to halt just before the point at which he reached out and pulled her into an embrace. Still, as he stood so near her, his arms twitched to do so.

He'd spent the entire afternoon too fearful for her danger and then too relieved for her safety to give a fig about propriety and what right he had to touch and hold her, even in front of others. Now he was once again bound by the restraints of proper behavior and found they chafed.

"You look lovely," he said, once he realized she'd been staring up at him, waiting for him to speak. "How are you feeling? Are you well enough to sit through a lengthy meal?"

She smiled and must have thought he was overly concerned, but someone had to have a care for her well-being.

"I shall be fine," she said.

"If you find you are not, simply say so, and someone will take you to your room. There is no need for you to endure the entire meal if you are unwell."

Juliana smiled at him, but her eyes cast to where the marquess stood with his wife, reminding Michael that he may be a bit too attentive for everyone's comfort.

"We are assembled. Shall we go in to dinner then?" the marchioness said. Michael was beginning to recognize the slightly higher pitch of her speech that signaled her efforts to be diplomatic in uncomfortable situations. She seemed well practiced.

When she received no response, the marchioness simply took her husband's arm and forced him to lead the way into the dining room.

"I'm very glad that you were well enough to join us, Miss Crawford," the marchioness said as they were seated. "I often think company, as opposed to solitude, is best for recovery from a difficult time."

"I'm sure you're right, Lady Rosevear." Judging by Juliana's expression, she did not believe it one bit. Company, Michael mused, was perhaps a comfort. An audience was another matter altogether.

As soon as they were all seated and the first course was served, Michael realized the dinner was a mistake for Juliana. Easy conversation was not a particular skill for her in any situation, and their group of four assembled in the large and unforgivingly formal dining room of Willow House could not have made it easier. Spaced apart as they were, each person was isolated yet entirely on display to the others. It no doubt added considerably to Juliana's discomfort to know she was continually watched.

It surely added to Michael's discomfort, for he found it impossible not to watch her—every motion, every expression, the curve of her neck, the movement of her mouth as she ate. What had this woman done to him?

Seeing her in danger had affected him in a way he could not understand and could not manage to control.

"Do tell us, Miss Crawford, where do you hail from, or is London your home?" the marchioness asked.

"My home is in a small village in Derbyshire, My Lady," Juliana answered. She met Michael's eyes as she said it and it was the first time Michael realized that her village—her father's home—was the one place to where she could not return. She could not go back to where everyone knew her and live alone as an unmarried woman.

"Do you have family in London then?" the marquess asked. Of course he would be primarily concerned with Juliana's ability to impose upon someone else's hospitality.

"I do not, my lord."

"Then you are visiting?" the marchioness asked. "With your parents, perhaps?"

Juliana looked down at her plate and Michael answered in her stead. "Miss Crawford's parents are not living."

"I am very sorry, dear," the marchioness said softly.

"What brings you to London then?" the marquess pressed, not possessing the same sympathies as his wife.

"As I've explained, Father, Miss Crawford has had a trying day. I don't believe an interrogation is called for just now."

"Certainly not," the marchioness agreed.

"I am sorry, Miss Crawford," Michael said, glaring at his father. "You should not be subjected to such questioning."

Juliana lifted her chin. The directness of her gaze was surprising as she faced all three of them. "Please do not apologize," she said firmly, all the uncertainty gone from her tone and countenance. "As you have most graciously opened your home to me, you have every right to know who I am and how I have come to be here."

Michael stilled, wondering how much of her story she would tell. The marquess and marchioness stilled also, waiting to learn whatever information she offered.

"My mother is no longer living, but her family, with whom I am not acquainted, have left me a small inheritance that I may collect now that I have reached the age of five and twenty." She addressed the other occupants of the table, each in turn, as she spoke, never shying from their direct attention. "I traveled to London on my own to do just that. I am certain you think it inappropriate and ill-advised for me to do so and you would be correct. The events of earlier today are the clearest evidence of that truth. To my great fortune, Mr. Rosevear,"—she smiled—"and the brave Gelert, came to my aid. I do not wish to cause any trouble for you," she said, addressing Michael directly. "Rather, I owe you a great debt. You saved my life. I will not forget it."

Michael could not look away from the intensity of her regard and her declaration. He knew not how the others reacted to it and found he did not care. He had believed her too insecure, too shy, to field questions but once again she had shown an inner vein of strength. Would he always underestimate her fortitude? After all that she had endured in her life, how could he ever question that beneath her ethereal timidity was an iron frame, sturdy and unyielding?

# Chapter Twenty-Four

Juliana allowed herself one final look in the glass before she removed the green dress. She had liked the dress far too much—the way Michael had looked at her while she was wearing it. Dinner had finished quietly and all had retired for the evening, leaving her alone in the unfamiliar and beautiful house. She draped the dress carefully over the chair in the corner so she could return it in the morning in the condition in which she had received it.

Tomorrow she would return to Mrs. Stone's.

The decision had not taken all that much consideration. She had briefly pondered accepting Lucy's offer, but in the end knew she could not. If the Brantwoods took her in, they would be just as entitled to explanations as Lord and Lady Rosevear were for accepting her at Willow House.

She would not do that to Michael. There was no way to provide satisfactory explanations without implicating Michael in her compromising situation and she had no way to predict what the consequences of those revelations might be. She had meant what she'd said at dinner. She owed Michael a great debt. She would not repay it by becoming a complication that threatened his plans and his desire for Rose Hall.

When she lay in the luxurious bed that evening, under the delicately embroidered coverlet, she expected to be assaulted with visions of the trauma of the day. And she was, for a time. She saw mostly her father—the hatred in his eyes as he claimed responsibility for her mother's disappearance. He was vile. She should mourn the loss of a father, but she could not. She was glad Michael had hidden the truth of his death. She did not want to wear black for him.

By natural progression, the memories of the day shifted to Michael— his fierce defense of her, his decisive action in protecting her. As she had begun to accept as inevitable, the thoughts of his actions that day gave way to memories of a different sort—the memories he had promised she would carry forever. She closed her eyes and let them consume her. She was glad now that she had them. They were a thing to cherish and keep.

"Juliana."

The whisper startled her and her eyes snapped open. The speed of her racing heart began to subside immediately when she registered that the voice was Michael's. He stood near the door—inside the door—in trousers and untucked shirt.

How had she not heard him?

He began walking toward her. When his steps made no sound, she looked down. He was barefoot.

She sat up in bed. "Why are you here? Is something wrong? Someone may have seen you."

Michael shook his head. "I don't care if they see me. I wanted to be sure you were all right." He lit a candle on the bureau and carried to the bed, casting its light over her. "Are you very sore?"

She was very sore, particularly in her back, but she didn't want him to worry, so she said, "Only a little."

"I know you well enough to know that if you've admitted to a little, it is a considerable amount." He set the candlestick on the bedside table. "Roll over."

"What?"

"Roll over. I want to look at your back."

"But the doctor said it's fine." She didn't think that was a wise idea at all. The very thing that had distracted her from noticing his entry had been her fantasies of him and the things they had done when she'd been undressed. Flushed and breathless indeed. And now he wanted her to undress and lie bare before him so that he could look at her, maybe even run his hands over her.

Oh, Lord, she was a wanton, wasn't she? She was allowing her imagination to wander too freely.

"I don't think—"

Michael cut her off. "I shan't leave you be until I am satisfied."

Slowly, she rolled over, but did not remove her borrowed nightrail. Once she was lying on her stomach, he slowly pulled the coverlet down all the way to the back of her knees. She felt the loss of its warmth with only the thin nightrail to cover her. That was soon lost as well as she felt Michael pull the garment up, tugging gently where she lay upon it, to bring it high enough to bunch underneath her arms, baring her back. It bared all of her, as she wore nothing underneath it.

"My God, Juliana," he breathed. "If I could, I would kill him again."

She'd imagined from the discomfort she felt that the bruise was large and unsightly. Michael's reaction confirmed her supposition.

"Does it hurt for you to lie on it?" he asked.

"No. The bed is soft."

"The chair at dinner must have been torture."

No. This was torture—lying there on her stomach with her eyes closed, knowing he was looking down at all of her. Her body hummed with the knowledge of it. His fingers touched her shoulder and she started.

"Have I hurt you?"

"No. I was only surprised."

Fingers became a splayed palm that skimmed with a feather-light touch down her back. He slowed and his touch became the barest hint of contact as he reached the spot from which the ache emanated.

"I should have shot sooner," he said fervently. "I should never have left you alone in the first place. I could have prevented this."

Juliana rolled to her side, pulling the nightrail down as she did. "It will heal. It will only be a memory, like every other time."

He stared into her eyes until she felt she had no secrets left. "Your spoon," he said. "It was his weapon, wasn't it."

She closed her eyes and nodded, ashamed that he should know the whole of it.

"No one will ever touch you that way again." When he said it, his voice was low, unyielding, and she believed him. Despite knowing full well he would not be by her side to prevent it, she believed him. He sat next to her on the bed and reached his hand to lift her face. "I have been tortured wondering what you're feeling, what you're thinking, Juliana," he said gravely. "Do you mourn him?"

Juliana held his eyes, hoping he would recognize the honesty in them as she said, "You should not suffer a minute's torture, Michael. I meant what I said at dinner. You were my savior today and I will always be grateful." She looked away a moment to examine her feelings. She tried to find a place within that could mourn for her father, but she couldn't find it. "I don't mourn him," she said, a little surprised at herself. "I suppose I should feel something as his daughter—at least regret for the way it all happened—but I don't. Not for him. I only feel relieved, as though I've been walking on tip toe and holding my breath for twenty-five years and now I can exhale." She did exactly that, letting out a long slow breath. "If I am mournful, it is for my mother."

"Your mother?"

Juliana recalled then that Michael had not witnessed her father's revelation. She hadn't told him, so of course he couldn't know, yet it bothered her. He knew more about her than anyone ever had and this seemed a significant missing piece. "I think he killed her."

Michael's lips pressed together. "There is that possibility. After today, I cannot deny he was capable of it."

"It is more than just a possibility," Juliana explained. "He said so today. Not directly, I suppose, but his meaning was clear."

"Are you sure?"

She nodded. She could feel the intensity of Michael's watchfulness—even more vigilant now that she'd revealed this new facet to the day's trauma. "I'm all right," she said, reassuring him. "I know it's odd to be all right, but I am. Knowing that truth—it helps, somehow." She gave a slight shake of her head, frustrated at her inability to articulate her feelings. "I am sad and furious on her behalf, but at the same time relieved to know that she did not mean to abandon me." She toyed with the embroidered coverlet. "Am I selfish and uncaring to feel relieved?"

"No." His response was swift and firm. "You should feel relief. Your burden was unfairly heavy." He sat on the edge of the bed and drew her hand into his, running his thumb across her knuckles. He looked down at their hands when he spoke. "I can't explain what it did to me today, seeing you threatened. For my own sanity," he whispered, "I can never allow anyone to hurt you again."

She expelled a sad laugh that sounded more like a sigh. "I believe you when you say that."

"You should. I would have battled anything to get to you today. I've never felt that way before."

She was lost in the intensity radiating from him as he whispered these things to her, else she would not have told him, "I wanted you with me more than anything. Before you were there, I wished for you."

Her admission broke a dam and he was with her, sweeping down to take her mouth with a possessive, hungry kiss. Her arms wrapped around his neck, and she responded with equal desperation, clinging to the comfort he offered, thrilled to have what she'd thought could only be fantasy for her now. Their moment of abandon in the carriage ride from the docks to Willow House had not come close to unleashing all that she had pent up inside her, and she released all of it now. She poured all of the anxiety and turmoil and worshipful gratitude out into their embrace like tossing so much wood on a fire and she knew he did the same. He stretched alongside her and her frantic hands slid under his shirt, itching to find contact with his warm skin. His did the same, slipping hands under her nightrail to slide along her thigh and close over her backside, kneading her there as he held their bodies close together.He lifted his mouth from hers. "Does this hurt you?" he asked.

"No," she said, frantic to have his mouth back to hers, frantic to have more. "Nothing hurts," she breathed. His caresses drew pain and turmoil from her until there was nothing left to feel but want. She thought she might die of the want that spiraled though her. "Just...please." Her hands slid around his torso to hold him to her. "It only hurts when you stop touching me."

He groaned and kissed her again. She could feel him straining against his trousers and her hands went there, first feeling him through the fabric and then fumbling at the laces.

"Wait," he said, but she didn't want to wait. Impatience coursed through her. He slid from the bed. Standing, he tugged his shirt over his head and pushed down his trousers. He stepped out of them. When he was fully undressed, he crooked a finger at her. "Come here and I will help you," he said, wicked promise in his dark eyes.

Held by that promise, she did as he asked, tucking her legs under her and rising until she stood tall on bent knees at the edge of the bed as all the while her body thrummed with anticipation. He grabbed hold of the nightrail and lifted it as she lifted her arms. Then the thing was gone and, with it, her patience. She slid her hands to the nape of his neck and pressed herself to him, loving how the hair of his firm chest teased her as her breasts crushed against him. His hand began exploring again—her arms, her hips, the backs of her thighs. Everywhere but the middle of her back. He was careful of her even in his passion, but surely she was numb to all feelings other than the intense desire that seemed to originate somewhere in her midsection and spider outward to every part of her—places of which she'd never been aware before. The feeling left her wanting to shout her demand that it be sated, but at the same time, it felt so marvelous, she never wanted it to end.

"I'm afraid," Michael said, "that I will lose my ability to be gentle with you."

"I don't want you to be gentle," she said, reaching down to touch him. She felt that he strained for her too and she loved knowing it. She closed her hand around him, feeling the pulse of the strain, and he groaned.

He pressed his forehead to hers. "Juliana," he exhaled her name.

"I don't want you to be gentle," she repeated. "I want you to be inside me, the way that you were before."

\* \* \* \*

The softly spoken wish was all Michael needed to hear. He slid an arm behind her knees and lifted her, laying her gently but quickly onto her back. He hovered over her, knees straddling her, and lavished kisses on her stomach, her breasts, and her shoulders. He splayed his hand across her stomach then slid downward, covering the mound of soft curls where her legs parted.

She squirmed under his hand. "Please, Michael."

He traced inside her crease, toying with her there until she responded with sounds instead of words. He dipped a finger inside her, loving the way she was warm and ready for him.

He stroked her with a steadily increasing rhythm until her moans became short, panting breaths and her fists clutched at the bed linens. He circled his thumb until her hips lifted and she turned her face into the pillow. He persisted until she called out, sending his name into the candlelit room, and echoing down the hall for all he cared.

Only then did he do as she asked, leaning lower and guiding himself inside her as she still quaked from her release. She clutched at him as he pressed into her and, God help him, he loved that her hunger for him was as fierce as his.

She bent her knees, sending him deeper into her, and he died a little with the pleasure. He retreated and plunged again, reveling in the feel of her and the sounds she made—so much that he did it again and again— over and over until he was no longer master of it, sweeping both of them toward the end they sought. He had just enough presence of mind as he neared his climax to plunge one last time and withdraw, collapsing on top of her as he contracted with his final release.

As soon as he'd done it, he regretted not finishing inside her, and the thought brought startling clarity. He didn't care about the consequences.

No.

He wasn't *frightened* of the consequences.

It didn't matter if there was a child this time. If not this time, the next, or the time after that. There would eventually be a child, because it would be unavoidable given the number of times he expected to repeat what they had just done.

He smiled at the thought. He smiled wider at the prospect of telling her so. He found a linen cloth and wiped away the trigger of his musings then stretched out beside her. "How do you feel?" he asked.

"Perfect," she murmured, her voice and eyes sleepy as she curled into him.

"You should," he said. "You are perfect. It was perfectly improbable that we met, Juliana, but I cannot fathom what possibly occupied my consciousness before you filled it."

She pulled slightly away from him, just enough to lift her eyes to his. They were wide with question.

"Can you doubt it?" he asked.

* * * *

Juliana couldn't answer. She could doubt so much. She was afraid to hope for more.

He shook his head, bemused. "We're not just going to be together tonight, Juliana. I love you. We belong together always."

At his words, her heart swelled. She felt a blissful weightlessness, as though the knowledge that he loved her had wrapped around her and lifted her, hovering, above the spot where she'd been.

"I love you." He said it again and she basked in it. What a lovely thing. What a beautiful, perfect thing to be looked upon the way that Michael was looking at her now. She couldn't imagine anything more wonderful than becoming accustomed over a lifetime to his looks, his touches, and his declarations of love. What a different vision she saw compared to the frightened and lonely future to which she'd been running.

She looked into Michael's eyes then, searching to know what he envisioned. The buoyancy his declaration had triggered faltered a bit as she considered Michael's future. Juliana would happily abandon her prior expectations—had already abandoned them—but what of Michael's? Suddenly conscious of everywhere that her body touched his, Juliana slowly placed distance between them. The entire reason he had come to London was to bargain for his place—for Rose Hall—to become owner of his accomplishments, both past and future. The only currency with which he had to bargain was his hand in marriage.

She looked down at his hand as it reached for her. It was large and strong and slightly roughened. If he gave it to Juliana, he could not purchase with it the thing he most wanted to acquire.

The beautiful, weightless feeling left her entirely. Its replacement was heavy enough to crush her soul.

He reached out to stop her from moving away, but she halted him. "No, Michael."

"What is it?" he asked, lifting himself to sit up as he peered at her.

She turned away and fumbled for something with which to cover herself. Her hands shook and she thought she might be physically ill.

"Juliana."

His confusion tore at her. He could not have failed to notice that she had not returned his declaration. She wanted so badly to give to him the same perfect feeling she'd experienced, but how could she? How could she tell him that she loved him more desperately than her next breath and then ask him to sacrifice everything for her? It would be wrong of her to take what he offered and so she would not. She pulled one corner of the quilt to her body, covering herself the best she could, wishing she could hide under it forever and never face him.

She did face him though. His expression was as miserable as her heart. "I'm sorry, Michael, but we cannot be together." Delivering the words hurt her more than any blow she had ever received from her father.

His brows pinched. Anger blended with misery. "What?"

She looked away because she had no more courage to face him, not when his expression accused her of the worst betrayal. "We are not meant to be together, Michael. I think if you consider it for a time, you will realize I am right."

"Meant to be together?" he asked, his voice rising. "Who is ever 'meant' to be together? We were not 'meant' to even meet, but for the interference of chance. We choose our path, Juliana, and I have chosen you. I assumed our wishes were aligned."

"Your path leads to Rose Hall, Michael. Mine does not."

"Your path leads to me, and mine you." He spat the words that should have been a gentle declaration of commitment.

She shook her head. "You have a place where you belong and I don't belong there."

He gripped her shoulders. "What if belonging is not a place, at all?" he asked. She could feel his eyes boring into her, begging her to see. "What if belonging is a person—one person—who has the ability to make everything else insignificant?"

She wished she could allow herself to be convinced by his words, moved by the power in them to forget every rational objection, but she could not be so selfish. After all that Michael had done for her, she could not. The only thing he had ever asked of her from the very beginning was that she not interfere with his plans—his chance to have something of his own. He had feared she would somehow find a way to keep him from getting the thing he wanted most and he had been right . He was offering to toss it away for her. She could not let him do it. It would be his greatest regret and hers.

Tears formed in her eyes amidst her denials and he must have thought she was going mad.

"Don't you see, Juliana?" He reached for her hands. "You are that person. Nothing else matters, so long as we are together. Everything that's happened today has made that perfectly clear." He peered at her and his pleading expression slowly killed the painful hammering in her heart until she was numb with grief and loss. "Clear to me, anyway," he added. "Isn't it clear to you?"

She looked down, avoiding his eyes, and heard him exhale as though she had struck him.

"Juliana," he said one more time.

She brought a hand to her face and swiped clumsily at the tears. She inhaled deeply and blew the air out slowly. She lifted her eyes. "No, Michael," she said, staring forward but not meeting his gaze. "I will not marry you. I told you before I mean to never marry and that was the truth. My feelings have not changed."

*Liar!* Her feelings had not changed? She was unrecognizable from the woman who'd departed Beadwell, so altered was she by his entry into her life.

Michael closed his eyes and she watched her lie settle over him like a chill that no fire could warm.

Silently, Michael rose from the bed and pulled on his trousers. With unhurried and deliberate motions, he located his crumpled shirt, shook it out, and put it on. Once dressed, he looked back at her. She could only weep. In an action that felt irreversibly final to Juliana, Michael snuffed the candle and left the room.

# Chapter Twenty-Five

"I have made a decision," Michael announced to the marquess and marchioness at the breakfast table.

He'd risen early that morning. Denying the initial listlessness into which he'd awakened, he took a bracingly cool bath to start his day. He was not particularly hungry, but made his way to the breakfast room from habit, and the desire to speak to his father. He'd found both the marquess and the marchioness there, which was just as well. Better to address them both. He'd bid them good morning, filled a small plate for which he had little appetite, and seated himself at the table.

"In what regard?" his father asked in response to his announcement.

"In regard to Alexander."

This drew their immediate curiosity. The marchioness lowered her cup to its saucer. The marquess leaned back in his chair and crossed his arms over his chest.

"I accept your terms," Michael told him. "I will marry Miss Thatcher and I will serve as trustee for the marquessate until Alexander comes of age, provided Rose Hall is transferred to me as a wedding gift." The words came more tersely than he'd intended, but they were well received despite his tone. The marquess began nodding as soon as the words 'I accept' had left Michael's lips.

"That is good news," the marquess said, clapping his hands on the table top. A footman started forward from the corner of the room, unsure if the motion was a summons. Michael shook his head to send him back to his post. "Come to my study this afternoon and we shall manage the details." the old man said, smiling. "We should invite Thatcher and his daughter to dine again," he directed the marchioness.

She'd been quiet since Michael's announcement. She studied him and he waited, unsure what she thought to find. "Perhaps in a few days would be a better time," she said finally.

"No point in waiting," the marquess insisted. "It's not as though we're rushing things. Thatcher is expecting a proposal. It's already been discussed."

The marchioness was unruffled by her husband's impatience. "Still, I think not this evening."

The marchioness was trying to avoid having both Miss Crawford and Miss Thatcher together at dinner. Michael was able to solve that dilemma easily. "If you are thinking of Miss Crawford, you should know she will be leaving today."

"Will she?" The marchioness lifted a delicate brow. "Where will she be going?"

In truth, the answer to that question was no longer Michael's concern, but he'd assumed she would go to Mrs. Brantwood's house. "To a friend," he said. He would speak to Juliana after breakfast. He would calmly inform her that she would be better to stay elsewhere, just as she had calmly informed him that her feelings had not changed.

"I see," the marchioness said, still studying him.

She could stare all she wanted and conclude whatever she wanted. Michael had said what he had come to say.

How trivial everything seemed all of a sudden. He rose. "Invite Miss Thatcher for this evening and I will propose tonight. I agree with father. There is no reason to delay."

He left then, leaving his father to his victory and the marchioness to her curiosity.

* * * *

Michael found Albert in the mews behind the house. A carriage had been readied and a pair of horses already hitched. Albert was bent over brushing one of them down.

Good, Michael thought. All the better that he was waiting and ready.

"Morning," Albert said, glancing up from brushing the horse's flank as Michael approached.

"Good morning, Albert. I have an errand for you today."

Albert continued brushing. "What is that, sir?"

"Miss Crawford will be leaving. She will need to be delivered to the home of Mr. and Mrs. Brantwood. I believe she has the direction."

Albert halted his task and faced Michael with an odd assessing expression. Was everyone determined to puzzle him out today? "You seem confused Albert," he said, frustration clipping his tone. "I should think that a fairly simple instruction."

Any other coachman would have accepted the rebuke, apologized, and gone about the task with extra haste. Albert did not. He crossed his arms in front of his chest and tilted his head to one side. "It would be simple," he said, "if she were still here. Since she's not, it's a bit more complicated."

Michael stiffened. She was already gone? No one had told him. *She* had not told him. Had she slipped away like some criminal in the predawn hours of the morning?

"When?" he asked.

"Just got back," Albert said.

"Fine." Michael nodded. "Thank you." He returned to the house.

Very well. So it was done. Juliana Crawford was gone and his life would proceed as though he had never met her.

# Chapter Twenty-Six

Michael went to his father's study early that afternoon, eager to have the entire matter of his marriage and future settled and eager to know that Rose Hall would be his.

"Come in. Come in," his father urged when he appeared in the doorway. "Sit."

"I intend to depart for Rose Hall tomorrow," Michael said as he sat, not seeing any reason to waste words on idle chatter when they were here for a specific purpose.

"Tomorrow?" his father echoed.

"I shall settle matters with Miss Thatcher this evening. I assume the wedding plans will require weeks, or even a few months. I will not remain in London during that time. I have matters that require my attention at Rose Hall, especially if I am to be there less often in the future."

The marquess scoffed. "You can't just propose and disappear, boy. How will that look for the bride? Ladies expect some courting and attention even after they've accepted you, you know."

"Miss Thatcher did not seem particularly foolish to me. She is well aware of the reasons for our partnership. I will not disrespect her by falsely declaring I have developed an undying devotion to her over a single meal and an aborted ride in the park." As soon as the words were out, Michael heard the parallel in them. How long had he known Juliana? Hadn't he declared his undying devotion to her? In retrospect, it *was* foolish. She'd been right to refuse.

"I am adamant for tomorrow's departure, Father," he said. "Let us discuss the other arrangements."

His father opened his mouth to speak but shut it again, looking beyond Michael's shoulder. Michael turned to look as well. The marchioness had entered, sailing into the room with an air of great import.

"How convenient that you are together," she said, clapping her hands together. "There is a matter I wish to discuss."

The marquess looked to her and sighed heavily. "Can it wait, dear? We were discussing another matter, just now." He gave her a significant look, clearly meant to suggest that she should know what *other* matter he referenced.

"That is precisely the matter I wish to discuss."

The marquess registered surprise, but indicated the chair next to Michael. "Then by all means, join us."

"Thank you." She sat and turned to Michael, reaching out to lay her hand over his. "Michael, dear, I know what he asks of you—for Alexander—is horribly unfair. Not only will you not inherit, despite the fact that you are the first son, but now you are asked to become caretaker of the inheritance you shall not have, only to turn it over to Alexander's care when he comes of age. I told your father it was too much to ask."

The marquess coughed. "You could not be my heir, but you have always been my son, Michael, and I have always been proud of you."

"Thank you," Michael said, appreciative of their recognition, at least. "But I have agreed to this arrangement and I will honor my word."

"I expected you would," the marchioness said. "That is not the bit I wish to address."

"What is the bit you wish to address?" the marquess blustered.

"Miss Thatcher," she said.

"What about her?" father asked.

"Michael can't marry her."

Father's fist pounded the desk. "Why the devil not?"

"Oh Edward!" she cried, spreading her hands wide. "He is clearly in love with Miss Crawford. Any fool can see that."

The marquess looked in surprise at his wife who had, in essence, just called him a fool.

The marchioness was not a fool. In fact, she was more perceptive than Michael realized, but she had failed to learn one very important point in the matter of Miss Crawford.

"She doesn't want to marry me," Michael said.

Both of the others looked at him.

The marchioness rolled her eyes. "Of course she does. Any fool could see *that*." She cut Michael a look indicating that *he* was now the one with questionable intelligence.

Michael straightened in his chair, finding this conversation not entirely comfortable. "She has already refused me."

"You proposed marriage to the girl?" the marquess asked, throwing his hands up in exasperation.

Ignoring her husband, the marchioness tilted away in surprise. "Has she?"

"Yes."

She considered, perplexed for a moment then asked, "Does she know of your father's arrangement?"

"Yes."

"Ah," she said, nodding happily. "There it is. She loves you more than I thought." She patted his hand again. "I'm very happy for you, Michael."

He peered at her. Was she daft? "I'm afraid I don't follow, ma'am."

The marchioness gave a delicate shrug. "It's obvious she is refusing you because she knows you must choose between her and all the rest of it—your father, your brother, Brinn Abbey, Rose Hall."

Could she be correct? Juliana said she didn't want to marry. She said she didn't belong at Rose Hall. Had she meant that she didn't belong there because she prevented Michael from having it? Could she truly love him so much that she refused to marry him only to be self-sacrificing?

*Damn it.* He could believe it of her. That was precisely the sort of thing she might do.

The marchioness turned to her husband and tapped one fingertip to her chin. "Now if only he could have all of those things *and* Miss Crawford," she mused.

The marquess threw up his hands. "The settlement from Thatcher was to be for you and Alexander, to make sure you're taken care of after I'm gone," he blustered.

The marchioness rose and rounded the desk to where her husband sat. She bent and placed a kiss on the top of his head. "We shall be well taken care of without Miss Thatcher's fortune, darling. Michael will see to it." She smiled across at him. "Won't you Michael?"

"I will, ma'am." He would. He *could.* He had meant what he said to Juliana. He didn't care if their lives were spent at Rose Hall or Brinn Abbey, or a tiny stone cookhouse in the middle of the Derbyshire countryside. He wanted to spend his life with her and if he needed to manage two estates and an underage marquess to do it, he would. He would manage the whole damned country if he needed to. He turned to his father. "I promise, I will care for your family,"—he looked to the marchioness—"my family," he amended, "after you are gone. You have my word."

The marquess sighed. "It will be more difficult. There is work to be done, improvements to be made. Those will have to come slowly without the settlement. You will have a challenge on your hands, Michael."

"I accept it, Father." The weight in his chest began to shift. It was no longer resignation. As he sat and listened to the marchioness it had become a burning need to know the truth. If Juliana had refused him to save his dream of Rose Hall, if she did love him after all—he needed to know immediately. The answer to that question became more important than all other things. "I need to find Juliana," he said, stupidly, as though they all did not already know it.

The marquess sipped his whiskey then shook his head. "I believe this should make our evening dinner plans decidedly uncomfortable," he said to the marchioness.

His wife smiled. "I've made no arrangements for dinner, dear."

Michael stared at them both then abruptly stood. "Excuse me," he said and left with no other explanation, knowing the reason was fairly obvious.

# Chapter Twenty-Seven

Albert took Michael to the address to which he'd delivered Miss Crawford early that morning. Michael darted out of the carriage before it fully stopped, disregarding the pain in his leg at his hard landing, and raced up the steps. He rapped upon the black painted front door.

Despite his urgency, the door opened slowly. It eventually revealed a pinch-faced woman with hair scraped severely back into a white lace cap. She glared at him as though he'd offended her by simply appearing at her employer's doorstep.

"Is Mrs. Brantwood at home?" he asked the sour-faced housekeeper. "I'm here to call upon her guest, Miss Crawford. She arrived this morning."

She stared a moment then said, "I don't allow gentleman callers," and began to shut the door.

*What the devil...?*

He reached his hand out and stopped the door before it shut. Shock crossed her expression briefly then narrowed into a glare. "Go cause your trouble somewhere else."

She wasn't going to let him in? Like hell, she wasn't. "Where is your employer? I demand to speak to Mr. or Mrs. Brantwood."

"You're at the wrong house. I'm the proprietress here. Kindly remove your hand from my door and be on your way." There was nothing kind about her request.

Wrong house? He looked back at Albert, seated in the coachman's box, settling the horses as they stood in the street. Proprietress?

It hit him then. "Are you Mrs. Stone?"

"I am," she said it as a dare. Of course. She'd gone to the boarding house. Michael changed tack. He steadied his voice and gave a reassuring smile. "I am very sorry, madame. I was confused, but I understand now. I am here to see a woman who is staying here. A Miss Crawford."

She eyed his hand still on the door. He removed it.

"I don't allow gentleman callers."

Frustration roared within him, but he worked to keep his tone conciliatory. "This is very important. I must speak with her."

"She knows the rules here. You can't come in."

"Then send her out," he blurted, unable to rein his frustration any longer.

"The front step is no better than the front parlor. The rule is firm."

"Mrs. Stone, please be reasonable. I have to see her. She is going to be my wife."

This declaration did nothing to budge the stubborn woman. "If that's the case, she will know where to find you, but you'll not come courting here, do you understand?"

My God, he wanted to shake her. He was so close. Juliana was in there somewhere and he had to know what she was thinking. If the marchioness was correct, she was as devastated as he. He had to get to her. "Mrs. Stone," he began again.

He was cut off by a loud crash from inside the house that sounded distinctly like a large item breaking.

Mrs. Stone's eyes widened at the sound. She looked over her shoulder toward a place he couldn't see.

"Mrs. Stone, come quickly," a female voice called from behind her.

She turned back to Michael. "Good day, sir," she said forcefully, and shut the door in his face.

*Damn it.*

He raised his fist to knock again, already preparing to shove her aside and tear the house apart until he found Juliana. To hell with the bloody rules.

His fist never met the door. It flung open. Mrs. Stone was gone and in her place was a buxom young woman with dark hair and even darker eyes. She grabbed his coat sleeve and tugged him inside. "You'll have to hurry," she whispered forcefully. "The vase didn't shatter as badly as I'd hoped, so it won't take long to pick up the pieces." She pulled him toward the staircase. "Second floor. Last room on the right."

"Thank you," he blurted out, vowing to find some way to repay the girl for her assistance, then he flew up the steps two at a time.

\* \* \* \*

Juliana had cried several times that day. To an observer, it might have seemed that she had succumbed to one long session of weeping, but she knew better. Each time was unique because it was triggered by a different reason. First, she'd cried for Michael, for the betrayal he so clearly felt when she'd refused him. Then she cried for herself, thinking of how the light of morning had likely brought a return of common sense and he was already relieved she'd said no. Then she cried at the thought that perhaps he wasn't relieved, but truly heartbroken. Then she cried because *she* was heartbroken. Finally, and most thoroughly, she wept because she had begun to wonder if he had been right after all. What if belonging meant finding the person with whom you belonged and nothing else mattered beyond that?

If that were true, she was the stupidest fool in the history of fools. And that was something to cry about.

It was only after she had spent all her tears that she slept, exhausted by emotion and lack of sleep. She awoke with a start when her door was flung open. She sat up in bed and gaped.

Michael filled the doorway. She rubbed her eyes. Was it really him, or had her dreams taken a realistic turn? "Michael. Are you real?"

Then he was next to her bed. "What else would I be?" he asked.

"A dream," she said.

He searched her face, tenderness in his dark eyes. "Do you dream about me?"

"You know that I do."

He took her hand and held it in his own. "If you dream about me, why do you refuse to be with me, Juliana?"

She started to speak, but didn't know what she should tell him.

"Don't answer yet." Michael lifted a staying hand. "Alexander's mother thinks you refused me because your love is selfless and you don't want me to make a choice between you and Rose Hall."

Juliana stared at him, neither disputing or agreeing to this truth.

"I have to know if that is true, darling, because if you truly don't want to marry me, I will let you alone. But you must know, I dream about you as well, Juliana—in sleep and awake."

"You have other dreams as well," she whispered, her objection as weak as her resolve to deny him.

He knelt low. "Is it true, then? The marchioness said you refused me because you love me *too* much to ask me to choose." His gaze searched hers. "Do you love me?"

Juliana lowered her eyes. She could not lie to him. She wanted to ask him to choose her. She was no longer even certain that she shouldn't.

"If that is your objection," Michael continued, "know that the choice is removed. Rose Hall will be mine no matter who I marry. My father has confirmed it."

Juliana lifted her eyes to his again, hope lightening her heart. "Is that true?" She needed to hear him say it again.

"Yes," Michael said, gripping her hand as he spoke earnestly, "but I need for you to know his decision does not change mine. There was never any choice for me but you. I am glad for his concession if it clears away your objection, Juliana. I chose you before and I will choose you always, if you will have me."

"Michael." She didn't know where to begin. So many words and emotions demanded release in that moment she couldn't find order or comprehension in them. She smiled and started with, "I was stupid, Michael." Once she said it, an irrational laughter bubbled up within her. Her grin widened. "I am an idiot."

He stood and reached for her, lifting her from the bed and into his arms. "Do you mean it?"

"Yes. Yes." She laughed as she said it, burying her face in the crook of his neck. "I was so worried you would choose me and later regret it. I walked away from the thing I wanted most because I didn't trust you to know your own mind."

She leaned away from him—enough to look up into his face as she told him, "I should have taken it, Michael. I should have clutched at what you offered and spent every day making certain you did not regret it. I should have vowed right then to spend the rest of my days showing you all the wonder and gratitude that are inside me because somehow you love me. Because I love you, Michael. I've never felt love. I don't know that I've ever even seen it, but I know that's what this is. When you asked for my hand, I should have given you everything—my hand, my heart, my gratitude and my devotion."

"Then give it now," he said. He crushed her to him. "Let me ask for it again, only tell me yes."

"Yes!" she said without hesitation, then repeated it for good measure. "Yes."

He kissed her then, as she'd wanted to beg him to do from the moment he appeared. Everything she'd failed to explain, all of her love and apology, she poured it into returning his kiss.

Noise sounded in the hall and Michael lifted his head. "I should tell you," he said, "I think you are likely to be expelled by Mrs. Stone."

"I'm not surprised," Juliana said. She smiled against Michael's throat. "She has very strict rules about gentleman callers."

"I think," Michael said, tilting her face up to hers and brushing his lips across hers, "you have had enough rules for one lifetime." He nibbled at her lower lip. "But if it would help, I don't have to behave like a gentleman."

Juliana closed her eyes, allowing the feel of his embrace and the knowledge that she belonged there to settle into her soul. "I hope that you won't, Michael."

# Epilogue

"It's as though the clouds have been banished," Lucy announced, peering up at the perfectly unblemished sky.

"The sun feels so splendid, I want to throw my bonnet off and let my face brown," Juliana declared closing her eyes and tilting her face up to the warmth.

Emma smiled at her. "You should." She meant it sincerely. Juliana had not spent enough hours in the sun in her life, to Emma's mind. She belonged in the light and anyone who found fault with a sun-browned face could go to the devil.

No one would, of course, for they were not in London. The three ladies sat in the center of Emma's garden in Beadwell and there would be no unwanted intrusions in their sanctuary. Not today, anyway. This day was for surrounding themselves with the peace and beauty of the garden.

Tomorrow would be less peaceful.

"Are you sure you don't mind returning?" Lucy asked Juliana, echoing Emma's thoughts. "I'm certain Emma and I could find a way to sort things out without you. We'll have a great deal of help—my parents, the Browns, Simon."

Juliana's smile was appreciative. "Thank you, but it's important that I help. Returning to the house may not be easy," she said, reaching down to tangle her fingers in the wiry fur of Gelert. Emma could not recall a single time in the past months that she had seen Juliana without her canine shadow. "Still, I can't avoid it forever, not if I'm to be an equal partner."

She was right, of course. The women had arrived in Beadwell to sort out Mr. Crawford's house together because it was to become the site of their joint project. The former home of the nastiest man Emma had ever had the misfortune to know was to become a special sort of boarding house for women who needed a place of refuge and had nowhere else to go.

The idea had been Juliana's. She had fled to London and found a place at Mrs. Stone's, but not every woman who needed help had the wherewithal to get to London or the ability to provide a respectable letter of introduction for sticklers such as the formidable Mrs. Stone. Juliana had introduced the idea to Lucy who had, in turn, presented it to Emma and the three of them had made the necessary plans.

Most of the planning and arranging had not appeared to be difficult for Juliana—completing the formalities of her inheritance, interviewing women to oversee the house—but all that had been accomplished from London. The last task necessary to bring their plans to fruition was the preparation of the house itself—a task Juliana insisted she could not leave to others.

"I feel very different from the girl who lived in that house," Juliana said. "Besides, Michael will be there."

Emma liked the way Juliana made the declaration, as though she was certain of her love's ability to ensure her peace and happiness even when faced with the prospect of sorting through grim memories.

"The sooner we can have the house ready, the better," Lucy announced. "My mother has found our first resident—*residents* actually. The woman would come with her twelve-year-old daughter."

Juliana sat up. "Already? How did she learn of us?"

"My mother spoke of our project to the wife of the vicar in Bradenton. When Mrs. Lewis heard the story, she immediately told my mother of a woman in her parish who is being mistreated by her husband. Mrs. Lewis had tried to help in whatever way she can, but she feels the only way this woman and her daughter would be safe would be to leave her husband's home."

"That's awful," Emma declared. "Of course we shall help."

Juliana rose from her chair. Her canine companion followed suit. "I think I shall start cleaning the house today. Now that I know someone awaits our help, I can't enjoy an afternoon of idleness."

Lucy stood as well. "You're right, of course. We should begin immediately."

Emma stood from her chair to complete the trio. "I agree."

Juliana beamed back at the other two ladies. "Thank you," she said, emotion welling in her eyes.

"Don't be emotional yet," Lucy teased, taking Juliana by the arm. "We haven't even started."

Emma stepped forward to take Juliana's other arm. "I think it shouldn't take very long to sort through what is there, if all three of us work together."

Juliana looked to one woman and then the other and gave a slight befuddled shake of her head. "Do you know," she said, "I think I might actually be looking forward to it."

Emma gave a nod of approval at the same time that Lucy announced, "Good," and the three ladies set off, arm in arm, to cross the garden and take on the task of converting the legacy of one Mr. Samuel Crawford to one that benefitted women for years to come.

# Meet the Author

the 2015 winner in the Historical Category of the Romance Writers of America® Golden Heart® contest, Sara has been a finalist and winner in several other writing competitions. A daughter of the Midwest, Sara was born in Illinois, grew up in Michigan, and currently lives in Ohio. In addition to her writing endeavors, Sara is a wife and mother in a large, blended family.

Visit her at www.saraportman.com.

## Love the Beadwell Brides?

Don't miss Emma and Lucy's stories

### The Reunion and The Offer

Available now wherever books are sold!

# THE REUNION

*An inconvenient engagement turns a marriage of convenience into so much more in this sparkling new series from award-winning author Sara Portman . . .*

Lady Emmaline Shaw's reputation was irreparably damaged when her fiancé, John Brantwood, disappeared immediately after their engagement four years ago. Since then, she's grown from a shy, uncertain girl to a woman who knows her own mind. And what she knows is that London society holds nothing for her.

Rumor has it that John ran off to war and died in battle. Now, as the new Duke of Worley, his shocking resurrection throws the ton into a tizzy and makes him one of England's most sought after bachelors—except that he's already engaged.

John needs a wife capable of smoothing his beloved sister's introduction into society. But though Emma appily grants him his freedom, her fiery beauty and resilient spirit hold him captive. In fact, John has no intention of letting her go. Her fate is now in his hands, but will her heart be safe there as well?

# THE OFFER

*The award-winning author of The Reunion continues her dazzling new series with a novel of one woman's fall from saint to sinner...*

Lucy Betancourt's future looks bleak. The daughter of an ailing vicar in a village with no eligible bachelors, her only hope is to find employment as a governess or companion. As she helps her childhood friend, the new Duchess of Worley, through her pregnancy, the ever-practical Lucy makes her plans. But life—in the way of the dashing Bex Brantwood—has something else in store for Lucy...

Upon meeting Bex, the duke's cousin, Lucy offers herself up to him. But Bex is no family man looking for a governess. And Lucy is not exactly mistress material. Still, the misunderstanding ends in a kiss neither can forget . . .

Bex finds the proper vicar's daughter and her most improper proposal endlessly amusing—and attractive. But, saddled with debt, he's in no position to keep a woman, much less marry one, which is what a woman like Lucy deserves. Little does he know that even with her reputation at stake, Lucy will take the biggest gamble of her life by following her heart—straight into his arms . . .

CPSIA information can be obtained
at www.ICGtesting.com
Printed in the USA
LVOW11s0841121117
555908LV00006B/135/P

*In this thrilling romance from award-wi... ...... ......... .... ......, the illegitimate son of a nobleman an... ... .......... ......... .. .... their fate on the Lond...*

According to his father's terms, Michael Rosevear's duty is to be ignored until such time as he is useful. Now that the earldom is in need of fun Michael is to be sold off in marriage to the daughter of a crass but wealt merchant willing to pay for any connection to nobility—even one from t wrong side of the blanket . . .

En route to his fate in London, Michael does not plan to board an ext passenger. Yet there is something in the young miss's desperate plea that tu at his conscience—though he is certain her story is a fabrication . . .

Juliana Crawford has fled her father's cruel home. Using a false name to eva pursuit, she must find a private traveler with whom to complete her escap Chance matches her with a dark and wounded young lord who guards h own secrets just as carefully. The unlikely pair embark on a journey fill with revelations and unexpected adventure—one that may lead them question whether to part at their destination—or change course entirely .

## Also in this series

Visit us at www.kensingtonbooks.com

ISBN-13: 978-1-5161-0054-5
ISBN-10: 1-5161-0054-9

5 1 5 0 0

9 781516 100545

LYRICAL PRESS
KENSINGTON
U.S. $15.00
PRINTED IN THE U.S.A.